Some things didn't add up.

Hannah was smart, and in her industry, she'd been an expert on nitrogen mustard compound. So why had she walked away from such a high-paying job? First, he had other questions.

"If someone got these chemicals," he asked, "how much would it take to kill a person?"

"Not much. They're highly toxic."

As she explained, Owen o̶_____ Her hands moved as she spoke _____ g to her neck, as if sh_____ ____ore a turtleneck in _____ _____iding?

Owen trie_____ _____eath. A woman's n___ _____ng—that sensitive spot under t___ _____ned his tongue tracing her skin. He c____ ___ally hear her breathless moans.

"Owen?"

He snapped out of his reverie and forced himself to tear his gaze away.

It was too many hours on this case, too many cups of coffee, too little sleep. Throw in a beautiful woman and his brain went haywire, concocting a fantasy. A fantasy he had no business enjoying. Not when there were bodies piling up.

* * *

Dear Reader,

One of my favorite things about being a writer is that I get to take a normal, everyday situation and let my imagination run wild. In this book, my heroine, Hannah, is a chemistry professor who used to work at a pharmaceutical company. I happen to be a biology professor who used to work at a pharmaceutical company, but I can tell you the similarities stop there. While my jobs were routine, even mundane at times, Hannah finds herself on the adventure of a lifetime when she steps up to help a police investigation. And while I had a blast writing her story, I'm glad I never lived through these experiences myself!

Writing and reading are such a fun way to escape, to explore wild and even dangerous situations without actually having to deal with them in real life. It's one of the reasons I love romantic suspense, and I imagine it's the same for you, too!

So sit back, get comfy and let Owen and Hannah take you on an exciting journey! As always, thanks for reading!

Lara Lacombe

KILLER EXPOSURE

Lara Lacombe

HARLEQUIN®ROMANTIC SUSPENSE

Recycling programs
for this product may
not exist in your area.

ISBN-13: 978-0-373-27919-7

Killer Exposure

Copyright © 2015 by Lara Kingeter

Printed in U.S.A.

LARA LACOMBE

I earned my PhD in microbiology and immunology and worked in several labs across the country before moving into the classroom. My day job as a college science professor gives me time to pursue my other love—writing fast-paced romantic suspense with smart, nerdy heroines and dangerously attractive heroes. I love to hear from readers! Find me on the web or contact me at laralacombewriter@gmail.com.

Books by Lara Lacombe

HARLEQUIN ROMANTIC SUSPENSE

Deadly Contact
Fatal Fallout
Lethal Lies
Killer Exposure

Visit Lara's Author Profile page at Harlequin.com or laralacombe.blogspot.com for more titles.

This one is for June.

Chapter 1

"Dr. Baker, is this going to be on the test?"

Hannah sighed quietly, her hand pausing in its journey across the chalkboard. *One...two...three...*

When she made it to five, she turned to face the class. Twenty-four faces watched her, their expressions running the gamut from drowsy boredom to bright-eyed interest. She was gratified to find that most of the students were awake, but she knew from experience they weren't all paying attention. The endless distractions of the internet were but a click away, and most kids couldn't resist the temptation of their phones for the full hour of class.

How times have changed. She felt like a stick-in-the-mud for even thinking it, but when she had been in college, she had come to class prepared, asked questions and paid attention. Now students howled in protest whenever an assignment was given, and spent more time trying to figure out how to get out of studying than they spent in class. It was a fact that amused and exasperated her in equal measures.

"You know I'm not going to answer that," she replied, smiling a little to soften the blow. "Like I told you on the first day of class, if I'm talking about something, it means I think it's important. And if I think it's important, you should, too."

"There's just so much material," another student piped up. "How are we supposed to know what to study?"

Hannah felt her smile grow thin. "Study all of it."

"All of it!" Despair was almost a palpable thing in the room, hovering over the students' heads like a gray storm cloud. "But that's not fair!"

"It's not that bad," she said, smiling at them before delivering her final coup. "You have all of spring break to study."

A loud groan rose from the mass of students, and she chuckled, a small part of her enjoying their over-the-top reaction. If chemistry didn't pan out for them, they all had a promising future in acting. She glanced at the clock. Almost time to end for the day. Recognizing she wouldn't be able to pull them back on track with so little time left, she decided to cut her losses. "Remember, you can always email me over the break if you have questions while you're studying. Try to do a little bit of work every day, rather than leaving it until the end and trying to cram. That never works." She started to gather up her papers, and the students, recognizing their cue to leave, began to do the same. "Have a good break," she said, raising her voice to be heard over the din of books thumping shut, bags zipping closed and phones beeping as they were switched off of silent mode.

She checked her own phone as the students filed out, a little surprised to find a missed call and message from her friend Gabby. Gabriella Whitman had been her roommate in college, and the two stayed in touch after going their separate ways, Gabby to medical school and Hannah to graduate school. Now that they were both back in the same city, they made it a point to have dinner together once a month.

Hannah slipped the phone into her pocket, deciding to wait until she was in her office before checking the message. Gabby probably just needed to reschedule their upcoming girls' night. She worked long hours as the county medical examiner, and it wasn't always possible for her to get away. Since Hannah's schedule was more flexible, she didn't mind adjusting to accommodate her friend.

She moved on autopilot back to her office, her mind already turning to the exams she needed to work on over the upcoming break. Then there were the letters of recommendation she had agreed to write for students applying to summer research programs or professional schools. She felt a surge of pride when she considered the number of references that were due. It was always gratifying to help a student succeed, and she had to admit, it made her feel good when a current or former student asked her to help them. Brian's letter was due next week, so she really needed to finish it and send it off well before the deadline…

"Are you Hannah Baker?"

She stopped a few feet away from her office door,

taken aback by the question. Two men stood in the hall, one tall and one about her height. The shorter man continued his perusal of the students walking by, apparently not particularly interested in her. The taller man, however, ran his gaze slowly over her body, seemingly evaluating her appearance and comparing it to some mental standard. Hannah felt her face heat, and her skin tingled in the wake of his blatant scrutiny. It had been a long time—*too long*, her hormones chided— since a man had paid her any attention. Especially a handsome man. And there was no denying her mystery questioner was attractive.

"Yes," she replied, taking a moment to return his stare. He was tall and lean, but she'd bet almost anything his body was rock solid underneath the green polo and khaki pants. He carried himself with the confidence of a man who could handle any physical threat that came his way, his stance relaxed but not soft. His dark brown hair was short and clipped, threaded with a few silver strands that caught the light of the hall. His cheeks were stubbled, giving him the look of a man who had rolled out of bed and come to work. She had the insane urge to run her fingertip across his face, to feel the sandpaper softness of his whiskers against her skin. Would it tickle against her chest, her stomach? *Whoa*, she thought, shutting down the crazy daydream before it could go further. Her cheeks grew even warmer, and his dark blue gaze filled with lazy satisfaction, as if he knew exactly what she was thinking.

She cleared her throat and swallowed, needing to steer herself back onto professional ground. She didn't know who these men were. They didn't look like the usual textbook reps; they lacked the ready smile and casual friendliness exhibited by so many of those sales-people. But no matter their identity, standing in the hall gawking at one of them was no way for a professor to behave. "How can I help you?"

"I'm Detective Owen Randall with the Houston po-lice department." He pulled a shiny badge from his pocket and showed it to her, then gestured to the shorter man. "This is my partner, Nate Gallagher." The other man nodded at her in acknowledgment before return-ing his gaze to the stream of people walking past. "May we have a minute of your time, please?"

"Of course." Her fingers fumbled with the keys, and it took her several attempts to find and insert the correct one into the lock of her office door. She wasn't used to having an audience, particularly an audience of handsome police officers. What on earth could they want with her?

Her stomach dropped as she pushed open the door. Was one of her students in trouble? Everyone had been in class today, and she didn't recall any missing faces in yesterday's classes, either. But she only saw them for an hour at a time, which gave them ample opportu-nity to get up to something. While most of her students were good kids, no one was perfect. Besides, how well did she really know them?

Hannah rounded her desk and sat, discreetly adjust-ing the fabric of the turtleneck she wore to make sure it fully covered her neck. She usually left her shoulder-length hair down as an added layer of concealment, which made it unlikely that Detective Randall or his partner had gotten a look at her scars. Still, her vanity demanded she check. Although she'd made her peace with the burn scars on her back and neck, she still didn't like others to see the marks. She'd had enough pity, and she didn't like answering questions about them, no matter how well-meaning the intentions of the other person.

The two men settled into chairs on the other side of her desk. Detective Gallagher, deprived of his view of the activity in the hall, turned his attention to her office, his eyes roaming across the walls and shelves, pausing here to take in her stack of books, there to examine the antique lab instruments she kept on her desk. Detective Randall was more direct, keeping his focus on her. She shifted slightly, then forced herself to stop. She was a professor, for crying out loud! She was used to demanding and commanding the attention of dozens, if not scores, of students at a time. She could handle being the center of attention of one man.

Even if he was the most handsome man she'd ever seen in real life.

"How can I help you gentlemen?"

"How long did you work for ChemCure Industries?"

She leaned back, surprised by the question. Of all the things Detective Randall could have asked, inquiring about her career in the pharmaceutical industry was the last thing she'd expected. "Five years. Why?"

He ignored her question. "And during your tenure there, did you work with nitrogen mustard chemicals?"

"Yes," she said slowly.

Detective Gallagher spoke for the first time. "Isn't that the stuff they used during World War I? Mustard gas?"

Hannah reluctantly turned her gaze to him, keeping Detective Randall in her peripheral vision. For some reason, she wanted to monitor his reaction to her responses, even though his expression hadn't changed from the businesslike look he'd adopted once he'd started asking questions.

"The chemicals are related but different. The nitrogen mustards I worked with are used as chemotherapy drugs."

"Is that what you were researching?"

She turned back to fully face Detective Randall. "Yes. The drugs are fairly effective at treating leukemias and lymphomas. I was trying to determine if related compounds would have the same effects, with less toxicity."

"And did they?"

"There were a few promising compounds, but the side effects were too severe, so we didn't pursue them. Did you really come here to ask me about my previous work?"

The two men exchanged a glance. Detective Gallagher raised one shoulder in an almost imperceptible shrug, as if to say "all yours." Detective Randall seemed to sigh before turning back to her.

"We're investigating a series of suspicious deaths."

Hannah felt her eyebrows shoot up. "And you think I had something to do with them?" The question came out as a high squeak, making her sound like a cartoon mouse. *Real smooth*, she thought, struggling to rein in the reflexive alarm the detective's statement had triggered. Her brain kicked into overdrive, trying in vain to determine why two police officers would think to question her in regards to any kind of deaths.

Some of her panic must have shown on her face. "You're not a suspect," Detective Gallagher assured her. "We just need to get some information from you, to help us in our investigation."

"Oh." Then why the cloak-and-dagger routine? Annoyance sparked as the adrenaline rush of the scare faded, and she narrowed her eyes at Detective Randall, who stared back at her impassively. "Why didn't you say so in the first place? I'm happy to help in any way I can."

"We appreciate that," Detective Gallagher replied.

Detective Randall coughed meaningfully, as if to signal to his partner to shut up.

"Why did you come to me?" Had something happened in her neighborhood? Was that why they were asking her questions? She frowned, considering. She hadn't seen anything out of the ordinary lately, and these quiet, tree-lined streets weren't the sort that drew trouble. Surely her neighbors would have mentioned a string of deaths in the area. The older, close-knit community had an active neighborhood association, and this was just the sort of thing that would have triggered an emergency meeting, complete with notices to lock doors and be on the lookout for suspicious activity. Still, perhaps the police were keeping things quiet.

Apparently ignoring his partner's signal, Gallagher spoke up again. "The medical examiner, Dr. Whitman, suggested we speak with you."

"Gabby thought I could help you?" That explained the mystery phone call. She'd bet a year's supply of chocolate the message on her phone had something to do with the two men sitting in her office, and she kicked herself for not listening to it on the way back from class. Gabby had probably shared details with her, something the handsome, closed-off detective and his partner seemed reluctant to do.

"Why did you leave ChemCure Industries?"

The question took her off guard, and Hannah reflexively moved her hand to her neck, her fingers slipping under the fabric to brush across the raised smoothness of her scars. "It was time for me to move on," she said, dropping her gaze to her desk. "I was tired of working in the industry." *And I couldn't go back. Not after the accident.* "I'd always wanted to teach, and when this position opened up, I jumped at the chance."

"Did you leave on good terms?"

She thought of the nondisclosure agreement she'd signed, the weeks spent in the hospital and the months of physical therapy. The company had been quick to deny any responsibility for the explosion in the lab that had nearly killed her, but when her attorney had come knocking, they'd been even quicker to settle out of court, agreeing to pay her a nice lump sum and take care of all her current and future medical bills.

Had it been an amicable parting? Not really. But it could have been worse.

"It went about as well as these things go," she said, tugging up the neck of her shirt before letting her hand drift down to lie on the desk.

Detective Randall narrowed his eyes at her, his doubt plain. "They didn't think it was odd you would leave a high-paying career in industrial pharmaceuticals for a teaching position at a small college?" He glanced around her office, then back to her, his expression calculating. "That must have been quite a pay cut."

"It was." She held his gaze, kept her voice cool. "But there's more to life than money. Don't you agree?"

For the barest second, heat flared in his eyes, burning bright and hot. His mouth softened, becoming a seductive curve, and his eyelids dropped slightly, giving him the look of a man who had been well and truly satisfied. She shivered, her skin prickling at the wild thought that *she* had been the one to satisfy him.

Then his expression shifted, returning to an inscrutable mask she couldn't read. She shook herself free of the moment, still feeling a little dazed. *Get a grip!* she told herself. *He isn't the first handsome man you've talked to, and he won't be the last.* Besides, she had no business letting her libido run the show when he was here to question her about people dying.

"Can't argue with that," Detective Gallagher piped up. His smile was friendly, and she felt herself relax. "Still, people don't usually walk away from that much money without a good reason."

Hannah shrugged, trying to seem indifferent. "I had gotten burned out by the hours I was working. I wanted to slow down, find someone, start a family."

Detective Randall's eyes flicked to her left hand, then back to her face. "And have you?" His voice was so low the question was almost a rumble, making it seem even more personal.

A lump suddenly appeared in her throat, and she swallowed hard to push it down. "Not yet," she replied. Jake, her ex-fiancé, had left once he'd learned how long her recovery would take. She'd pushed the pain of his betrayal aside and directed all her energy toward healing, but now she was finding it hard to ignore. The worst part of all was the despair, a swirling black hole in her stomach that threatened to consume her soul. She felt scarred both inside and out, and it was becoming increasingly clear that she was destined to be alone. Who would want her? It was hard enough finding a man who wanted to date a chemist. The men she encountered seemed to be intimidated by her intelligence, a reaction that made it hard to get a second date. And even if she did manage to find a man who wasn't bothered by her intellect, there was no guarantee he'd be okay with the extensive scarring on her back. Pushing back the familiar feelings of loss and loneliness, Hannah pasted on a bright smile. "I'm sure you're not here to talk about my personal life, Detectives. Why don't you tell me what you think I can do to help you today."

She was smart, that much was obvious. They didn't just hand out PhD's in chemistry, and from what he knew of her work in industry, Hannah Baker had been the leading expert on nitrogen mustard compounds. Why had she walked away from such a high-paying job? Her story about wanting to slow down just didn't ring true—it sounded too rehearsed, as if she was trying to convince herself as much as him. He made a mental note to ask Dr. Whitman, the medical examiner, for more details. He knew the two of them were friends. Perhaps she could shed more light on why Hannah Baker had dropped out of the corporate world to hide at this small college.

"Are these chemicals commonly available?" Nate leaned forward slightly, shifting in the chair. Dr. Baker turned her attention to him, and her shoulders relaxed a bit. He glanced at Nate, but the other man showed no reaction.

"Not really." She frowned slightly. "There are companies that supply chemicals for research, and you could purchase some of the compounds from them. But there are certain restrictions in place that prevent an individual from ordering chemicals."

"How hard would it be to falsify information, to skirt around the supplier's security?"

Her hazel eyes were steady on his, but he didn't miss the subtle tightening at the corners of her mouth and eyes. "I don't know. I've never tried. You'd have to ask them."

"Let's say someone did manage to order these chemicals," Nate broke in. "How much would it take to kill a person?"

"Not much. They're highly toxic."

"Tell me about how they work," Nate encouraged.

She was reluctant at first, but after a few moments, she warmed to her subject, and her enthusiasm began to shine through. She was a patient and thorough teacher, answering questions and explaining complicated topics with ease, and Owen was forced to admit that regardless of her real reasons for taking the job, Hannah Baker had a gift for teaching.

He was content to let Nate steer the questioning. For some reason, Dr. Baker seemed more comfortable interacting with the other man. Her obvious preference for his new partner irked him a little, but he wasn't about to let his ego get in the way of collecting information. With the way this case was going, they needed all the help they could get.

The woman was animated, her slender, graceful hands moving in a fluid series of gestures as she spoke. Every once in a while, one of those hands would briefly land on her neck before taking flight again. It was a gesture he'd noticed before, her seeming preoccupation with the collar of her turtleneck. Why was that? Was she nervous? Was she trying to hide something?

She sounded genuine, he mused. She answered Nate's questions without hesitation, showing no signs of evasion or lying. Why, then, did she keep fiddling with the neck of her sweater? And who wore a turtleneck during a Houston spring? The temperatures were already in the mideighties, with the humidity so high it made him wish he had gills. Most people were breaking out the shorts, skirts and sleeveless tops, not turtleneck sweaters. What was she hiding?

Owen focused on her neck, trying to catch a glimpse of the skin underneath. It wasn't a bad way to spend a few minutes, studying the smooth column of skin, the elegant lines. That spot just under the ear, so sensitive to his mouth. He let his thoughts drift, imagined peeling down the fabric of Dr. Baker's sweater, exposing the pale expanse of her throat. He'd use his tongue to trace along her skin, down to her collarbone. She probably had nice collarbones, he thought. Gentle, sloping lines begging for his touch. He could practically *feel* them under his lips, hear her breathless moans as he slowly stripped away her clothes. She was so prim and put together, it would be a real pleasure to find out what she was concealing underneath that sweater.

"Owen?"

The sound of his name snapped him out of his reverie, and he shook his head slightly, focusing on his partner. Nate and Dr. Baker were both staring at him, their expressions making it clear they'd been trying to get his attention for some time. Damn.

"What?"

Dr. Baker tensed, and he mentally cursed himself for being so gruff. "Sorry, I was thinking about something else for a moment. What do you need?"

Nate didn't press, but he could see the concern in the other man's eyes. Great. He'd heard the rumors swirling, knew Nate had, as well. After Owen's partner had died in the line of duty six months ago, he'd taken a leave of absence to handle the loss. A lot of people thought he shouldn't have come back. Was his new partner one of them?

"Dr. Baker was just offering to look at the chemical signatures of the compounds found in our victims."

"If I can see what they had in their systems, I can tell you if the drug was purchased from a company, or if someone modified the compounds to create something even more potent," she said.

"That would be great," he replied. "Thank you."

She nodded, her cheeks taking on a pretty, pale pink color. Her hand found her neck again, and he forced himself to tear his gaze away before he slipped back into his highly inappropriate daydream.

It was fatigue, he decided. Too many hours focused on this case, too many cups of coffee, too little sleep. Throw in a beautiful woman, and his brain took the path of least resistance, concocting a fantasy he had no business enjoying when there were bodies piling up.

Time to go, before he did something stupid.

He stood, and a second later, Nate did the same. "Thank you for your time, Doctor." He offered her his hand, tried not to notice the smooth softness of her skin when she took it. "We'll be in touch."

"Let me know what else I can do to help," she said.

Nate nodded, and they walked out of her office, leaving her standing behind her desk watching them go, her hand at her neck.

"She's prettier than I expected."

Owen bristled at his partner's casual remark. While Nate Gallagher was by all accounts a good guy, he didn't like the thought that the other man had noticed Hannah Baker in anything other than a professional capacity. *Like you should talk*, he thought wryly.

Biting his tongue to contain the reflexive retort, Owen settled for a grunt, hoping Nate would drop the subject.

He didn't take the hint.

"I mean, I didn't expect her to be so young. Silly of me, since Doc Whitman isn't that old herself. But I heard the word *professor* and pictured some gray-haired woman in support hose. Know what I mean?"

Owen grunted again, refusing to engage.

"Do you think she's seeing anyone?"

"How should I know?" He sounded sour, even to his own ears, but Nate carried on as if he hadn't noticed.

"I think she likes me. It felt like we had a connection back there. Maybe I should ask her out."

Owen's grip tightened on the steering wheel. "No," he said quietly.

"What do you mean, no?"

He cut a glance over to his partner. "It wouldn't be professional of you. Besides, she might somehow be involved in all this."

"Oh, please," Nate scoffed. "You and I both know that she's not a suspect. There's no conflict of interest here. Besides," he added, his voice taking on a smug note, "I wasn't the one daydreaming about her during the questioning."

Damn. It had been obvious, then. Still, his pride wouldn't let him admit his partner was right. "I don't know what you're talking about."

"Sure you do," Nate said. "We've been partners now for over two months, and in all that time, you've never once mentioned a wife, a girlfriend or even a one-night stand. You're lonely. Would it be so bad if you let your guard down and enjoyed the company of a beautiful woman?"

"There's no time."

"So multitask. Take the professor out for dinner and ask her about the chemicals. That's got to be every woman's dream date."

Owen rolled his eyes. "I thought you were going to ask her out."

"Nah. I was just trying to yank your chain. Besides, she's not interested in me."

"What makes you think she's interested in me?" As soon as the words were out, Owen wished he could take them back. This wasn't junior high, and he really shouldn't care if Hannah Baker liked him.

But he did care. And he wanted to hear confirmation that his attraction to her wasn't one-sided. It was juvenile of him, but he needed that reassurance. Nate was right—he was lonely. And even though he had no intention of starting anything with the woman, it would be nice to know he had the option.

"For starters, she kept watching you. You were too spaced out to notice, but the whole time she was talking to me, she was glancing at you, looking for your reaction to what she was saying. And she kept touching her neck."

"You noticed that, too?"

He saw Nate nod out of the corner of his eye. "Yeah. But what's with the turtleneck? Kind of a strange choice, given the weather we've been having."

Owen tapped his fingers against the wheel. "I was wondering that myself. Think she's hiding something?"

Nate considered the question for a moment. "Could be. But I don't see her being involved in these deaths. We've been fishing bodies out of the bayou every seven days like clockwork. And while she may have the upper-body strength to overpower the smaller victims, there's no way she could have handled that bruiser we found two days ago."

"Good point. But she could have had help."

"Besides," Nate went on, ignoring him, "what these victims went through after they died…" He shuddered briefly. "It takes a lot of isolated space to inflict that kind of damage. Not to mention time. And she hasn't been missing work, or acting unusual."

"Again, she could have a partner." Owen didn't believe it, either, but they did have to consider every possibility, no matter how remote.

Nate gave him a droll look. "Uh-huh. And I have a Lamborghini in the garage."

Owen merely shrugged.

"You know as well as I do that she's not involved. She doesn't have it in her to do that to someone."

"I hope you're right. We still need to look into it though."

His partner let out an inelegant snort. "Don't sound so broken up about it."

Owen ignored the gibe, but he didn't try to hide the smile that curved his lips. The thought of seeing the lovely professor again gave him something to look forward to, and given the way this case was going, he'd take his pleasure where he could find it.

Chapter 2

The Harris County Institute of Forensic Science was a six-story redbrick cube on a tree-lined street near the Medical City area of Houston. Hannah parked in one of the visitor spaces and made her way to Gabby's office, where she found her friend typing madly and staring at her computer monitor wearing an expression of fierce concentration.

Hannah hovered in the doorway, waiting for a break to interrupt Gabby. It didn't take long. With a few muttered curses, Gabby punched at the keyboard, then leaned back, her brows drawn down in a frown. Seeing her chance, Hannah coughed quietly.

Gabby looked up, her scowl melting into a smile when she saw Hannah. "Hey! Come on in."

Hannah stepped into the small office and extended her arm, offering Gabby the extra cup of coffee she'd brought. "You sure I'm not interrupting?"

Her friend took the cup and gestured to a chair across from her desk. "Saving me, more like. I'm up to my eyeballs in reports." She took a sip, closed her eyes in appreciation. "Thanks for this."

"No problem. I figured you could use some caffeine."

"You know it. So how'd it go yesterday?"

Hannah sat in the lumpy chair and shifted to find a comfortable position. "It would have gone a lot better if I'd listened to your message first. I was totally thrown by the whole thing."

Gabby grimaced in sympathy. "Sorry about that. I should have texted you, too, but I didn't have time. Were they at least nice to you?"

"I suppose. One more than the other."

"Let me guess—Detective Gallagher was friendlier?"

"You got it."

Gabby nodded and set her cup on the desk. "I figured. Detective Randall can be a little…intense."

"That's one way of putting it." Goose bumps broke out on her arms as she recalled the feeling of his dark blue eyes on her. "What's his story?" She tried to make the question sound casual, but she and Gabby had been friends for a long time, and the other woman didn't miss a trick.

"Oh, so it's like that?" she teased. Hannah rolled her eyes and looked away, shaking her head.

"Seriously, Hannah. I'm glad you're showing some interest. How long has it been since you've gone on a date?"

"I don't know," she replied, exasperation bleeding into her voice. "About a year, maybe?"

"Probably more like a year and a half," Gabby retorted. "I know you haven't seen anyone since Jake the Snake left." She took a sip of her coffee and muttered, "Good riddance."

Hannah smiled despite the pang that stabbed through her chest at the thought of her ex-fiancé. "Since when are you so obsessed with my love life?"

"Since you're my friend and I care about you." Gabby gave her a level stare, then smiled. "I just want you to be happy. And while I don't know much about Detective Broody McGrumpyPants, he is handsome. You could definitely do worse."

"I didn't say I was going to be doing anything," Hannah protested weakly.

Gabby gave her a wicked smile. "Oh, but you should. *Doing* things can be so much fun."

"Gabby!" Hannah chastised. "Don't be so vulgar."

Her friend's laugh was full-throated and rich, and it filled the room in a warm wave of sound. "Oh, honey. We're not in a British period piece. Lighten up a bit." She picked up her coffee and winked at her. "You're too young to be so prim."

Hannah focused on her own coffee, hoping the steam would explain the sudden redness in her cheeks. Gabby had always been the more outgoing one, quick with a clever comeback or play on words. Sometimes Hannah envied her friend's ability to think on her feet. She was more deliberate, more cautious in her approach to conversations. Where Gabby was outgoing and friendly, Hannah was reserved and shy. More than once, she had marveled at their unlikely friendship, but at the end of the day, she knew their bond was unbreakable.

"Why don't you tell me about these victims?"

Gabby leaned back in her chair, her playful smile fading as she turned her focus to business. "I don't have much to share, unfortunately. There have been six deaths so far, one every week, and the pathology findings suggest they're linked."

"In what way?"

"The victims all suffered extensive trauma, and a lot of it occurred after death." She shook her head. "I've seen some pretty terrible things in my job, but these victims really take the cake."

Hannah grimaced, revulsion making her stomach roil. "If the injuries were that severe, why did you look for chemical traces?"

"Because I think the extensive external injuries were inflicted to distract from the real cause of death."

"And you found something?" It was a silly question—of course she had. That's why the detectives had paid her a visit yesterday.

Gabby bared her teeth in a fierce grin. "Yep. I'm really good at my job."

Hannah couldn't help but smile in return. "So if they didn't die from physical injuries, you think it was the chemical that killed them?"

Her friend tapped her index finger on the tip of her nose. "It's the only way I can explain the internal findings. As if the external injuries weren't bad enough, when I opened them up, things got really strange."

"How so?"

"Their lungs were totally wrecked. They didn't even look like lungs anymore—they were disintegrating before my eyes."

Hannah leaned forward a bit. "What do you mean?"

Gabby frowned and stared at the table. She cupped her hands and pantomimed a scooping gesture. "The chest cavity was filled with fluid. Like their lung tissue had dissolved." She shook her head. "I've never seen anything like it."

A frisson of memory jolted through Hannah, making the fine hairs at the nape of her neck rise. "Was there a smell?" she whispered.

Gabby's gaze jerked up, her eyes narrowing. "Yeah. Kind of like rotten fruit with some garlic tossed in for good measure. Definitely not the usual cadaver smell I'm used to." She cocked her head to the side. "How did you know?"

Hannah shook her head, dismissing the question. "And how did you feel after the autopsies?"

Her friend leaned back, considering. "I got a headache," she said thoughtfully. "But I just chalked it up to the weather. You know I get headaches whenever we have a storm system move through."

"Any trouble breathing?"

Gabby shook her head. "No. What's going on, Hannah? What do you know?"

"Excellent question, Doctor" came a deep voice from the doorway. "I can't wait to hear the answer."

Damn, Owen thought, watching the way Hannah flinched at the sound of his voice. She turned to face him, her eyes wide and troubled, and his stomach dropped. *She is involved.*

Disappointment settled over him like a heavy blanket. He'd been so sure that she wasn't connected to these cases, but the fear shining in her eyes dashed his hopes.

How could he have misread the situation so badly? Were his instincts really deserting him? He'd heard the whispered comments, the remarks made behind his back. A lot of people thought he was weak for taking a leave of absence after John's death. Even his captain had recommended working through the pain, saying the distraction of the job was the best way to deal with the loss of his partner. But Owen couldn't bring himself to do the job without his friend, and he'd needed the time to get his head on straight and figure out if he still wanted to be a cop. How could he go on without his best friend? But in the end, he'd come back. Being a cop was the only thing he knew how to do, and quitting felt like a betrayal of John's memory.

It was hard, though. Some days, he felt like a rookie all over again, and he spent a lot of time questioning decisions that would have been automatic before John's death. The realization that Hannah Baker was indeed connected to this case, when yesterday he'd been so sure she wasn't, did nothing for his shaky confidence.

"Please, Dr. Baker. You were saying?"

She swallowed hard and closed her eyes for a second, as if calling up some inner strength. "It's probably nothing," she began, but Dr. Whitman cut her off.

"How did you know about the smell? And about my headaches?"

Hannah shook her head. "Lucky guess?"

Owen cleared his throat. "Try again, please."

"The findings you described…" She trailed off. "I saw a similar pathology a few years ago, when I worked at ChemCure Industries."

"What do you mean? I thought you didn't do human experiments." Dr. Whitman leaned back in her chair and crossed her arms across her chest, frowning slightly. Owen felt a flash of gratitude at the woman's presence. Since she and Hannah had a history, Dr. Whitman's questions added to his understanding of Hannah and her possible involvement in the case.

"I didn't," Hannah replied. "These were findings from some animal studies. We were testing a drug that had performed beautifully in cell lines, but cells in a dish are a far cry from cells in a person. The next step was animal testing, and we abandoned the compound after we found out it destroyed the lungs." She shook her head, her gaze turning inward, as if she were reliving the experiments. "It was the strangest thing. The lungs were completely wiped out—just a puddle of goo in the chest. And the smell." She shuddered, wrinkling her nose.

"Dr. Whitman," Owen said, keeping his gaze on Hannah, "do you have the chemical signatures from the samples you sent to Toxicology?" His pulse accelerated as adrenaline leaked into his system. This could be the break he'd been waiting for. If Dr. Baker recognized the chemical signatures, then the chemicals had to have come from ChemCure Industries. And if that was the case, he could use her to gain access to the company and the people who worked on that project.

"Yes." He heard her rummage through pages on her desk. "Here you go." She picked up a manila folder and held it out.

Hannah stared at the folder as if afraid it might bite her. Then she extended a hand and took it, holding it in her lap.

"I had the police contact you when I saw the signature for nitrogen mustard compounds," Dr. Whitman explained. "I thought you might be able to give them some background information on the chemicals."

"If this says what I'm afraid it does, I think we're way beyond background information." With a glance in his direction, Hannah sighed heavily and opened the folder.

He held his breath as she examined the printed reports, trying to read her expression for clues. Did she recognize the chemicals? Could she tell him where they had come from?

Her brows drew together as she scanned the papers, and her hand moved to her neck in that unconscious gesture he was beginning to associate with her. She wasn't wearing a turtleneck today, he noted, but rather a collared shirt and gauzy scarf. While this outfit was more weather appropriate, the effect was the same— the skin of her neck was completely covered. Why did she insist on doing that? Was she overly modest, or was she trying to cover up some kind of scar?

Focus, he told himself. Now was not the time to get distracted by irrelevant questions, no matter how intriguing.

When she looked up and met his eyes, he knew. She recognized the compounds. He swallowed hard to keep from shouting in triumph, instead settling for what he hoped was an encouraging expression. "Do you know these chemicals?"

Hannah nodded, her features downcast. "I do," she said, sounding miserable. "They're the same ones I worked with at ChemCure Industries."

"Can they be bought from a company?" *Please say no...* If the chemicals were unique, it would be easier to track down the source.

She shook her head. "No. We modified them for our studies. We were trying to develop a new chemotherapy drug that could be taken by inhaler—it was going to revolutionize the treatment of lung cancer."

Owen felt his eyebrows shoot up. "Like an asthma inhaler?"

"Something like that. The hope was that by delivering the drugs straight to the lungs, the patient would experience fewer side effects."

"But you never made it to human trials?" Dr. Whitman interjected.

"No. Not after the results of the animal studies."

The room fell silent as everyone retreated to their own thoughts. After a moment, Owen cleared his throat. "I need to phone this in to my partner. Dr. Baker, I'll need you to accompany me to ChemCure Industries. Are you free this afternoon?"

"I suppose I am now." She smiled ruefully, but he could see the worry in her eyes.

He nodded. "Thanks. I'll be right back."

Owen pulled his phone from his pocket as he walked down the hall, heading for a small, closet-sized coffee station. He stepped inside, grateful for the added privacy. He didn't think his voice would carry all the way back to Dr. Whitman's office, but he didn't want to take any chances.

His partner answered on the third ring. "Gallagher. What's up?"

"I've got a lead." He tried to keep the excitement from his voice, not wanting to sound too eager. But this was the best break they'd had after weeks of investigating. While he knew it was due to timing rather than his own skills as a detective, a small part of him was proud of being the one to bring this information to the table. Maybe it would even help silence some of his critics.

"What have you got?" Nate's tone was urgent, hopeful even. He'd been waiting for this, too.

"I'm at the ME's office. Dr. Baker is here, as well. She recognized the chemical signatures of the compounds isolated from our victims. Said they're the same as the stuff she used to work with at ChemCure Industries."

"Hot damn," Nate breathed. "That is good news. Can she tell you if the chemicals are from the same batches she worked with herself?"

Owen frowned, wishing he'd thought to ask that. "I'm not sure. I'll ask her. In the meantime, I'm taking her to ChemCure Industries. I'm going to ask a few questions about their nitrogen mustard program, see if I can come up with any more connections between the company and our bodies."

"Need any help?"

The offer was tempting. Having a second set of eyes and ears was never a bad idea, particularly when questioning people. But Owen felt a little protective of this lead, and while he knew Nate wasn't the kind of guy to swoop in and steal credit, he wanted to look into this one himself, at least for the time being.

"Not right now. As far as ChemCure Industries is concerned, I'm just there to ask background questions. Nothing that's going to raise any alarms. Besides, I need you to keep digging for a connection between our victims. Found anything yet?"

"Maybe." There was a rustle of papers before Nate spoke again. "Several of the victims were patients at the free clinic down off Thomas Street. They had appointment cards in their wallets."

Owen closed his eyes, pulling up his mental map of Houston. "That's several miles north of Buffalo Bayou, where they were found." He leaned against the wall and focused on the blinking red light of the coffeemaker. "That means it's even more likely these were dump jobs."

"Yep. The Little Whiteoak Bayou runs right behind the clinic, but according to Doc Whitman, the bodies weren't in the water long enough for them to have floated downstream that far."

"So we have a serial killer who is trying to get the evidence as far away from himself as possible," Owen mused, thinking out loud. "Are you going to check out the clinic today?" Could there be some connection between the clinic and ChemCure Industries? He made a mental note to ask Hannah if the company gave any donations to the free clinics in Houston. Perhaps a bad batch of drugs had gotten through?

"That's my plan."

"Do me a favor, will you? Get the names of all the employees at the clinic, from the doctors all the way down to the guy who takes out the trash. I want to see if there's any connection between ChemCure Industries and the workers there."

"Will do. Anything else?"

"Just keep me posted. I'll do the same."

"Roger that."

Owen ended the call and returned the phone to his pocket, then ran a hand through his hair. This new connection between his case and ChemCure Industries was big, but he couldn't figure out how just yet.

It was like hiking in the dark through a field littered with land mines. He needed to tread carefully, or he would blow the whole thing and his career would tank.

With a sigh, he stepped back into the hall and made his way toward the ME's office, his mind already focused on the questions he wanted to ask. He had to be careful to set the right tone, or the company would throw up so many roadblocks he'd never be able to get close again.

The hum of feminine voices drifted out of the office, and he paused, considering the best way to ensure Hannah Baker cooperated. She'd sounded distinctly unhappy about the need to visit the company this afternoon. Was she worried about her former coworkers' possible involvement in these murders? Or had her departure not been as amicable as she'd indicated yesterday?

"You need to stop touching your neck." Dr. Whitman's voice was firm but kind. "I know you don't always realize you're doing it, but it's making him suspicious."

"Do you think he's noticed?" Hannah sounded faintly alarmed. Owen took a step closer, straining to hear. She had been hiding something after all. But what?

"It's hard not to, the way you're constantly tugging at your shirt."

"I can't help it. I'm just nervous."

"I know," Dr. Whitman said. "But I promise, no one can see anything."

"I suppose you're right." Her admission sounded reluctant, as if she didn't really believe her friend but was simply playing along to avoid an argument.

"Just try to relax," Dr. Whitman suggested. "I know

he's a bit…intense, but he is a good guy." Owen felt the tips of his ears warm at her pronouncement, and he resisted the urge to hang his head and shuffle his feet. Coming from any other person, the observation would have filled him with pride. He was a detective— intensity was part of the package. But the idea that his attitude scared Hannah Baker gave him pause.

"I know," Hannah replied. "He's just a tough person to read. I can't figure out what he's thinking, and it makes me nervous."

"I understand. Just be yourself. You'll get to know him in time, as you two work together. And if you decide to have a little fun while you're at it…"

Was it warm in here? He tugged at the collar of his shirt, suddenly feeling hot.

"Gabby!"

The reproach in Hannah's voice cooled him off somewhat, but he had to admit, he liked the idea of the buttoned-up professor having some fun with him. And as much as he hated to admit it, Nate might be onto something. He'd felt so disconnected from everything and everyone since John's death. Maybe a fling, however brief, was just what he needed to start feeling again. After John's shooting, Owen had welcomed the numbness that exhaustion and grief had brought. Now, in his darker moments, he wondered if that numbness was becoming a permanent part of him, a cancer growing and spreading, destroying him in the process. Would he wake up one day to find he could feel nothing?

"I just hope you don't let the accident keep you from enjoying the rest of your life. You lost so much time to recovering, it would be a shame for you to lose any more to fear."

"I know. But even though he's attractive, it wouldn't be right for me to try to start something while he's working on this case."

A surge of respect flowed through him, and Owen found himself nodding in agreement. Exactly. Good to know they were on the same page. And since both of them had no intention of being anything other than professional, it was time for him to stop eavesdropping.

Even though he was more curious than ever when it came to Hannah Baker.

Moving quietly, he retreated a few steps down the hall, then turned and walked heavily toward the office, making noise so the women would know he was coming. They both looked at him when he stepped into the room. Hannah's cheeks were the light pink of a fading blush, while Dr. Whitman had a knowing look in her eyes. Did she realize he'd been eavesdropping? He gave a mental shrug, dismissing the question. It didn't matter—if she knew, she didn't look inclined to share the information, and if she didn't know, he didn't want to raise her suspicions by acting guilty. Better to act as if everything was normal.

He offered Hannah a small smile. "Nate, my partner, is following up some leads at a medical clinic this afternoon. That means it's just going to be you and me heading over to ChemCure Industries."

"Okay." She nodded and reached for her bag, then stood. "Do you want to go now?"

"That would be great," he said, a little surprised by her apparent change of heart. Just a few minutes ago she'd seemed reluctant to go back to ChemCure Industries, but now she was practically running for the door. Had she gotten over her initial shock at the company's apparent involvement? Or was she just eager to get this over with so she could return to her normal life?

He pushed the thought aside and nodded at Dr. Whitman. "Please call me if you find anything else on the victims."

"Of course." She stood as they moved toward the door, but didn't come out from behind her desk. "Good luck at ChemCure. I'll talk to you later, Hannah?"

"Yeah."

He led her to his car, trying not to read too much into her silence. *Focus on the case.* Nothing else mattered. Later, when he'd solved these murders, he could relax and indulge in an exploration of his attraction for the professor. Maybe he could even talk her into a fun, no-strings-attached celebration. But for now, it was strictly business between them.

She climbed into the front seat of the car, and he caught a whiff of lavender as she moved to fasten her seat belt. He closed his eyes briefly, enjoying the soft scent that was filling the small space of the car. Of course she smelled good. How could she not? With a quiet sigh of resignation, Owen twisted the key in the ignition.

It was going to be a long ride.

Chapter 3

He was quiet as they started out for ChemCure Industries. It was a quality that Hannah appreciated, as she wasn't much of a talker herself. Over the years, she'd learned that most people weren't comfortable with silence, and would chatter on about anything and everything in an attempt to fill the void. Very rarely, she would come across another person who didn't mind the quiet, and she always enjoyed spending time with them. It was exhausting trying to come up with small talk with someone she didn't know very well. Apparently, Detective Randall felt the same way, and her estimation of him went up a notch or two.

What made it even better was the quality of the silence. It wasn't the cold, closed-off sensation that came from being ignored. Nor was it the awkward, prickly feeling she got when there were things to be said but neither person knew how to start. This was the cozy, peaceful silence of familiarity, which was strange, seeing as how they'd just met yesterday.

It was odd, feeling so comfortable around a relative stranger. It usually took Hannah weeks, if not months, to let down her guard after meeting someone new. But there was something about him that made her feel safe and secure, protected even. It was a comforting sensation, and it gave her the courage to consider approaching him when his case was resolved. He didn't seem the type to be put off by a smart woman, and it would be nice to go out on a date again.

Hannah's stomach fluttered, and she cast a sidelong glance at Detective Randall, wondering if he could sense the direction of her thoughts. His expression was relaxed as he navigated Houston's permanent traffic. The intensity she'd first noticed about him was banked but still there, lurking under the surface. This was a man who was passionate about his job, that much was clear. Would he apply that same passion to his relationships?

Doesn't matter, she thought, shivering slightly. *This isn't the time to ask him out.* She ran her hands briskly over her arms, trying to rub away the goose bumps.

"Cold?" His deep voice cut through the silence, making her jump. He reached over with one hand to adjust the knobs on the dash, and the airflow slowed. "I always crank it into the subzero range when I'm in the car. I forget not everyone likes to be frozen out."

"It's okay," she said, offering him a smile. "I'd rather be cold than hot."

"Me, too." He grinned back, dimples winking from his stubbled cheeks. Hannah's breath caught in her throat. *Oh, my.* With a smile like that, he had to have a trail of drooling women following him around.

He returned his focus to the road, and Hannah swallowed hard, determined to ignore the residual zings arcing through her system.

"We should be there soon," he said.

Hannah glanced around at the parking lot that was I-45. "Uh-huh," she said. "Don't you think that's rather optimistic?"

"Maybe a little," he admitted. "Why don't you tell me about ChemCure Industries while we wait."

"What do you want to know?"

"Were you the only one working with nitrogen mustard compounds?"

She shook her head. "No, I was one of a team. There were five of us working on this particular project."

"Only five?" He frowned slightly. "I thought this was a big company—wouldn't the working group have been larger?"

"ChemCure Industries is a large company," she explained. "But there are multiple divisions in the company, and each division worked on different projects. I worked in one of the chemotherapy divisions, and that division was further divided into smaller teams. My team worked on the aerosolized nitrogen mustard project, while other teams worked on drug discovery or other delivery projects."

"I see. Who was the head of your team?"

"Ah. That would be me." He cut her a glance, one eyebrow raised, and she shifted slightly under the scrutiny. "I was the senior scientist on the project."

"What were your responsibilities?"

"I essentially steered the direction of the research.

I designed experiments for the techs to complete, and used the data collected to guide the next steps."

"Did you do any experiments yourself?"

She shrugged. "Some. But not as many as the techs."

"So the techs would have the most access to the compounds?"

Hannah considered the question. "Yes. But they're not the only ones. The division manager, Marcia Foley, would also have access, as would anyone else who walked into the lab."

He jerked his head around to face her, his brows lifted and eyes wide with shock. "Are you telling me that the dangerous chemicals you worked with weren't under some kind of restricted access?"

She frowned back at him, puzzled by his reaction. "There wasn't a need."

"How is that even safe?"

"Well," she began, struggling to find the words to explain lab culture to an outsider. "We didn't advertise what we were working with, so it was unlikely anyone outside the team really knew what chemicals we had in the lab. Besides," she said, stalling his objection, "it's considered very poor form, not to mention dangerous, for someone to walk into your lab and start rooting around."

"And I suppose everyone in the company obeyed this unspoken rule?" His tone made it clear exactly what he thought of *that* arrangement, and she bristled slightly at the underlying accusation.

"I certainly never saw someone enter the lab without an escort."

"I'm sure you didn't," he said, a little more gently. "But you weren't there 24/7. Isn't it possible someone could have gained access to the chemicals without your knowledge?"

The cars in the lane next to them began to move, and the detective merged smoothly into the stream. "I guess it's possible," she admitted, taking a deep breath as they rolled past the rows of vehicles. "But we kept detailed records—who accessed the chemicals, how much they used, for what experiments, that kind of thing. That way, we could always account for where the chemicals went."

"And are you certain those records were well maintained after you left the company?" He let the suggestion hang between them as he drove.

Before the accident, Hannah would have said yes without any hesitation. But it was someone else's mistake, someone else's sloppy science that had nearly gotten her killed. She had trusted her coworkers without reservation, and it had nearly cost her her life.

Her hand moved up reflexively to touch her scars before she remembered Gabby's warning. She dropped the offending limb into her lap and glanced at Detective Randall from the corner of her eye, but he kept his gaze on the road ahead. If he'd noticed her gesture, he gave no indication of it.

"Anything is possible," she said softly.

"Did anyone show a particular interest in your project and the compounds you worked with?"

She scrunched her brows together as she considered his question. "Not that I recall. Sorry," she added, almost as an afterthought.

"Why are you apologizing to me?" A faint smile touched the corner of his mouth, and an answering warmth kindled to life in her chest.

"I feel bad that I'm not more help to you," she explained.

He let out a quick huff of a laugh. "Believe me, you've been a great help. More than what I'm used to getting. I really appreciate you coming with me today."

She felt her face warm, and hoped she wasn't blushing too darkly. She fought the urge to squirm in her seat with embarrassed pleasure, and instead turned her head to focus on the scenery zipping by her window. "I'm happy to assist in any way I can," she said.

After clearing the initial snarl of traffic, it didn't take long to arrive at ChemCure Industries's gates. Hannah's stomach twisted when they pulled into the visitors' lane and Detective Randall rolled down his window. She hadn't been here since the accident, and the once-familiar beige buildings now seemed forbidding and cold.

A security guard walked over to the car. "Can I help you?"

Detective Randall removed his badge and showed it to the officer. "We're here to see Marcia Foley."

The guard frowned. "Do you have an appointment?"

Detective Randall shook his head. "I'm afraid not."

"Wait here, please. I'll see if she's available." The guard walked back to his post and picked up a phone.

"She won't see us, Detective," Hannah said. "Marcia Foley is the living, breathing definition of control freak. She has to be in charge, and she won't want to meet with you unless she can plan it well in advance."

He turned to look at her fully. "That's quite a character analysis," he said drily.

Hannah shrugged. "I worked with the woman for five years. You learn a lot about a person in that time."

"True enough," he murmured. He was quiet for a beat, then shrugged, as if he was shaking himself free of memories. "I appreciate the heads-up. And since we'll be working together for the foreseeable future, why don't you just call me Owen and I'll call you Hannah." He flashed another one of those heart-stopping grins, and she found herself nodding dumbly in response.

Get it together, she chided herself. *One smile, and you turn into a bobblehead doll!*

The security guard walked over and leaned down to address them. "I'm sorry, but Ms. Foley is gone for the day. You'll have to make an appointment and come back another time."

Owen turned and shot her a questioning look. *Does she leave early?*

Hannah shook her head.

Owen turned back to the guard. "That's fine," he said. He leaned over and pulled out a small notepad and pen from the center console. "In the meantime, I'm going to need your name and address."

The guard frowned at him. "Why?"

Owen didn't bother to look up, but instead kept his gaze on the small book as he flipped through to find a clean page. "I'm going to issue you a citation for interfering in my investigation."

"But…" the guard sputtered. "You can't be serious!"

Owen did look up then, his pen poised above the page. "Try me."

"But I haven't done anything!"

"You're preventing me from doing my job, and I have a real problem with that." Owen cocked his head to the side, studying the man. "Tell me something. Is protecting her worth your job? Because I don't think the company will look too kindly on this infraction. The State of Texas and the City of Houston tend to come down pretty hard on people who interfere in a murder investigation."

The guard went pale under his tan. "Murder?" he whispered.

"That's what I said. Now, your name?"

The man took a step back. "Uh, listen. I was just trying to do my job, you understand? I call, they tell me who can come in."

"Sure."

"But since you're a cop and all, I should probably follow your instructions."

The corner of Owen's mouth twitched, but he kept his smile hidden. "That seems like a good idea to me."

Hannah watched this exchange with a growing sense of amusement and admiration. Owen could have gotten bent out of shape and angry at the guard's initial refusal to let them pass, but instead of trying to bully the man into cooperating, he'd used calm reason and a touch of intimidation. It was a potent combination, as evidenced by the guard's babbled apology-cum-explanation as he lifted the gate and waved them through.

Hannah waited until they'd cleared the checkpoint before turning to look at Owen. "Were you really going to arrest him?"

"No," he replied, pulling smoothly into a parking space. "But what he doesn't know won't hurt him." Then he winked at her, triggering an electric wave of awareness through her system.

Hannah shook her head as she climbed out of the

car. Not only did the detective have a sexy grin, but he winked at people, too? It just wasn't fair.

The more she saw of his personality, the more she felt drawn to him. It was going to be hard for her to keep her attraction to him under wraps until his case was closed.

But it was for the best.

It was obvious she didn't want to be here. With her arms wrapped tightly around her waist and the thin lines of strain fanning from the corners of her mouth, she looked absolutely miserable. It was clear that no matter what she'd told him about amicable partings, Hannah was haunted by something at ChemCure Industries.

But what? And did it possibly tie in to his investigation?

If she'd discovered something amiss, it was entirely possible the company had acted quickly to silence her. They may have offered her money to buy her off, tried to legally tie her hands so she couldn't report her suspicions to the authorities.

He glanced at her while they walked down the hall. *No,* he thought, dismissing that notion. Whatever else she may be, Hannah Baker was not the type of person to stand by when a wrong was being done. She hadn't hesitated to jump in and offer assistance when she discovered the topic of his investigation. That wasn't the action of a woman who was legally bound to remain silent. Besides, if the company was doing something wrong, they couldn't force her to keep quiet. No court would uphold a company-issued gag order where illegal or immoral activities were concerned.

Why, then, did she look as if she'd seen a ghost?

She slowed, and he adjusted his pace accordingly. "Do you mind if I just duck in here?" She pointed to the restroom door. "It took a little longer than I thought to get here."

"No problem," he replied. "Take your time."

She emerged a few minutes later, a bit more color on her cheeks. She'd applied lipstick, too, he noticed. Her mouth had a faint pink sheen to it, as though she'd just eaten ripe berries. A wave of lust slammed into him and he rocked forward, wanting to find out if her lips tasted as good as they looked.

Her eyes widened when she met his gaze, but there was no fear in her expression. Encouraged, he leaned closer, gratified to hear the soft hiss of her indrawn breath. *She feels it, too.*

This close, he could see her pulse beating, faster and faster under the delicate skin of her neck. He licked his lips, wanting to put the tip of his tongue just *there*, to feel the thrum of her excitement as he tasted the salty tang of her skin. His own heart rate kicked up a notch in response, and he sucked in a deep breath, trying to rein in his body's automatic response to being close to such a beautiful woman.

Not here.

Owen jerked back, shaking his head to clear the fog of arousal that had threatened to obscure his better judgment. Hannah watched him, her hazel eyes a swirl of blue and green and yellow. He could get lost in those eyes, if he let himself.

"Sorry about that," he muttered, reaching up to run a hand through his hair. The short strands tickled his palm, chasing away the last of his lust and redirecting his focus to the job.

She offered him a shy smile. "Don't worry about it." There was a wistful note to her voice, as if she was disappointed that the moment had passed.

Not knowing what to say, Owen held up his arm. "Shall we?"

She nodded, but before they could take a step, a loud voice rang out.

"Hannah Baker, is that you?"

Hannah froze in place, and he could tell by the way her shoulders tensed that whoever this new woman was, she wasn't happy to see her.

"Oh my gosh, it is you! How have you been? It's been ages since I've seen you!" The newcomer, a plump woman who appeared to be in her forties, approached and threw her arms around Hannah, then drew back, beaming. "You know, I was just thinking about you the other day. Tim and I were wondering what happened to you after the accident, hoping you were okay. You are okay, aren't you? I mean, it was just horrible, that fire—"

"I'm fine, thanks," Hannah cut in. She aimed a pained smile at the woman and indicated Owen. "Let me introduce you to my friend. Shelly Newman, meet Owen Randall. Owen, this is Shelly. She's a former coworker."

"Nice to meet you," Owen said, offering his hand. He was grateful Hannah had introduced him as a friend and not a detective. Shelly appeared to be a bit of a gossip, and if she knew the real reason he was here, it would be all over the building before they'd even made it to Marcia's office.

Shelly gave him a quick once-over before turning her focus back to Hannah. She pushed a wayward curl out of her brown eyes and reached up to pat Hannah's shoulder. "It just hasn't been the same around here since your accident. We all miss you so much. Did you come to see the new lab? They totally renovated it after the explosion—brand-new everything. You can't even tell!" She sounded so proud, like a mom bragging about her kid's latest accomplishment.

Owen felt his brows raise and fought to keep his expression neutral. Had Hannah been involved in some kind of explosion? It sounded like it, if Shelly's ramblings were to be believed. The woman prattled on, oblivious to Hannah's strained expression and Owen's presence. He listened closely, absorbing all the news and piecing it together to make a complete picture.

Apparently, Hannah's lab had been ruined due to a lab accident a few years ago—"Just terrible! You should have seen the aftermath—glass everywhere. I thought they were never going to find all the little pieces." Evidently, Hannah had been injured, although Shelly didn't seem to know how severe her injuries were. She kept asking Hannah leading questions, clearly hoping Hannah would fill in the blanks for her and give her a juicy story to share. But Hannah didn't cooperate, instead replying with monosyllabic replies and nodding. Undeterred, Shelly pressed on.

Owen narrowed his eyes when Hannah reached up to fiddle with her shirt. She tugged at the collar, pulling it up to cover more of her neck. *Her injuries*, he realized. *She must have scars.* Shelly had mentioned a fire—had Hannah been burned?

He mentally winced at the thought. He'd seen a few burn victims in his time on the job. Nasty stuff, and painful as hell, from what he'd heard. His heart clenched at the thought of Hannah suffering like that.

Had she left the company because of the accident? She wouldn't be the first person to shy away from returning to work after an injury. If the accident had been severe—and from what Shelly was saying, it had been—it made sense that Hannah wouldn't want to keep working in a lab. A pay cut like the one she'd taken was nothing compared to peace of mind.

"I'm on my way out the door. I have to pick up Jeffrey for soccer practice, but it was so good to see you!" Shelly went in for another hug, and Hannah shot him a "save me" look over her shoulder. Owen hid a smile, although the other woman continued to ignore him. "You should give me a call sometime. We need to grab lunch and catch up! I know Tim would love to see you, too."

Hannah smiled, but Owen noticed it didn't reach her eyes. "Sounds great. You take care."

Owen waited until Shelly was out of earshot before turning back to Hannah. "Having fun yet?"

Hannah huffed out a laugh. "Loads." She was quiet for a moment while they walked, then said very softly, "That's exactly why I didn't want to come here."

He cast about for something to say that would make her feel better but came up empty. "She seemed nice enough," he said lamely.

She shook her head. "Shelly's harmless. I just didn't want to stir things up again."

"I'm sorry," he replied. It was the truth. From what he could gather, she'd already been through a lot, and he didn't like forcing her to relive some of the worst moments of her life. But he had a case to solve, and all clues pointed in this direction. Hannah was his best shot at cutting through the red tape, and he had to take advantage of that.

Even if it did make him feel about two inches tall.

She shrugged off his apology. "Not your fault. Let's do this." Drawing up her shoulders like a woman preparing to do battle, she led him down a white corridor. Small windows high on the walls allowed glimpses of laboratory space behind closed doors, but he couldn't see enough to form a complete picture. Many of the rooms were dark, their occupants having gone home for the weekend.

At the end of the hall sat a large glass enclosure. Hannah led them inside, and they approached an older woman sitting behind a desk. She glanced up but didn't stop typing, the *click* of her keys the only sound in the otherwise silent room.

"What do you need?"

"We're here to see Marcia Foley," Hannah said.

The secretary returned her focus to her computer monitor. "She's not available right now."

Owen stepped forward, pulling out his badge. "Sure she is."

The woman's hands paused, the only indication of her surprise. She reached for the phone. "Let me tell her you're here."

"Don't worry," Owen said, walking past her desk. He grabbed Hannah's hand as he went, enjoying the feel of her soft skin against his palm. "We'll show ourselves in."

Chapter 4

Hannah blinked, too stunned to do anything but trail along in Owen's wake. How long had it been since a man had held her hand? It felt good, too good, having that warmth surround her. It was something she could get used to, and fast.

He'd been so casual about it, reaching out and grabbing her with strong, gentle fingers. Even now, his hand was wrapped protectively around hers, his grip solid and sure. It felt natural to be touching him like this, and the realization made her stomach do a little flip.

Marcia's office hadn't changed in the three years since Hannah had left the company. A huge glass-and-brushed-chrome desk dominated the space, centered in front of an abstract painting done in swirls of gray and white. Two skeletal metal chairs sat in front of the desk, looking cold and unfriendly. It was clear their presence was a mere formality, and that the owner of the office did not encourage her visitors to stay long. Overall, the ultramodern furniture and white carpet gave the room a cold, sterile feel. Hannah had always thought it was an accurate reflection of Marcia's personality: aloof and icy.

The woman herself sat at her desk, which was clear of anything but her silver computer. Her back was ramrod straight, her ankles crossed on the floor and tucked under her chair. She was the very picture of a cool and composed executive.

"Detective," she said, not bothering to look up. "This is highly unorthodox."

"I just have a few questions for you," Owen replied, dropping Hannah's hand and crossing his arms. He presented an imposing figure, and Hannah was glad she wasn't on the receiving end of his stare. Once had been quite enough.

"Questions that couldn't wait for an appointment? My time is valuable."

"As is mine. So let's get started."

Marcia lifted her head then, the strands of her platinum-blond bob swaying gently with the motion. "Please, have a seat." She gestured to the metal chairs with a polite smile. Then her ice-blue gaze cut to Hannah. "Dr. Baker, what a nice surprise. I see you've recovered from your injuries."

Hannah nodded, not trusting her voice. Bad enough they had run into Shelly—the last thing she wanted was for Marcia to fill in the details about her injuries.

Marcia returned her focus to Owen. "What is it you think I can do for you?"

He pulled a notebook from his back pocket before

settling into one of the chairs. Hannah took the other, and immediately wished she hadn't. The cold metal bit into her legs and back, but no matter how she moved, she couldn't find a comfortable position. She glanced at Owen, who sat perfectly still. Either he didn't have the same problem, or he was too stubborn to show any kind of discomfort in front of Marcia. Given what she knew about him so far, she figured it was the latter.

"I'm investigating a series of suspicious deaths that have occurred over the last several weeks," he began.

Marcia quickly cut him off. "Then I'm sure I can't help you." She softened her words with a smile, but it didn't reach her eyes. "I can assure you, I have nothing to do with people dying."

Owen flashed her a quick smile of his own, and Hannah felt a spike of jealousy. He hadn't smiled at *her* like that when he'd come to her office asking questions. Why was the Ice Princess getting such special treatment?

It seemed Hannah was not the only one who appreciated the gesture. Marcia's shoulders relaxed slightly, and her eyes took on a warmer glow. She leaned forward, the movement smooth and graceful.

If Owen noticed the effect he had on her, he didn't show it. "I'm confident you're not involved," he said. His voice was deep and smooth, almost like a caress. Even though he wasn't talking to her, Hannah felt goose bumps rise on her arms. "I just want to talk to you about the chemicals your company works with, as the evidence shows a related compound was found in the bodies of the victims."

Marcia swallowed. "I see." She wet her lips with the tip of her tongue. On anyone else, the gesture would have seemed like a reflex. But Hannah thought it was a bit too calculated to be real. Unless she missed her guess, Marcia was playing the part of a seductress. She was being subtle about it, but the vibe was definitely there. Was she trying to deflect suspicion? Or had she simply realized Owen was an attractive man and she wanted to get closer to him?

Marcia lifted her hand and ran a finger under the edge of her collar, down to where the buttons of her suit jacket closed across her breasts. Then she stood and rounded her desk, coming to a stop in front of Owen. She leaned back, crossed her legs and placed her hands on the desk. The position showed off her slim figure and thrust her breasts forward for display. Hannah resisted the temptation to roll her eyes. Could the woman be any more obvious?

She glanced over at Owen, expecting to see a flat, bored look on his face. Instead, he cocked one eyebrow, and his mouth curved up in a sexy grin of pure male satisfaction.

Hannah's stomach dropped. Was he really falling for this act? Surely he was smarter than that!

She studied him as he continued to question Marcia. He appeared to be relaxed and enjoying the show the other woman was putting on, but Hannah caught the way he kept tapping his pen against the side of his leg. It was a small gesture, but it made Hannah think he wasn't as affected as Marcia would like him to be.

"I can assure you we have stringent tracking measures in place to document the uses of all our chemicals," Marcia said, practically cooing. "I'd be happy to show you around if you like, or if you'd rather, we could discuss this further over dinner?"

Owen smiled up at her. "Your offer is very tempting, but I'm afraid I'll have to take a rain check."

The corners of Marcia's mouth turned down in disappointment. "Very well." She sighed, then reached into her suit pocket and withdrew a business card. She took the pen from Owen's hand and scribbled on it, then leaned forward and tucked it into the pocket of Owen's shirt, her fingers lingering against his chest. "All of my contact information is there, including my personal number. I hope you'll use it."

Owen reached for his pen, his fingers sliding across Marcia's in a gentle caress that made Hannah frown. "You should expect to hear from me soon." He stood, but Marcia didn't move to give him room, so they wound up only inches apart. "Thank you for your time," Owen said, smiling down at her.

Marcia nodded. "Of course," she murmured. Then she rose to her tiptoes and pressed a kiss to Owen's cheek. "Call me anytime, day or night." Hannah heard the slight emphasis on the word *night* and clenched her jaw. How tacky could the woman get?

Before Owen could reply to the invitation, Hannah jumped up from her chair. "Good to see you again, Marcia," she said, faking a cheer she didn't feel. "You take care now." Not bothering to wait for a response, Hannah marched over to the door and flung it open. The secretary let out a startled squeak, but Hannah didn't stop to apologize. She strode down the hall, her shoes clicking out a fast rhythm on the tile floor.

She heard Owen start after her, but she didn't slow down. She needed to get as far away from Marcia as possible—she'd had enough of the woman's cloying presence. Seeing her again had reminded Hannah of all the things she'd hated about working with Marcia to begin with. The woman was a ruthless, coldhearted snake who manipulated people and situations to her advantage without compunction. Hannah had seen her befriend people, only to betray them later when it suited Marcia's needs. She was a toxic person, one Hannah hadn't been sorry to leave after her accident.

It didn't take long for Owen to catch her, not with those long legs eating up the distance between them. His hand was warm on her arm, pulling her gently until she stopped and turned toward him. His expression of concern was so earnest and sincere it made her heart clench, and she had the sudden desire to press herself against him, to feel him hold her so she could put ChemCure and Marcia and her accident out of her mind. Being back here had stirred up emotions she'd buried long ago, and it was difficult for her to pretend everything was fine when she wanted nothing more than to run away.

"Are you okay?"

She nodded, swallowing hard before trying to speak. "I'm good. I just needed some fresh air."

His brows relaxed, but his eyes remained watchful. "Does it upset you to be back here again? If I'd known about your accident..." He trailed off, but the apology was clear.

Hannah smiled faintly, acknowledging his point. "It's okay. It's just a little hard. Being here brings back some memories I'd rather not revisit."

Owen nodded and didn't press for more details. "Let's get going, then."

She waited until they were back in the car before asking, "Did Marcia tell you anything useful?" Hopefully this hadn't been a wasted trip. She really didn't want to come back.

Owen huffed out a laugh. "Oh, yeah. She's a real piece of work."

Hannah turned to look at him, feeling her stomach sink. Did he need to question her again? "What?"

"Let me ask you something—does she normally lay it on that thick? Or am I just special?"

"Um. You're just special, I guess."

"Turns out my mom was right, then." He winked at her before returning his focus to the road, and Hannah realized what his interactions with Marcia had been missing: warmth.

He hadn't been rude to Marcia, but there was definitely more depth to his tone now that it was just the two of them. Hannah couldn't help but feel special, as though she was seeing a side of him not everyone knew was there.

After all, yesterday *she* hadn't even known he was capable of teasing.

"Did this help your case?" She needed to keep talking, needed to distract herself from the bad memories dredged up by this visit. After all, the last time she'd been here, she'd left in an ambulance.

Her hand drifted up to her neck, and her fingertips brushed along the smooth, raised scar tissue under her collar. Still there. Sometimes she forgot about the accident and her painful injuries, and she felt normal again. The sensation never lasted long, and it always hurt when reality came crashing down on her. After being back at ChemCure Industries and seeing Shelly and Marcia, Hannah knew it would be a long time before the memories of that time receded.

"Marcia didn't say much, but it was the things she didn't say that make me think she's hiding something."

"Oh?" Hannah didn't know whether to be disturbed by the possibility her former boss was involved in these deaths or happy that Owen had discovered a clue that might help him solve his case. It was a little far-fetched, though. Marcia was definitely not the type to get her hands dirty, although she had no problem delegating to others. Who, though, would help her kill people? And more important, why?

"Did you notice how she went right to seduction?" Owen asked, keeping his eyes on the road. "I barely got my first question out before she started flirting with me."

"So it was obvious to you, too?"

Owen gave her an arch glance. "Please. I know what I look like. I'm no Quasimodo, but I'm a pretty average looking guy. Women typically don't fall all over themselves when I open my mouth, and in my experience, the ones that do are hiding something."

Hannah made a noncommittal noise, but a part of her brightened at the implication that the detective didn't date much. Something they had in common, apparently.

"What do you think she's trying to hide?"

He shrugged. "I'm not sure. But based on the way she tried to deflect all my questions, I'm guessing the chemicals found in the bodies are somehow connected to ChemCure Industries. And I think she knows about it."

"How did you get all that from a kiss on the cheek and an invitation to dinner?"

Owen's tone was thoughtful, and Hannah got the

impression he was thinking out loud. "Because if she hadn't known about the chemicals, she would have gone straight to denial not distraction. She would have called in the company lawyers and had me thrown out on my ass. But she didn't. She wanted me to think she's cooperating, but what she's really doing is finding out what I know and what I suspect. Those aren't the actions of someone who is blameless."

"Wow." Hannah felt as if the breath had been knocked out of her. As much as she hated to admit it, Owen's logic made a sick kind of sense. And while Hannah had never liked Marcia, she would never in a million years have dreamed the other woman was capable of murder. "I can't believe it," she said quietly.

"It's still a theory," Owen cautioned. "But the more I think about it, the more I'm convinced that woman is hiding something."

"Do you think it's just her? Or is the company itself dirty?" Who else knew? Shelly? Tim? Nausea curdled in her stomach at the thought that the people she'd once considered friends were somehow involved. They had seemed so nice, so trustworthy. But what if they weren't? What if that was just the face they presented to the world?

What other parts of her life were not what they seemed?

Owen's words broke into her reverie. "I'm not sure, but I think if it were a widespread thing, she would have run to the company for cover. She didn't, so it might just be her."

Hannah nodded, not knowing what to say. The car picked up speed as it rolled along the freeway. This late in the day, traffic had died down and they moved easily, orbiting the city like a tiny planet. She was glad of it, because it meant they'd get back to her car soon. She needed to spend some time alone tonight to re-group and process the day's events. Nothing like hear-ing your former boss and coworkers were potentially involved in a string of murders to make a girl reevalu-ate her life choices.

"Are you okay?" His voice was soft and comforting, like a cozy blanket. She wanted to wrap herself in the sound and tune out the world.

"I just need some time to think," she replied.

Owen was silent for a moment. Then he took a deep breath, as if preparing himself to say something impor-tant. "I know this has been a difficult day for you. And I just want you to know, I appreciate you coming with me. I'm sorry if it stirred up bad memories for you."

Sudden tears prickled Hannah's eyes, and she blinked, turning away to look out the window so Owen didn't see. "I'm fine," she said, waving off his concern. "Nothing a hot bath and a glass of wine won't fix."

He swallowed hard, and his knuckles whitened as he tightened his grip on the steering wheel. Had she said something wrong? Maybe he was just stressed and worried about the case. After all, now that he had a potential lead, he had to decide what to do next. She didn't envy his job—it seemed like a giant ball of knots that he had to untangle, one by one.

Owen was quiet for the rest of the drive, and Han-nah let him think. While she was curious to know what he planned to do next, it was better if she stayed out of it. She'd done her part today by taking him to Chem-Cure Industries and introducing him to Marcia. The rest was up to him.

"Say, would you like to grab a bite to eat?"

Hannah blinked, taken aback by his question. She'd assumed he was lost in thought, focused on his case, but apparently he hadn't forgotten she was there after all.

Dinner sounded appealing. It had been too long since she'd eaten a meal with an attractive man. Even if he'd only made the offer to be polite, it would be a nice way to end the evening.

And it would give her a chance to get to know him better. He was intriguing, to say the least, and before she went out on a limb and asked him out, it would be good to know if they were compatible.

She opened her mouth to reply, but her stomach interrupted, growling loudly in the otherwise quiet car. He grinned, and she felt her face heat.

"Should I take that as a yes?"

"What did you have in mind?"

"There's a little Mexican place a few blocks away. They make a corn enchilada that will change your life."

Hannah couldn't help but smile at that description. "Well, when you put it like that, how can I refuse?"

"Great!" He sounded genuinely pleased, and a warm glow spread through Hannah's chest at the thought of spending more time with him. Apparently, he felt the same way, which likely meant he was attracted to her, too. Maybe she wasn't as rusty at the whole dating thing as she'd thought? She fought to hide a smile. Gabby would be proud of her.

He pulled up to a small, plain white house wedged between two office buildings and scored the last parking space in the tiny lot. The smell of tortillas and spices hit her as she climbed from the car, and she inhaled appreciatively.

Owen caught her reaction and smiled. "Just wait," he told her. "It's even better inside." He stretched his arms above his head and arched his back, sighing in pleasure. The movement pulled his shirt up, and Hannah caught a tantalizing glimpse of his stomach and the line of dark hair that disappeared into the waistband of his pants.

Her earlier guess had been correct—he appeared to be toned in all the right places.

He turned to face her, and she jerked her eyes up to meet his. Hopefully he hadn't caught her ogling him!

"After you," he said, waving her forward. She moved automatically, her brain still preoccupied as she pictured that teasing hint of his body. What would he look like without the shirt? Probably magnificent, she thought, if the preview was any indication.

She mentally shook herself, steering her thoughts onto safer ground. Yes, he was handsome, and yes, he had a nice body. But she was a grown woman, not a giggling teenager, and she needed to control herself so she didn't end up looking like a shallow idiot at dinner.

Besides, she had all night to relive the moment. Alone, in the privacy of her apartment.

The place was busy, but they were seated quickly at a small table in the back. A cluster of votive candles bathed the tiled tabletop in a warm glow, and the circle of soft light gave the illusion that they were alone in their own private space. The overall effect was rather romantic, and a small part of Hannah wondered if Owen had considered that when making his choice.

No, her practical side chimed in. *He's here for the food, not the ambience.*

Still, she couldn't help but notice how well the candlelight suited him, giving his skin a golden glow that made him look lit from within. It softened the rougher edges of his jaw and cheekbones, and he appeared relaxed. Approachable, even. A far cry from the quiet, imposing man who had visited her office yesterday.

A waiter brought glasses of water, a bowl of chips and two bowls of salsa. She smiled her thanks and was pleased to notice Owen did the same. She'd done some waitressing in high school, and to this day she was still amazed at how badly some people treated those who served food. Seeing Owen's polite gesture was just one more confirmation that he was a nice guy.

But Jake had seemed nice at first, too.

The thought of her ex drew her up short, and she frowned. Jake had no place in her life, and she wasn't going to let him ruin her chances at a nice dinner.

"Does anything look good?"

Pushing thoughts of Jake firmly out of her mind, Hannah glanced over the top of her menu to find Owen watching her.

"Your ringing endorsement of the corn enchiladas was pretty convincing," she said, quickly reading the description. "I think I have to give them a try."

Owen glanced up at the waiter. "Make that two orders, please."

The waiter nodded, collected their menus and left. Owen leaned forward and grabbed a chip, breaking it into two pieces before dipping into the salsa.

"So tell me about yourself," he said, popping the

chip into his mouth. "Where are you from? How'd you get into chemistry?"

Hannah reached for her water and took a sip. "I'm from Fort Worth, but I moved here for college and came back after graduate school. My parents still live in Fort Worth, and I try to visit them a few times a year."

He nodded. "And the chemistry?"

She smiled. "Is it really that strange of a career choice?"

Owen tilted his head, considering her question. "Not strange, no. But I've never met a chemist before. Makes me wonder how one goes about becoming one."

She reached for a chip, dipped into the salsa and took a cautious bite. It was fresh and tangy with just the right hint of spice, and she went back for another.

"I got a chemistry set at a rather formative age," she explained between bites. "Plus, I watched a lot of Sesame Street, and my favorite character was Beaker."

He was quiet a moment, then his face brightened. "The little guy with red hair who always got hurt?"

She nodded. "That's the one."

He laughed, a rich, pleasant sound. "I remember him. Poor little guy."

"He turned out okay in the end."

"I suppose." He reached for a chip of his own. "Well, with a childhood like that, I guess you had to be a chemist."

Hannah shrugged. "Pretty much. Now it's your turn. Why a cop?"

He chewed for a moment before responding. "My uncle," he said finally. "He was a cop, and I thought that was the coolest thing in the world. I was always so fascinated by his utility belt—all the tools and stuff attached. It was a powerful image that stuck with me."

She reached for a chip at the same time he did, and their hands accidentally brushed. It was nothing—a mere whisper of skin against skin—but the contact arced through her arm like lightning. She could have sworn she saw his eyes darken with heat, but it was probably just a trick of the candlelight.

"What did your parents think when you told them you wanted to become a police officer?" She had to keep him talking. It gave her something to focus on besides the butterflies in her stomach and the residual sparks tingling up her arm.

He shrugged, the movement drawing her attention to his broad shoulders. They looked even bigger now with the edges extending beyond the candlelight's glow.

"My dad was fine with it. He knew it was something I'd always wanted to do, and I think he expected it. My mom was a tougher sell."

"Did she think it was too dangerous?"

He nodded. "Exactly. She was convinced I was going to get killed on my first day. I think she still worries, but she's gotten better about keeping quiet."

The waiter returned, sliding two steaming plates on the table. He refilled the water glasses and then disappeared again.

Hannah inhaled appreciatively, the warm, tangy scent filling her nostrils and making her mouth water. "This looks amazing."

"Tastes even better," Owen replied. He waited while she cut a bite and kept his eyes on her face as she brought the fork to her mouth.

As soon as the food hit her tongue, she realized

he hadn't exaggerated. The enchilada was the perfect combination of sweet and spicy, and it tasted divine.

"Oh, my God," she breathed, closing her eyes to savor the flavor. When she opened them again, she found Owen watching her, a pleased smile on his face.

His expression made her catch her breath, and she had to remind herself to swallow. He seemed genuinely happy that she liked the food, and he still hadn't taken a bite of his own dinner. It was almost as if he wanted to see to her pleasure before taking care of himself.

The ramifications of *that* thought hit her hard, and she felt her face heat. "Aren't you going to eat?"

He nodded, the smile still in place. "Yep. Just wanted to make sure you like it first."

"I do," she said. "You were right—it's amazing."

They ate in silence for a moment, then Owen spoke again. "I bet your family was proud when you got the job at ChemCure."

Hannah nodded, a little surprised by his statement. It had been a steady job, sure, but it wasn't like she had put her life on the line every day to keep people safe.

"They were happy, yes. I think they were relieved that all the time I had spent in school had paid off."

"I bet."

He waited until she took another bite, then said, "And after the accident? Did they come help you out?"

Hannah chewed mechanically, the food turning to a lump in her mouth. The last thing she wanted to talk about was the accident. It had been hard enough going back to ChemCure, seeing Sandy and Marcia again. She had hoped this dinner was an indication that Owen was interested in her, but it seemed he was more interested in her connection to the chemicals found in his victims.

She swallowed, pushing her disappointment down. What did she expect? He was working a case that had few leads—of course he was going to want to question her about anything she might know.

"My parents came down for a bit to help me during my recovery," she said neutrally. "But I'd really rather not talk about it."

"I'm sorry," he replied. "I know this afternoon must have been hard on you. I didn't mean to make it worse."

"It's okay." She smiled, searching for something else to say. "So how long have you and Nate been partners? He seems nice."

It was Owen's turn to pause. "He's a good guy. We've only been working together for six months, but so far, I have no complaints."

"Did you have another partner before him?"

Owen winced like he was in pain, but covered it by clearing his throat. "Uh, yeah. I did."

"But something happened?" she asked quietly. It wasn't really a question—it was clear from his reaction that the thought of his old partner bothered him.

"Yeah." He looked down at his plate for a moment, aimlessly stirring his fork. Then he scooped up another bite and held it up in a salute. "So, best enchiladas you've ever had, or what?"

She heard the forced cheer in his voice, but accepted the change in topic. It seemed he had his own secrets to keep, and she could respect that.

"Most definitely." She took her own bite, and they chewed in silence for a moment. Even though he wasn't talking, she could tell by the set of his shoulders that

Owen's demeanor had changed. The mention of his old partner had cast a shadow over him, and she wanted to bring back his earlier ease.

Without stopping to think, she reached out and laid her hand over his. His eyes widened briefly and he stared at her hand over his, like he couldn't believe what he was seeing.

Feeling self-conscious, Hannah started to pull away. But before she could move, he lifted his hand up and threaded his fingers through hers, linking them together and keeping her in place.

Her heartbeat picked up speed when he slid his thumb over her fingers in a gentle caress. He continued to study their hands for a moment, and she felt her eyes pulled to the sight, as well. It felt so natural, so right, to be touching him like this. Their hands fit together perfectly, as if they were designed to make this connection. His skin was warm, and she enjoyed the slide of their fingers as they explored each other's touch.

After a few seconds, she looked up to find him watching her, a look of wonder on his face. There was a vulnerability in his eyes she'd never seen before, and she squeezed his hand, wanting him to know she was here.

He opened his mouth, but before he could speak the waiter returned, gathering their plates and clearing the table. They separated to give the man more room, and she immediately missed his touch.

"Will that be all?" the waiter asked. Owen nodded and shifted in his seat, reaching for his wallet. Hannah grabbed her bag as well, but before she could fish out her own wallet, Owen had handed the man a card.

"I didn't mean for you to pay for me," she said.

He waved away her objection. "It's my pleasure. It was the least I could do—you saved me from another frozen TV dinner."

"Well, thank you," she said. "I do appreciate it."

He signed the bill and looked up. "Ready?"

Was she? The meal was obviously over, but part of her wished they could stay at the table longer, to linger in the candlelight and hold hands again. It was silly, she knew, but it had been so nice to feel connected to a man again. She usually didn't feel lonely, but sharing that moment with Owen made her realize how much she really missed touching someone.

"Let's go," she said, reaching for her bag as she stood. The moment between them was gone, and no amount of wishing would bring it back. Better to move forward.

They were quiet as he drove her back to Gabby's office.

He pulled up next to her car and turned to face her. "Thanks again for your help today."

She smiled. "No problem."

"Let me give you my card. In case you think of anything else." He lifted the armrest between them and pulled out a card and a pen. In an echo of Marcia's earlier action, he wrote a number on the back. "My cell phone," he said, offering it to her with a mildly sheepish smile. "It's the easiest way to get in touch with me."

"Thanks." Hannah took it, careful to avoid touching his fingers. She didn't need a reminder of how nice it felt, and if she made contact now, she might never get out of the car.

"I may need to get in touch with you again," he said,

stalling her exit. "Just in case I have some additional questions," he continued.

"In that case, let me give you my personal number, as well. I'll be out of the office all next week for spring break." She dug through her purse, searching for a scrap of paper. Nothing but grocery receipts and gum wrappers—not the kind of thing she wanted to leave him with.

He let her struggle for a moment, then passed her his notepad and pen. She accepted with a smile, trying to ignore the fact that they were still warm from being pressed close to his body. *They probably smell like him, too,* she thought wryly.

She scribbled down her number quickly and passed it to him. She had to get out of the car, now, before she did something ridiculous like sniff his pen.

"Good luck with everything," she said, climbing out of the car and into the furnace that was a Houston evening. The muggy heat helped clear her head, and she breathed deeply, pulling in the heavy air with a sense of relief.

"Take care," Owen replied. He waited while she climbed into her own vehicle and started the engine. Only after she flipped on the lights and gave him a wave did he drive off. It was difficult to tell in the low light, but Hannah thought she saw him watching her in the rearview mirror as he pulled away.

The situation was rapidly spinning out of control.

Marcia pushed back from her desk and rubbed her eyes, too tired to care if she smeared her mascara. Besides, there was no one around to see it—everyone had left hours ago.

The detective's visit had rattled her. On some level, she'd known the police would eventually show up, asking questions about the chemicals used at ChemCure Industries. But she hadn't expected them to make the connection so soon. Her partners had assured her the evidence had been obscured, describing their actions in nightmare-inducing detail. They'd told her it would take weeks, if not longer, for the police to realize they weren't dealing with another garden-variety serial killer.

At least, that was how it was supposed to work.

She reached into her bag and withdrew a large bottle of antacids, shaking out several tablets. Lately, she'd been taking so many of the things that the chalky taste didn't even register anymore. It took several swallows to get the powder down, and then she leaned back in her chair and rested her hands on her roiling belly. Think, she had to think.

Her part in this operation was simple on paper. She supplied the chemicals, and she didn't ask questions. While she was curious to know what they were doing with the compounds, her innate self-preservation prevented her from asking for details. That didn't stop her partners from offering them, though. Sometimes she thought they wanted to make sure she knew everything as a kind of insurance policy. That way, if things went to hell, they'd take her down with them.

No honor among thieves.

She shuddered, wondering for the millionth time how things had gotten so twisted. When her boss, Dave Carlson, had approached her three years ago with a special project, she'd jumped at the opportunity, seeing it as a means of securing her position at the company.

At its heart, Big Pharma was still a good old boys' club, and Marcia knew if she wanted to succeed, she had to find a way to break in and make friends.

At first, she didn't really dwell on the fact he insisted she keep her work secret. Company audits usually were confidential, and since she was tasked with determining the success/fail rate of experiments, it made sense she wouldn't talk about it. The company scientists would raise a stink about all data being useful, would say that even the experiments that didn't yield the expected results were still meaningful. So she just assumed Dave wanted to keep things under wraps until the data was in and the project was complete. Besides, Marcia was used to keeping things close to the vest. Too many people had stolen her ideas and stepped on her neck as they climbed the corporate ladder for her to trust anyone.

But as time went on, she realized Dave insisted on secrecy because the project she was working on was outside the bounds of the company. While ChemCure Industries was trying to modify the nitrogen mustard compounds to make more effective drugs, Dave was only interested in the data from the failed experiments, the modifications that had increased the toxicity of the chemicals. She wasn't working on an internal audit to track company efficacy—she was compiling data that would allow someone to create highly destructive compounds.

But why?

She'd made the mistake of asking that very question. That night, the lab had exploded in a fiery blast of glass and metal and toxic fumes. She'd arrived at work the next morning to find a piece of shrapnel in her desk chair, with a note taped to the twisted metal.

Curiosity killed the cat. Do you want to be next?

Since then, Marcia hadn't had the guts to say no. Anything Dave asked for, she did, knowing that at any moment, he might decide she was no longer an asset to his "project." Fear was her constant companion, hanging around her neck like an invisible anvil. And while she was almost positive Hannah Baker had been collateral damage, Marcia knew if she asked, it would not end well for her. If Dave had no problem destroying the life of an innocent employee—what would he do to her?

She reached for her phone, gripping it hard to counteract the shaking of her hands. Her breaths were shallow as she waited for him to pick up. How would he respond to this development? Would he blame her?

"What?" He sounded impatient, and her stomach clenched in reflex.

"The police were here tonight asking questions about the nitrogen mustard compounds."

He was quiet for a moment, the silence heavy. "And how did you respond?"

"I denied any involvement and offered to assist in any way I could."

Dave didn't respond, and a flicker of fear danced across her skin. Had she done the wrong thing?

"That's good," he said finally. "Did they buy it?"

Marcia swallowed. "I think so. I tossed in a little flirting as well, which the detective seemed to enjoy."

"I'm sure he did." Dave's voice was smug and knowing, and Marcia felt her cheeks heat. "What is his name?"

"Owen Randall." She paused, unsure if she should reveal Hannah's presence, as well. Would Dave target her if he knew she was involved?

"Anyone else?" Dave asked.

In the end, self-preservation won. "Hannah Baker," she said, pushing aside the flare of guilt that accompanied her words.

"The same Hannah Baker that was injured three years ago?" he asked sharply.

"Yes." Marcia closed her eyes, knowing she was trapped.

"What does she know?" he demanded.

"I'm not sure. She didn't talk."

"But she was with the police," he mused. "Which means she knows something."

"I suppose."

"Very well." The words were crisp and clear, and she knew he had arrived at some sort of decision. "These complications will be dealt with. If this detective contacts you again, continue to distract him."

"And Hannah?" Dread settled over her, pushing her down into the chair with a relentless weight.

"I thought you didn't like to know the details," he taunted.

"I don't."

"Has that changed?"

She sighed. "No," she said quietly.

"Then don't ask."

He hung up, and Marcia lowered the phone to her desk. She was tired, so tired. And while she hated that the handsome detective and Hannah were now targets, she couldn't help but feel a small sense of relief.

Better them than me.

Chapter 5

Hannah stepped out of the shower to hear her phone ringing. The catchy jingle told her it was Gabby calling, and for the first time in a long time she decided not to answer. Gabby would want to know how the trip to ChemCure Industries had gone, and if she and Owen had found out anything to help the case. She'd also ask if anything had happened on a personal level, and *that* was a question Hannah wasn't ready to hear.

Especially because she didn't know how to answer it.

She ran a comb through her wet hair, working out the tangles as she thought. She couldn't deny she was drawn to Owen, but she didn't know what to make of her attraction. It had been years since she'd noticed a man in that way, and the fact that she was feeling this way now was a little unsettling. Things had been so much simpler before her accident—she'd gone on dates and even thought she'd found "the one." She had viewed men as interesting and entertaining companions, not people to shy away from out of fear and insecurity.

But the accident had destroyed more than the skin of her back. It had wrecked her confidence, as well. The cosmetic damage was bad enough, but in the wake of the explosion, she had questioned her actions in the lab that day, replaying her motions in an endless loop until she thought she'd go crazy. Had she left the chemicals out? Was the explosion her fault? She was normally so careful, so safety conscious. Never before had she made a mistake of that magnitude, but anything was possible.

ChemCure Industries hadn't helped. While they didn't blame her outright, the company made it clear they thought she was at fault. The added burden of their conviction made Hannah even more unsure. Although she knew better than to leave such volatile chemicals next to each other, she couldn't very well blame her coworkers when everyone was pointing the finger at her. And maybe they were right. The doctors said that short-term memory loss was common following a concussive injury. It was possible Hannah had left the chemicals out and had forgotten about it due to the explosion. It was a reasonable explanation, but deep in her gut, Hannah didn't fully believe it.

Still, it had taken a long time to get to a place where she no longer second-guessed her every move. She had thought those days were behind her, until she met Owen. He stirred up feelings in her that had long been dormant, and Hannah's nice, orderly world was once again in disarray. She felt as if she was standing on the deck of a ship, tossing and turning in the middle of a storm.

She wasn't going to bother pretending she wasn't attracted to him. But what she couldn't figure out, what had her on edge and feeling jumpy, was if Owen felt an attraction to her, as well.

He was friendly enough. His earlier gruff manner had thawed as they'd spent more time together, and his flashes of humor had left her feeling warm, as if she'd been standing in the summer sun. And then there was the dinner they had shared, and that loaded moment when they'd held hands. Those hadn't been the actions of a man who was only interested in his case.

Part of her wanted to throw caution to the wind. But while the thought of being so bold was tempting, fear kept her from acting. The fear of rejection. Or worse, the fear of delayed rejection. What if he did say yes but pushed her away after seeing her scars? No matter how strong she felt, no matter how tough she tried to be, Jake the Snake's retreat in the wake of her injuries had hurt her badly, and she didn't want to go through the experience again. After all, Jake had been her fiancé, the man who was prepared to stand in front of people and pledge his life to her. If he was so willing to walk away, what would stop Owen from doing the same?

Hannah crawled into bed, determined to stop thinking about bad memories and hypothetical scenarios. She ran her fingertips over the glass phoenix sculpture on her bedside table, drawing comfort from the cool, smooth figure. It had been her grandmother's, and she'd given it to Hannah soon after the accident.

"You'll rise again, my dear. This is just a temporary setback."

Years later, her grandmother's words still soothed her. As a child, Hannah had spent many hours gazing at the figurine and its swirls of red, orange and yellow glass. She couldn't count the number of times she'd begged to hear the story of the phoenix, that magical bird who rose anew from its ashes. It was a fascinating tale, one that held even more meaning for her now. And while she tried every day to put the explosion behind her, she could never truly forget it or the damage it had caused.

Maybe her attraction to Owen was a good thing, she reasoned. A sign she was really moving forward, heading toward the day when she could open herself up to the thrilling vulnerability of a relationship. Perhaps this crush was a way of taking those first tentative steps back into a full life again.

So why not ask Owen on a date? There was no law that said she had to show him her scars just because they shared a meal. She eyed his business card on her bedside table. Should she call him now? Or was it better to wait? After all, she didn't want to seem too desperate...

A glance at the clock made her decision. It was too late to call, and besides, waiting a few days was probably for the best. It would give her time to figure out what to say. Gabby would probably be all too happy to offer suggestions, and Hannah knew her friend would be thrilled to hear she was taking the plunge.

Hannah turned off the lamp on her bedside table and snuggled under the covers, smiling to herself. Tomorrow, she'd call Gabby and share her decision. Maybe they could take an afternoon and go shopping for date clothes—it would be great to have a girls' outing, especially for such a special occasion. She drifted off to sleep, enjoying the pleasant thrums of anticipation at the thought of what tomorrow would bring.

It was the sound that woke her. A faint, insistent scratching at her door. Hannah lay in bed for a moment, focusing on the noise. Was it just a tree branch outside her window? Or something more sinister?

She heard the unmistakable *click* of her dead bolt turning, and her breath froze in her chest. Someone was breaking into her apartment!

The door opened slowly, the squeaky hinge letting out a long whine of protest. She'd been meaning to oil it for months, but now she was grateful for the noise. Her heart began to gallop out a pounding rhythm, making it hard to hear over the rush of blood in her ears. Where was the intruder? Was he going to come closer, or just grab her TV and run?

A loud crash broke the silence of her apartment, and she strained to hear over the noise. Would the intruder run now that his presence was known?

But no. Whoever was in her apartment, they seemed to be hell-bent on destroying her things. She heard the bangs and thuds of furniture being turned over and the splintering of wood. She held her breath, not really trusting her own ears. Who was doing this? And why?

She churned her legs frantically, kicking the covers off so she could roll out of bed. Her feet hit the floor and her knees nearly buckled, but she grasped the bedside table for support. Now was not the time to fall apart!

With shaking fingers, she grabbed her cell phone. Something white fluttered to the floor, and she reflexively picked it up as she moved to the sliding glass door in her room. It opened onto a balcony, and while three stories up was too high for her to jump, there was a small storage closet tucked to the side. The door was flush with the wall and not easily seen, and she headed for it now, knowing it was her only chance.

Heavy footsteps on the wooden floor of the hallway made the bed shake. He was coming closer—she couldn't stay here any longer.

Hannah pushed open the door, holding her breath as it slid along its tracks. *Please don't make noise!* If the intruder heard her, he would know in an instant where she had gone. She knew it was only a matter of time until he found her—her apartment wasn't very big, and only had one entrance—but if she could stay hidden long enough, the police might arrive before he got to her.

She slipped through the opening and into the warm night air, forcing herself to slowly close the door behind her. It wouldn't do to leave a calling card directing him to her hiding place. She took a few quick steps and flung open the door to the storage closet, hesitating only a second before climbing inside. She hunkered down into the corner, trying hard to ignore the cobwebs and the millions of imagined bugs keeping her company.

Her phone screen was bright in the inky blackness of the closet. Would the light shine through the cracks around the door? She pressed the phone to her ear, hopefully dimming the glow.

"Nine-one-one, what is your emergency?"

"Someone has broken into my apartment," Hannah whispered.

"What is your address?"

Hannah rattled it off, keeping her eyes on the door and straining to hear. Was the intruder in her bedroom? Was he coming closer to the glass doors?

"Where are you now, ma'am?"

"I'm in a storage closet on my balcony. Please come quickly—I don't know how long it will take for him to find me."

"Police are on the way. Please stay on the line."

Hannah nodded, then remembered the operator couldn't see her. "Okay," she said, her voice shaky with fear and stress.

Gradually, she became aware of something pressing into the skin of her hand. She opened her fist to find the white paper she'd picked up on her way out of the bedroom. It was Owen's business card, now crumpled, the numbers he'd written on the back smeared with her sweat.

But still legible.

Moving on instinct, she accessed her text messages while keeping the operator on the line. There wasn't much time, and she didn't want to keep the phone away from her ear for longer than necessary. Even as she typed, she wasn't sure what she expected Owen to do. It wasn't as if he could ride to her rescue and banish the bad guy. But knowing he was there made her feel a little safer, something she wasn't going to question right now.

She pressed Send and settled back to wait, trying to focus on the steady stream of reassurances coming from the operator. The woman was so calm, so confident the police would arrive in time.

Hannah hoped she was right.

* * *

Owen had given up trying to sleep hours ago. What was the point? His brain wouldn't turn off, and he'd rather work than lie in bed and stare at the ceiling.

He'd chatted with Nate on the way home from the ME's office. Nate's initial interviews at the Thomas Street clinic hadn't turned up much, but that wasn't surprising. With over fifty employees, it was going to take time to question everyone.

"The culprit might not even be an employee," he'd said to Nate. "It could be a fellow patient."

"God," Nate groaned. "That's just what we need. Talk about searching for a needle in a haystack."

"I know," Owen replied. "But first things first. Let's clear the employees before we start eyeing the patients."

"Sounds good."

Owen had told Nate about Marcia's behavior and was gratified to hear his partner agreed that something was going on.

"But it might not be what we think—she could be hiding some other problem, like a stack of unpaid parking tickets," he'd suggested.

Owen hadn't considered that, and felt a surge of annoyance at having missed the possibility. "True. We can run a search on her tomorrow."

He'd arrived home and tried to zone out by watching the Astros game on TV. But no matter what he did, he couldn't stop thinking about the case. He was missing something, he was sure of it. But what?

He knew from experience that if he kept going over the facts he already had, he'd eventually see them in a different way. Something would click, and all the pieces would fall into place. But until he got to that point, he had to keep turning them over and over, examining each piece of information from all angles.

Times like this made him miss John even more than usual. His old partner had been a master at seeing patterns in a collection of disjointed facts. What he wouldn't give to talk to him about this case!

And, if he was really being honest with himself, he wished he could talk to John about Hannah Baker, as well.

There was just something about her, something that called to him. She seemed so fragile, but he'd seen the determination in her eyes today at ChemCure Industries. She hadn't hesitated to go back to the scene of what must have been a horrible accident, and he respected the hell out of her for it. Not many people would have been willing to dredge up painful memories to help someone they barely knew, but she'd done it. That simple act alone made him want to get to know her better.

He'd asked her to dinner on an impulse. Given how upset she'd been after the company visit, he'd half-expected her to refuse. But he was glad she hadn't.

He had really enjoyed sitting across from her, watching her reaction to the food. The way she'd closed her eyes and moaned a little after the first bite had been sexy as hell, even more so because she had no idea she'd done it.

In fact, he'd be willing to bet Hannah Baker had no idea how attractive she was.

Her accident probably had something to do with that, he mused. Even though she hadn't wanted to talk about it, he'd pieced together enough to know that she had been hurt badly. He couldn't tell if the injuries still caused her physical pain, but it was clear they affected her emotionally.

Of course, he knew all about that kind of suffering.

He flexed his hand, still feeling the echo of her touch. She hadn't hesitated to reach out and offer him comfort, something he hadn't expected. Normally, he kept his emotions bottled up, and on the rare occasions he let anything slip, he was quick to cover it up or pretend like it hadn't happened. But Hannah hadn't let him hide. She'd acknowledged the moment without making a big deal out of it, something he appreciated.

Her hand had been so small in his, but it had fit perfectly, as if it belonged there. It would be easy, too easy, to get wrapped up in this woman. To tease apart her defenses and learn her secrets. To share his own.

It was a powerful temptation. But one he couldn't risk. Not now.

Just focus on the case, he told himself. Thinking about Hannah Baker was a nice distraction, but that was all it would ever be. Maybe, when this was all over, he'd try to find out what was between them. But until he solved these murders, she was off-limits.

With a sigh, he grabbed a legal-size pad and divided it into columns—one for each of the victims. Then he started filling in details: name, age, sex, race, where they'd been found, their injuries. They were a disparate lot, but most of them had been patients at the Thomas Street clinic. He was willing to bet the other victims had some connection to the clinic as well—he just hadn't discovered it yet. He added a note to his growing to-do list: get the victims' medical records. Hopefully the clinic would surrender them without a warrant.

He flipped the page and wrote "nitrogen mustard," then drew a circle around it. Then he wrote "Chem-Cure" and linked it to the center circle with a line. It was so simple on paper, but until he figured out just how the company was connected to his victims, it was all just speculation.

Could he use Marcia Foley to get what he needed? The thought of spending more time with the woman made his skin crawl, but if it got him the information he needed, it would be worth it. She had been all too willing to play the part of the temptress. What would happen if he called her bluff?

He stared at her card, debating his next move. This could go one of two ways: he could call and suggest they meet again, over dinner, as she'd suggested. They'd share a meal, he'd talk her up and try to keep her expectations down, and he may or may not walk away with useful information. That was the extreme version of "good cop." The alternative was to set up an official meeting with Nate in tow, which would make it very clear he had no personal interest in her. It was probably the smarter thing to do, but if she felt as if he was blowing her off, she could retaliate by refusing to talk. He knew from experience that a scorned woman was not someone to be messed with—he'd seen several women who had turned in their husbands or boyfriends once they discovered the men in their lives had done them wrong.

Before he could make up his mind, his phone buzzed, signaling an incoming text. He glanced at the screen, frowning when he didn't recognize the number. But the message got his attention: Someone is in my apartment.—H

He shot forward in his chair, adrenaline spiking in his system. *H* had to be Hannah. She was in danger.

Without stopping to think, he grabbed his weapon and shoved his feet into his boots. He typed with one hand, hardly stopping to look at the screen. Address?

He held his breath while he waited for her to respond. If she didn't write back, did that mean the intruder had discovered her? And if that was the case, could he get there in time to keep her from being hurt?

A few seconds later, his phone buzzed again. Good. She didn't live too far away. It shouldn't take him too long to get there, but he knew better than most that in this type of situation, every second counted. He dialed in to the office while he drove, keeping one eye on the road so he didn't hit anyone.

"This is Detective Owen Randall, badge number 5921. I'm calling to report a break-in in progress." He rattled off Hannah's address. "I'm en route and request assistance."

"Roger that." He heard the clicking of a keyboard as the dispatcher worked. "There's a 911 call in progress from that address. Officers have already been dispatched."

A swell of satisfaction rose in Owen's chest. *Good job*, he thought, appreciating the fact that even in what had to be a terrifying situation, Hannah hadn't lost her head.

"Understood. Please alert the officers I'm on the way." The last thing he needed was to spook his own team and get shot for his troubles.

"Copy."

He hung up and pressed on the accelerator, speeding to beat the yellow light. He could put his light kit on the roof to give him an excuse to drive recklessly, but he didn't want the flashing strobe to alert the intruder to his presence. While he wanted Hannah to be safe, part of him hoped the intruder would still be there when the officers arrived. There was nothing quite as satisfying as catching a bad guy in the act.

I'll be there, he texted, hoping the message would reassure Hannah.

Hold on, he thought, banking hard around a corner. *Just hold on...*

Owen didn't bother to question the magnitude of his reaction after hearing Hannah was in danger. Later, when things had calmed down, he could stop to wonder just why he was so worried about a woman he barely knew. What it was about her that had broken through his professional detachment. But there was no time for that now. He had to get there, to try to protect her.

Before it was too late.

Chapter 6

Hannah huddled on the couch, trying to make herself as small as possible. Although the officers assured her there was no longer an intruder in her apartment, she didn't feel safe. Sitting in her living room made her feel exposed and vulnerable, and she desperately wanted to crawl into her bed and wrap up in the covers.

A female officer sat next to her and offered her a gentle smile. "Ms. Baker?" At Hannah's nod, she continued. "I'm Officer Benton. Can you tell me what happened here tonight?"

"Someone broke into my apartment," Hannah replied, her voice shaking. "And they did this—" She gestured with her hand, encompassing the mess the intruder had left behind.

Her television had been pulled off its table and smashed on the floor. The lamps had been knocked over, their shades dented and crushed. Even her furniture hadn't been spared—her kitchen table was on its side, and the chairs were in pieces. The floor was covered in a thin, sparkling layer of broken glass that crunched underfoot. *I'll never be able to clean up all the slivers*, she thought numbly.

Officer Benton winced sympathetically. "It does look like whoever did this was going for maximum damage. I know it's hard, but can you tell if anything is missing?"

Hannah glanced around, trying to see through the mess to determine if anything had been stolen. With so many things broken or out of place, it was almost impossible to know.

"I— I'm not sure," she said. How could she be expected to focus at a time like this? It was all she could do to keep from bursting into tears—asking her to account for all of her possessions was too much to handle right now.

"Okay." The officer's voice was soothing. "Can you tell me if you have any enemies? Anyone who would want to hurt you?"

Hannah blinked at her. Enemies? The thought was almost laughable. She was a college professor who led a quiet life. Sure, the occasional student would get angry over a grade, but they tended to vent their rage in scathing reviews, not by breaking into her home and trying to destroy everything she owned.

She settled for shaking her head. "No. Not that I know of. I can't imagine making anyone this angry." She glanced around the room again and shuddered. The destruction was methodical and total, as if someone had tried to erase her very existence by smashing her things.

It took a lot of rage to do that. And anger like that wasn't something a person could hide. Surely she would have noticed if someone had that kind of hatred for her.

Officer Benton looked as if she wanted to ask another question, but her attention shifted to the door of Hannah's apartment. Hannah followed her gaze, and her heart kicked into high gear when she heard what had distracted the officer: heavy footsteps in the hall, growing louder by the second.

Hannah shrank deeper into the cushions, desperately hoping the couch would swallow her up. She glanced over at Officer Benton. The other woman looked alert but not panicked, a fact that made Hannah feel a little better. After all, what were the odds the intruder would come back now that the police were here? It was probably just one of her neighbors, or maybe another officer coming to help. *Nothing to worry about*, she told herself, trying hard to believe it.

A moment later, Owen's tall frame filled the doorway. His eyes scanned the room, taking in every bit of the damage before landing on her. Hannah nearly cried out in relief at seeing him—in the aftermath of the police arriving, she had totally forgotten he was coming.

He crossed the room in a few long-legged strides and knelt in front of her. She reached out to grab on to him, and he folded her hands in his own. The feel of his warm skin against hers drove some of the chill from her body, and she felt her muscles relax. The tight band of panic that had kept her from drawing in a deep breath loosened and she inhaled, pulling in the comforting scents of summer night and warm male.

"Are you okay?" His voice was laced with concern, and her eyes prickled with unexpected tears. The thought that he genuinely cared about her welfare touched her deeply, and with her emotions already so close to the surface, it didn't take much to make her cry.

Hannah settled for a nod, not trusting her voice. She already felt weak and powerless, sitting on the couch in her robe in the middle of her destroyed apartment. If she started crying, she'd lose what little dignity she had left.

"You must be Detective Randall."

Owen spared the woman next to her a glance. "That's right. Have you found anything?"

Officer Benton shook her head. "The perp was gone by the time we got here. We can try to dust for prints, but in this mess..." She trailed off, and Hannah realized the problem. With so much damage, it would be hard for them to find any evidence. And even if they did, there was no guarantee the person who'd done this was in their system. Without fingerprints on file to match against, it would be next to impossible to discover who had wrecked her home.

"Give it a shot," Owen instructed. "I want to catch this guy." He rose to his feet and gave Hannah's hands a gentle tug. "I'm taking her with me so your team will have time and space to work."

Hannah gingerly put her feet on the carpet, scanning the ground for broken glass before she put her weight down. She didn't want to slice her foot open on a hidden sliver of glass. Owen noticed her hesitation, and before she realized what he was doing, he swept her up into his arms. The breath whooshed out of her, and her head spun from the quick change in position. "Which way to your bedroom?" His chest vibrated pleasantly against her side, and she fought the urge to squirm closer against him.

"Down the hall." She pointed helpfully and he set off, carrying her over the debris with practiced ease, as if he did this sort of thing all the time. Perhaps he did, but for Hannah it was a novel experience. She'd never been held like this before, never been carried in a man's arms or felt such a casual display of strength against her body. It was a heady sensation, and had the circumstances been different, she would have enjoyed it more.

Owen set her gently on the bed and took a step back. The loss of his body heat against her side left her cold, and she shivered slightly. Without even stopping to ask, he grabbed a blanket off the chair in the corner of the room and wrapped it around her shoulders. "Better?"

She didn't have the courage to tell him that her chill had nothing to do with the temperature of the room and everything to do with him. Instead, she nodded. "Much. Thank you."

"My pleasure." He looked around the room, and Hannah followed his gaze, trying to see it through his eyes. She'd never been much of a decorator, instead favoring simple patterns and neutral colors. Her bedroom was no exception. The curtains in front of the sliding glass door were the color of beach sand, and they matched her bedspread. The only splashes of color in the room were the sea blue blanket wrapped around her, and her grandmother's phoenix figurine.

"Doesn't look like the intruder had much time in this room before the cops scared him off."

It was true; her bedroom had been left largely intact, spared from the berserker destruction of the rest of her apartment. He had knocked a few books onto the floor, and her bedside table lamp was askew, but other than that—

Hannah sucked in a breath as she realized what she *wasn't* seeing. The phoenix.

Owen raised a brow at her expression. "What is it? What's wrong?"

She lifted her hand while she walked around the bed, her steps slowing as she approached. She knew what she would find, but if she didn't see it, she could still pretend everything was still okay.

Except it wasn't.

Her grandmother's phoenix sculpture lay in a glittering pile next to her bed. It had been smashed so completely, so thoroughly, there was no chance she could glue the pieces back together. Such a beautiful gift, gone in the space of a few careless seconds.

This time, Hannah didn't try to hide the tears. They coursed down her cheeks in warm, wet streaks to drip off her chin. Then came the sobs, loud, pitiful sounds that she couldn't stop. She was dimly aware of Owen's arms around her, of him guiding her away and then lowering her back onto the bed. She didn't try to fight, didn't care where he took her. Nothing could change the fact that her grandmother's gift, the symbol of her new life, had been wrecked into a million tiny pieces.

He probably thought she was silly to get so worked up over a broken glass figurine, but what he didn't understand, what she couldn't explain, was that it felt as if she had lost some of her fondest memories. Her grandmother had died not long after gifting the sculpture to her, and every time Hannah had looked at it, she'd felt the comfort of childhood memories wrapping around her. Now that was gone, and it felt as though she'd lost her grandmother all over again.

Gradually, Owen's presence pierced the fog of her emotions. He held her close, his hand stroking her head and down her back while he murmured words of comfort. She closed her eyes and allowed herself to savor the contact for a moment. He was such a perfect combination of gentle and strong, and she marveled at his ready display of those seemingly disparate qualities. Jake, her former fiancé, had hated it when she'd cried. He'd always gotten a deer-in-the-headlights look and had searched for any excuse to get away, claiming he found her tears upsetting. Never in a million years would he have gathered her up and held her close while whispering soothing nonsense words in her ear. But Owen—strong, stoic Owen—hadn't hesitated. He'd given her the space to cry and hadn't tried to make her stop by offering false comfort or telling her that her tears were unnecessary. He just accepted them, and her, with no sign of annoyance or impatience.

Hannah took a deep breath, and he loosened his grip. She leaned back, feeling suddenly shy. What could she say now?

"You're back."

She nodded. "I am. Sorry about that." She gestured to the floor with one hand while wiping her eyes with the other. "I don't know what came over me."

"You don't have to explain." His dark blue eyes were warm with understanding. "Sometimes you just have to let it all out."

She tilted her head to the side and offered him a

small smile. "You sound like you have some experience in that regard."

"I do."

Hannah remained quiet, hoping he would elaborate. When he didn't, she said, "I'm sorry to hear that."

He shrugged, as if it didn't matter. But she could tell by the set of his mouth that something had happened to him, something that had caused him to break down. And while she'd never want someone to experience pain, the fact that Owen had faced some kind of loss made her feel closer to him. He wasn't just a tough, hard-to-read cop. He was a man, one who let a woman cry on his shoulder and seemed to understand why she might need to.

"Why don't you get a bag packed. A few days' worth of clothes and toiletries should do it."

He was trying to change the subject and she let him, grateful for the distraction. "Where am I going?"

"There's an extended-stay hotel down the street. I thought you might be more comfortable there for the next few days, while we gather evidence here. Unless you'd rather go somewhere else?"

She considered the question for a moment. There really wasn't anywhere else for her to go. Her parents lived in Fort Worth, which was a six-hour drive north. And Gabby had just moved in with her long-term boyfriend—no way was Hannah going to crash on the couch while Gabby was setting up house. The hotel was as good an option as any.

"That will work," she said, moving to the closet to swipe blouses and pants off hangers. Owen stepped out of the room to give her some privacy while she packed, a fact she appreciated as it gave her a few moments to gather her composure.

She hadn't broken down like that since her accident, when she'd woken up in the hospital and the doctors had told her about her injuries. And while she normally hated to cry, she had to admit Owen was right—there was something cathartic about just letting all the emotion go. Definitely more healthy than trying to keep it all in.

The low rumble of Owen's voice drifted into her room while she packed. Even though she knew he was waiting on her, Hannah spared a moment to close her eyes and listen. He was too far away for her to make out what he was saying, but the sound of his voice was reassuring.

When did that happen? she wondered. When did she start finding comfort in a relative stranger's presence?

She shook her head. Now was not the time to worry about her growing dependence on Owen. After all, a stranger had invaded her home tonight and tried his level best to wreck everything she owned. Was it any wonder having a strong, protective man around made her feel better?

With a sigh, she zipped the duffel bag closed. Time to go to the hotel. Even though she felt too keyed up to sleep, it would be nice to spend some time in a quiet room, away from all this destruction.

"Ready to go?"

Hannah nodded, grabbing her bag as she turned to face the door and the man standing there.

Owen glanced at Hannah as he drove, trying not to be too obvious about it. She was quiet, so quiet he wondered if she was still functioning. Not that he would blame her if she had shut down. She'd had quite a scare tonight.

Officer Benton had pulled him aside while Hannah had been packing. Apparently, she and her partner had just missed catching the intruder. He'd taken off as they'd entered the building, and since no one had gotten a good look at him, didn't have a description to use for neighborhood canvassing. He'd held his temper, knowing it wasn't the officers' fault that the perp had escaped.

He was just glad Hannah was safe.

The destruction in her apartment was overwhelming in its scope. In his experience, random burglars didn't break into an apartment just to wreck stuff. That meant whoever had done this either knew Hannah or was trying to send her a message. But who would want to target her like that?

And what would have happened if the police hadn't arrived when they did?

He shuddered at the thought. Based on the evidence, the man had been methodically working his way through the apartment, room by room. He'd started with the living room, then made it to the kitchen before heading to her bedroom. The fact that he'd left her bedroom for last was telling—perhaps he hadn't meant to hurt her. After all, he had to know that Hannah would hear him breaking her things and try to get away.

But there's only one door.

That thought gave him pause. Hannah had escaped by hiding in a closet on her balcony, a closet that wasn't visible from the street, so the intruder had no way of knowing it was there. Because she had a third-floor apartment, the burglar had to know she couldn't jump.

As he considered all the facts, the pattern of destruction in her apartment took on a new, sinister meaning: Had the intruder deliberately started in the living room, knowing Hannah would wake and hear him? Had this all been a means of scaring her before he finally entered the bedroom to harm her?

Owen clenched his jaw at the thought. It took a special kind of sadist to get off on causing other people fear. And based on what Officer Benton had told him, Hannah hadn't been able to come up with any potential suspects. Of course, she was still recovering from the shock of the evening—maybe after she'd had time to think, something would jog her memory.

He pulled into the hotel parking lot and cut the engine. "I'm going to get you set up with a room," he said softly, so as not to startle her. "Do you want to wait in the car, or would you rather come with me?"

Hannah's hazel eyes were huge in her pale face. "I'd like to come with you, please." She wrapped her arms around herself before adding quietly, "I don't want to be alone right now."

His heart clenched at her admission, and he wanted nothing more than to gather her into his arms and hold her, to convince her with his body that she was safe and would stay that way. She had felt so nice in his arms as he'd carried her to her room. He actually hadn't wanted to let her go, and would have continued holding her if he could have gotten away with it. His body agreed with him, and even now, he felt a strong urge to find out exactly how well they would fit together in other ways...

Before he could embarrass himself, he climbed from the car and moved to the passenger door, holding it open for Hannah. She moved gingerly, as if her bones hurt. He glanced down to check her feet—had she cut herself, after all?—but it was too dark for him to tell. He offered her his arm, knowing she wouldn't appreciate being carried into the lobby. She wrapped her hand around his biceps, gripping tightly, as if she was afraid to lose him.

"Are you hurt?" he asked in a low voice. If she was injured, he might need to take her to a hospital rather than the hotel.

Hannah shook her head. "I just can't stop shaking."

He felt it now, the faint tremor that ran from her hand to his arm. No wonder she was moving slowly; she was probably afraid of falling over with each step. Not knowing what else to do, he covered her hand with his own. "This won't take long. We'll get you a room and then you can take a hot shower to try to relax." His libido was all too happy to imagine *that* scenario, and he tamped down hard on his burgeoning fantasy. *Now is not the time!*

Fortunately, it didn't take long to procure a room. At this time of night, there was no line at the front desk, and the clerk worked quickly. The young man gave him a knowing smile as he passed the key across the desk, but he blinked in the face of Owen's hard stare.

"Uh, here's your key, miss," he said.

Hannah seemed to focus on him for the first time. "Thank you," she murmured, reaching out to accept the card.

A few minutes later, Owen unlocked the door and carried Hannah's bag inside. The room was spacious, with a small kitchenette, a living area and a bedroom nook taken up by a king-size bed. It wasn't home, but it would fit the bill for a few days.

Hannah stood just inside the doorway, still hugging herself. Owen set her bag down on the coffee table and walked back to her. "You okay?"

She nodded jerkily. "Yes. Just…processing."

"It's a lot to take in." He reached up and brushed a stray cobweb out of her hair, a remnant of her time in the outdoor storage closet. "Want to take a shower?"

Her breath gusted out in a sigh. "God, yes."

"Bathroom looks to be over there."

She took a step forward then stopped, her expression stricken. "You'll be here when I get out?" Her voice was high and thin, on the edge of panic.

"If you want me to."

"I do."

He swallowed around the sudden lump in his throat. "Then I'll stay."

Hannah nodded and grabbed the bag on her way to the bathroom. The door clicked shut, and only then did Owen allow himself to sink onto the thin couch. *She wants me to stay.* He shook his head, recalling the expression on her face when he'd arrived at her door. She'd looked at him with such profound relief it had nearly brought him to his knees. In that moment, she had viewed him as a hero. It was such a heady sensation—he'd felt ten feet tall and bulletproof, convinced he could leap tall buildings in a single bound or fix anything that was broken with just a touch. If only that were true…

It had been forever since anyone had seen him as a source of comfort. He'd tried to be there for John's widow, but Casey had pushed him away. Her anger and grief had been overwhelming forces, and he'd been powerless to help her in the wake of John's death.

"Just go," she'd screamed at his last visit. "You can't give me back my husband, and that's all I want."

That's all I want, too, he'd thought. Still thought.

To his shame, he'd left Casey alone. Even though she had made it clear she wanted nothing to do with him, he still felt like he'd abandoned her and let John down. Several times over the past few months, he'd picked up the phone to call and check on her, only to put it down again without dialing her number. What could he say? It wasn't as if he was a shining example of coping.

"When this is over, I'm going to call her," he muttered. Maybe she'd hang up on him, maybe she'd scream at him again, but at least he'd know he tried.

The sound of running water brought his thoughts back to Hannah. She was holding up well, under the circumstances. Hopefully, the hot shower would go a little way toward restoring her peace of mind. Although he hated to do it, he was going to have to ask her some tough questions when she came out. She didn't seem like the type to make enemies, but someone was out to hurt her, and he needed to find out who.

Before it was too late.

Chapter 7

Hannah stood under the hot spray, letting the water cascade down her body in warm rivulets. She was still cold, but she no longer felt frozen through. Just a few more minutes, and then she'd climb out and face Owen again.

She knew he'd have questions for her, questions she couldn't answer. Ever since Officer Benton had asked if she had any enemies, she'd been obsessing over the people she knew, trying to determine who would be capable of such violence. And more important, why they would want to hurt her.

So far, she'd come up empty.

She turned, letting the water hit her back. The fire had destroyed many of the nerve endings there, so she didn't really feel the water hitting her scars. Still, old habits were hard to break.

The small bathroom was steamy and warm when she stepped out of the shower. Moving quickly, she patted herself dry and dug lotion out of her bag. Her scars dried out easily, and if she didn't keep them moisturized, she'd be plagued by itching. Not a distraction she needed while talking to Owen.

Part of her still marveled at the fact that he'd come so quickly. She wasn't his responsibility, and yet he hadn't hesitated to answer her call for help. She knew it was his job to respond to trouble, but she'd called him on his personal phone, when he was off duty. He didn't owe her anything, and yet he'd been there, striding into the apartment looking like a man on a mission.

Her hands tingled with the memory of being held by his. Something about his touch had burned through the fear that had surrounded her, melting it like the sun on snow. He made her feel as if things were going to be okay, a reassurance she desperately needed right now.

She shrugged into her robe and flipped the collar up to cover her neck, took a deep breath and entered the room on a cloud of steam. Owen turned to face her, triggering a wave of self-consciousness that made her want to squirm. She wasn't used to having a man watch her enter a room, especially when she was fresh from a shower.

"Feel better?" Had his voice gotten lower? Maybe it just seemed that way since she was in her pajamas and robe. There was something intimate about talking to a man in a hotel room, her hair still damp from the shower.

"Much. Thanks." And it was true. Even though she had never seen the intruder, having her home invaded had made her feel dirty somehow. The simple act of washing had done a lot to restore her composure.

"Good." He was silent a moment, then sighed before speaking again. "I have to ask you some questions. I'm sorry."

She shrugged. "That's all right—I figured you would. What do you want to know?"

He looked at her then, his eyes full of apology. "I need you to tell me about your accident at ChemCure Industries."

Her hand flew to her neck before she could stop it. "Why do you need to know about that?"

"Because I think tonight's events are connected to the explosion."

"I don't see how." Her stomach twisted, and her earlier sense of peace dissolved. Why, of all things, did he want to know about that?

"Try to see it from my perspective," he said, his tone gentle. "You're a college professor who leads a quiet life. By all accounts, you have no enemies, no one who would want to hurt you. But hours after your return to Chem-Cure, the scene of a horrific accident in your past, an intruder breaks into your apartment and starts destroying everything you own? That's quite a coincidence."

Put like that, it did seem like the two events were connected. But the accident had been so long ago— how could it be relevant today?

"The two events don't have to be connected," she pointed out weakly.

"True," he conceded. "But let's consider all the angles. There might be something about the accident that gives us a clue as to why you were targeted tonight. Will you tell me what happened at ChemCure? Please?"

It was the *please* that broke her resistance. After all, it was the least she could do, after everything that he'd done for her tonight.

She crossed to the sofa and sat, keeping a tight grip on the terry cloth of the robe.

"I'd been working at ChemCure Industries for five years. It was my first job after finishing graduate school, and I enjoyed it."

Owen whistled softly. "You must have been good at it to be head of the lab at such a young age."

Pleasure bloomed in her chest, spreading tendrils of warmth through her limbs. "I did all right for myself," she demurred.

He chuckled. "I'm sure you did."

"Anyway," she continued, "I had come back to the lab to check on something that night. I was running a timed experiment, and I needed to collect data."

"But you were the senior scientist," Owen interjected. "That sounds like something a more junior team member should do."

"Ordinarily, yes. But this was a special experiment. I was testing the toxicity of a new compound, one we had high hopes for. I wanted to make sure everything was perfect, so I insisted on doing it myself."

"How did people respond to that? Was there any resentment to your taking over on that experiment? Did people feel snubbed?"

She frowned, trying to remember. "Not that I recall. We all knew this was a big deal. If anything, the other team members were happy for me to take the lead. That way, if the drug didn't work like we wanted, their performance wouldn't be scrutinized."

"I see. Did you notice anything unusual when you came back to the lab?"

"No. But I wasn't really paying attention. I was focused on my experiment so I could collect the data and go home." She shrugged. "As much as I liked my job, I still didn't want to live in the lab."

He grinned. "I can understand that. Did you get your data?"

"I don't know. I heard a hissing sound behind me, and the next thing I remember is waking up in the hospital." *In terrible pain.*

"So the explosion was behind you?"

"Yes."

"How bad were your injuries?"

Hannah lifted one shoulder, trying to seem nonchalant. "I had third-degree burns all across my back and neck." Unbidden, the doctor's voice popped into her head: *Miss Baker, I'm so sorry to have to tell you this...*

"But not your legs?" Owen looked confused.

"The doctors thought the force of the explosion was at the level of my back, which is why my legs weren't affected." *Almost complete destruction of the skin... Skin grafts are required... Physical therapy will be extensive...*

"My God," he said softly. "That must have been incredibly painful."

What an understatement! The first time she'd had to undergo debridement to remove the dead skin off her back, she'd screamed until her voice had given out. She offered him a faint smile. "What doesn't kill you and all that."

He studied her for a moment, his expression serious. "Was there anyone there to help you?"

Hannah swallowed hard. "My parents came down from Fort Worth."

"That's not what I meant," he said so softly she could barely hear him.

She dropped her head, not wanting to meet his gaze when she confessed this next part. "No. My fiancé took one look at my injuries and left. He couldn't handle it."

Owen cursed, long and low. "I'm so sorry."

"Don't be," she replied, hating the sting of his pity. "I'm fine."

"Yes, you seem to be," he said slowly.

"What is that supposed to mean?"

He spoke deliberately, as if he was choosing his words with care. "I think whoever he was, he hurt you more than you care to admit."

Was she that transparent? Apparently so. Her pride smarted at the news that three years after the fact, the pain caused by Jake's abandonment was still plain for others to see.

Hannah cleared her throat, needing to change the subject. The last thing she wanted was for Owen to start seeing her as a victim. "So how do you think the explosion is linked to the intruder?"

He sighed and ran a hand through his hair. "I'm not sure. Like I said, it was a hunch. Did ChemCure ever figure out what caused the explosion?"

"Two volatile chemicals had been left next to each other on one of the countertops. It was only a matter of time before they reacted."

"Any idea who put them there?"

She shook her head. "Not really. They said I must have been the one to do it, but I honestly don't remember making that kind of mistake."

"Can you think back to the days before the explosion? Did anyone seem angry with you, or was anyone acting strangely?"

She'd asked herself that very question hundreds of times. "No, not really. Nothing stands out to me as being odd—everything was business as usual. That's what makes it so frustrating." She stood and began to pace, needing to move, to release the tension that had been building ever since Owen had asked her to talk about the accident. "I've tried so hard to find a reason for why this happened to me but I can't. As hard as it is for me to say it, I think it really was just a random accident, and I was in the wrong place at the wrong time."

"And that bothers you?"

"Hell, yes! Do you have any idea how frustrating it is to have your life turned completely upside down with no warning or explanation? To wake up one morning to find that life as you know it is over, and your new reality involves pain like you've never imagined it? Of course I want to know why it happened!" She stopped, feeling strangely empty after the outburst. "But life isn't like that."

"No, it's not." Owen rose to his feet and moved until he was standing in front of her. Hannah kept her gaze on his chest, not wanting to meet his eyes and see the pity she was sure would be there. She probably sounded crazy to him. A deranged, bitter woman railing against life and looking for someone to blame for her troubles. *Way to make an impression*, she thought sadly.

"Believe it or not, I do have some idea of what you're talking about," he said softly. His breath was a warm caress across her face, and she closed her eyes, savoring the sensation. It might be the last time a man got so close to her, and she wanted to remember every second of it.

"You do?" Was that her voice, sounding breathy and low? She'd never spoken like that in her life, didn't even know she could.

"I do. And let me tell you—" Was he getting closer? She felt warmer, as if she had stepped out of the shade and into the sun. "You are one hell of a woman, Hannah Baker."

That made her eyes fly open, and she looked up, certain he'd be smirking down at her. But he wasn't. His expression was serious, his deep blue eyes filled with an intense emotion she couldn't name. Was it longing? Surely not. She was probably just imagining it, projecting her own desires onto him.

Her doubt must have shown on her face. He chuckled softly. "Don't believe me? What am I going to have to do to prove it to you?"

Before she could gather a response, he lowered his head and pressed his lips to hers.

Hannah stiffened, the contact arcing through her like a bolt of electricity. His kiss was soft and gentle, his lips gliding across hers in a sweet exploration that had her wanting more. But she didn't know how to respond. Shock froze her muscles and shorted out her brain, and it was all she could do to remember to breathe.

Owen drew back a little, and she immediately missed the feel of his mouth on hers. "I'd really like to keep kissing you," he murmured. "But only if you want this as much as I do."

His words broke her paralysis, and Hannah lifted her hands to cup his head. She didn't know what to say, and her brain wasn't helping her come up with some clever response. Instead, she rose to her tiptoes and captured his bottom lip between her own. It was warm and wet, and he hummed appreciatively when she slid the tip of her tongue along the slick surface.

She wasn't aware of his arms banding around her until she was pressed up against his chest, her breasts pinned against his muscles. The contact thrummed through her, and she felt her limbs go warm and soft as he continued kissing her, continued exploring her mouth and caressing her body.

The knot of her robe dug into her stomach, an annoying obstacle that prevented her from fully connecting with Owen. She released his head to tug at the belt with short, desperate pulls until the fabric parted. She pressed against him with a sigh, enjoying the feel of his flat, hard torso against her body. He felt so perfect, so *right*.

Owen took full advantage of the access her open robe granted. He ran his hands inside the robe and tugged up her nightshirt until his fingertips caressed the skin underneath. An effervescent tingling spread through her in the aftermath of his touch, making her shiver.

Through it all, he kissed her. Gentle, teasing, demanding—his kisses captivated her, made her forget about ChemCure Industries, the intruder, everything. Her whole awareness shrank to this room, this moment. This man.

Slowly, so slowly, his hands left her waist and circled round to her back. His touch was questioning, tentative, as if he was asking permission before crossing a border. Hannah sucked in a breath, a black swirl of uncertainty entering the kaleidoscope of sensations surrounding her. This was the moment of truth. What if he felt her scars and was repulsed? Could she handle that rejection, after everything else that had happened tonight?

He traced one fingertip down her side, trailing along the ridge that demarcated the healthy skin of her side from the scar tissue that covered her back. She went still, suddenly feeling like a rabbit caught out in the open.

Owen drew back slightly, just enough to free his mouth from hers. "You are so beautiful," he whispered. His lips were warm against her brows, her cheeks, her chin. "Just lovely," he murmured, working down the front of her neck.

His words unlocked emotions she couldn't name. Jake had never tried to make her feel special, never been so patient with her. He hadn't been a bad guy, but it wasn't in his nature to go slow, to make sure she was enjoying herself as much as he was. With Owen, it was different. He made her feel as if she was the only woman in the world. Like she was cherished.

Warmth rose in her chest, flowing out into her arms and legs with every beat of her heart. With it came a powerful urge to give back, to make Owen feel as appreciated as she did in this moment.

She lowered her hands until she found his, still hovering at her sides, waiting for permission to touch her. With careful deliberation, she placed her hands over his, guiding his palms until they pressed flat against her lower back. He froze, his mouth on her neck. Then the breath gusted out of him on a long sigh.

"Hannah," he said softly.

She kept her eyes closed, focusing on the contact

of his body against hers. What was he thinking? Was he turned off by the unnatural feel of her scars? Or was he so aroused he didn't even notice? It was hard to ignore the evidence of his desire pressing against her belly. Perhaps he was too preoccupied to register anything else.

After a few endless seconds, his hands began to roam, moving up and down her back with exquisite gentleness. She released the breath she hadn't realized she'd been holding in a shuddering sigh, then tilted her face up to find his lips again.

Owen continued his exploration while he kissed her, his touch both inquisitive and playful at the same time. Hannah smiled against his mouth, reveling in the joy of this moment. Before, she'd always felt as if her scars would be a huge turnoff, that no one would ever want her again. But Owen was quickly disproving that theory, and she'd never been so happy to be wrong.

He pulled back again to look at her, his lids heavy with arousal. "Hannah—" he began, then broke off quickly, an almost comic expression of disbelief taking over his features. "You've got to be kidding me," he murmured, reaching into his pocket and withdrawing his phone.

"Randall," he said sharply. His eyes widened, and he glanced at her before he moved a few steps away.

His abrupt change in demeanor left Hannah feeling exposed. Moving quickly, she tugged her nightshirt down and pulled the fabric of her robe together, knotting the belt tight with fumbling fingers.

Owen turned back to face her, shoving the phone into his pocket. His brows drew together when he saw she had put herself back together. "That was my partner, Nate. You met him yesterday."

Hannah nodded. "Is everything okay?"

"No." He ran a hand through his hair. "Another body has washed up. I have to go work the scene."

"I understand." She swallowed hard and offered him a faint smile.

He studied her for a moment, his eyes growing warm. "I'm sorry to have to leave you," he said, his voice dropping as he moved closer. "Believe me, I would much rather finish what we started."

Hannah felt her face heat and fought the urge to squirm under his scrutiny. "Some—some other time," she managed to say.

A slow, lazy grin stretched across his face. "You can count on it." He was right in front of her now, invading her space, leaving her nowhere to hide. Before she could respond, he bent and pressed a swift, searing kiss to her mouth. Then he pulled back, keeping his eyes locked on hers.

"This isn't over, Hannah. Don't try to run from me. From this."

She nodded, not trusting her voice. Was he in her head? How did he know her insecurities came rushing back the second he stopped touching her?

"I'll call you later. Try to get some sleep—you'll be safe here. I'll phone in and have an officer sit in the parking lot, just to make sure."

"Thank you," she said. She stood and walked him to the door. "Please be careful," she blurted out. Maybe the events of the evening had made her jumpy, but the thought of Owen attending a crime scene in the middle of the night made her nervous.

He gave her another heart-melting grin. "Don't worry. Nate will protect me." He stepped outside, stopping on the threshold to turn back. "I want to hear you lock up."

She snorted. "After tonight's events, I'm not likely to forget."

"Humor me. I'll feel better."

"Well, when you put it that way..." He winked at her as she shut the door, making her heart jump in response. She turned the dead bolt and swung the privacy bar into place, trying to be extra loud so he would be sure to hear. Then she turned around and pressed her back to the door, sliding slowly down until her butt hit the floor.

Wow. Just wow. Her head was still spinning at tonight's turn of events. She'd gone from one emotional extreme to another in the space of a few hours, and she was left feeling uncertain and out of sorts. It was a sensation that was uncomfortably close to the way she'd felt in the aftermath of her accident, when she'd woken in the hospital with no knowledge of where she was or what had happened.

It was enough to make her want to hop in the car and drive, to leave the confusion and emotion and arousal and sheer terror of the night behind. She would have, too, had Owen's voice not been in her head. He had gotten under her skin, and although their future was still a big question mark, her curiosity insisted she stick around and discover how things played out.

She raised her fingers to her still-swollen lips, marveling at the memory of his kisses. Her slumbering libido, which had been dormant for so long Hannah had assumed it was in permanent hibernation, was now fully awake and cheering for more. And there would be more, if Owen's dark promise was any indication.

Goose bumps of anticipation rose along her skin, and Hannah rubbed her hands up and down her arms to dispel the chilly tingle. She rose to her feet and walked the few steps to the bed, drawing back the covers to slide inside. She still felt too keyed up to sleep, but at least now it was memories of Owen keeping her awake rather than the faceless intruder.

Marcia fumbled for her phone, one eye on the alarm clock on her bedside table. It took her a second to shake off sleep and register the glowing red numbers: 3:00 a.m. Nothing good ever happened at three in the morning.

She cleared her throat, trying to sound more awake than she was. "Yes?"

"We've entered into phase two of the program. The first patient was discarded tonight."

"Why are you telling me this?" she demanded, hoping Dave mistook her shaky voice as annoyance rather than nerves.

"You need to distract the detective. Point him in the wrong direction."

"What do you want me to say?" Better to get it verbatim from the source so she couldn't be accused of making a mistake later.

"Be creative. I'm sure you'll come up with something."

She sighed, trying to keep the disappointment out of her voice. "Very well. I'll call him in the morning."

"Good. And one more thing."

"Yes?"

"The woman. Hannah Baker."

Nausea coiled in her stomach like a writhing snake. "What about her?"

"She managed to evade our first attempt. Make sure she doesn't escape a second time."

"But what am I supposed to—" The steady drone of a dial tone interrupted her, the sound loud in her ear.

Marcia slammed the phone down and leaned back against her pillow, her breaths coming shallow and fast. Why did they keep calling her when things went wrong? What the hell did they think she could do about it? She was a corporate shark, not a criminal mastermind!

She flipped on the light, knowing she was done sleeping for the night. She had to come up with some way to distract the detective, a task that wasn't as easy as it sounded. If she came on too strong, it would rouse his suspicions. If she was too subtle about it, he wouldn't notice her at all. She had to strike just the right balance, like an acrobat walking a tightrope.

And if that wasn't difficult enough, she was now expected to ensure Hannah Baker stayed in one place long enough to be "dealt with," whatever that meant. A chill danced across her skin as the implication of those two seemingly innocent words sank in. Poor Hannah. Hadn't the woman been through enough already?

I could warn her, she thought wildly. *Encourage her to take an extended vacation until the danger had passed.* As soon as the ridiculous thought crossed her mind, she dismissed it as impossible. The danger would never pass, not as long as Dave Carlson and his ilk thought Hannah knew something. If they suspected Marcia had helped Hannah evade them, there would be no end to the damage they did in the name of revenge.

She reached for the bottle of antacids on her bedside table and shook two tablets into her palm. She knew from experience that they wouldn't take away the constant pain gnawing at her belly, but they should dull it enough that she could think.

She glanced at the clock again. Three-thirty. It would be several hours before she could legitimately call the detective. Plenty of time for her to come up with some kind of workable plan.

But what if I can't?

The thought sent a frisson of fear down her spine. If she couldn't figure anything out, she'd have to start running.

And hope they didn't catch her.

Chapter 8

The sky was the color of orange sherbet by the time
Nate and Owen rolled into the morgue's parking lot.
The technicians had moved the body hours ago, and
Owen and Nate had left the scene, not wanting to in-
terfere while the crime scene investigators collected
evidence.

Not that there was much to find. From all appearances, it was another dump job. Still, Owen held out
hope that this time the perpetrator had made a mistake
and left behind some clue that would lead them to his
door. It was a long shot, but they needed a break.

He cut the engine and turned to look at his partner.
"Do you get the feeling we're spinning our wheels with
this investigation?"

Nate nodded. "Oh, yeah. Big-time."

"I just have this nagging feeling that we're missing

something—that the answer is right in front of us, but we haven't seen it yet."

"I know what you mean. Hopefully, the doc can give us some answers."

Owen swallowed a mouthful of lukewarm coffee, needing the caffeine. "You and me both."

They found Dr. Whitman standing behind her desk, rummaging through files.

"You're already done with the autopsy?" Owen couldn't keep the surprise out of his voice. Normally, it took her most of a day to complete the procedure. For her to be finished so soon was unusual.

She glanced up, acknowledging them with a nod before returning her focus to her desk. "Not yet. I've completed my external exam, and from what I can tell, this victim was treated the same as the others. Extreme postmortem mutilation, most likely to obscure evidence. Look here." She held out a file, opened to images of the first victim. "See the cuts along the torso and neck? They're the same as today's body." She pointed to another set of images on her desk, inviting them to look.

Owen grimaced, the coffee in his stomach turning to lead. He was no stranger to death, but the damage done to these poor people was extreme. "You're sure this was all done after death?"

She nodded, sharing his expression. "Fortunately for them, yes. Whoever you're after, they're not doing this because they get off on torture."

"So why did you stop after the external exam?" Nate asked. "Needed a break before you opened them up?"

Dr. Whitman shook her head. "No. I'm waiting for my consultant to arrive."

"Consultant?" Owen said. "You've never needed a consultant before."

"Every case is different," she replied calmly.

"Who's your consultant?" he asked, raising a brow. He had a sneaking suspicion he knew just who she had called, and he didn't like it one bit.

"That's not really your concern, Detective," she said evenly. His other brow shot up, and he felt his irritation rise to the surface.

"It is if your 'consultant' jeopardizes my case," he retorted.

He felt his partner's hand on his shoulder. "Owen," Nate said quietly. "Take it down a notch."

He took a step back, embarrassment flooding through him. Way to be a professional. Was it any wonder people still questioned his ability to do his job, when he kept letting his emotions get the best of him?

"I'm sorry," he said, running a hand through his hair. "That was out of line."

"Yes, it was," Dr. Whitman said, giving him a hard stare. "But I'll let it slide because I know you're exhausted." She looked past him, to the door of her office. "Come on in."

"Are you sure? I don't want to interrupt your meeting."

Owen closed his eyes at the sound of Hannah's voice. He hated being right, especially now. He inhaled slowly through his nose, digging deep for the patience he didn't feel. "I don't think this is a good idea."

"Why not? I need her to tell me if the lungs of your victims show the same kind of pathology as her failed experiments."

"She had a rough night. She can't have gotten much sleep. Besides, she doesn't need to see that right now."

"'She' is right here, so you can stop talking about me like I'm invisible," Hannah said. "And I'm fine, thanks."

"What happened, Hannah?" Doc Whitman rounded her desk to stand by her friend.

Hannah shifted on her feet and looked down, clearly uncomfortable with the question. Owen stepped in. "Her apartment was broken into last night, and the intruder did a lot of damage. I took her to a hotel down the street so she could rest and feel safe."

"Hannah! Why didn't you call me?"

Hannah shot him a quick glare before responding to Gabby. "You just moved in with Brett. I'm not going to crash on your couch when you're still in the honeymoon phase."

"Don't be ridiculous. You know you're always welcome." Dr. Whitman frowned at Hannah. "But he's right—are you sure you're up for this today?"

"I'm fine," Hannah said, irritation giving her voice a sharp edge. "I'm not a child that has to be coddled."

"Can't you have her look at pictures or something?" Owen put in. "Does she have to be there when you cut them open?"

"I'm afraid so," the doctor replied slowly. "I need her there so she can help me decide which samples to take for analysis."

"I don't like it," he muttered. He hated the thought of Hannah being exposed to this side of his life. He'd built up a tough, emotional callus so that the sight of the victims didn't really bother him on a personal level anymore. But it had taken him years to get to that point. Hannah had no experience cultivating that kind of reserve, and her defenses were already down after the events of last night. He admired her desire to help, but not if it cost her her peace of mind.

"I'll be fine," she said, resting her hand on his arm. The contact arced through him, a visceral reminder of the feel of her skin against his own.

"I don't want you exposed to this." He placed his hand over hers and met her eyes, trying to make her understand. "This isn't like dissecting a lab rat. And after what was done to the body…" He trailed off, not wanting to go any further.

"I'm not looking forward to it," she said wryly. "But if my being there helps Gabby find something, some clue that will help you solve this case…" She shrugged. "Then I have to do it."

The selfish part of him wanted her to do it. Wanted to suit her up himself and shove her into the room so she could give him the information he needed. If only it were that easy!

"Okay," he said finally, knowing she was going to do it no matter what he said. The least he could do was be supportive. "I'll stay here until you're done."

"You will?" Nate sounded surprised, and Owen realized he was right. It would be hours before she finished, hours he couldn't afford to spend twiddling his thumbs in the hall.

"I'll come back for you," he amended.

She gave him a faint smile, and he had the distinct impression she was humoring him. "That sounds good." Then she turned to Doc Whitman. "Ready?"

The doctor glanced from Owen to Hannah, speculation gleaming in her eyes. "Sure," she replied easily. "Let's get to it." She grabbed her keys off her desk and gestured for everyone to walk out ahead of her.

Owen stepped into the hall and caught his partner's expression. Nate's grin was obnoxiously large, and it was clear he had something to say. *Please, not now...*

Fortunately, Nate had the decency to wait until the women were halfway down the hall before starting in. "So," he began, sounding positively gleeful. "Big night, huh?"

"It wasn't like that."

"Really? Then why are your ears so red?"

Owen reflexively reached up, only to quickly drop his hand at Nate's burst of laughter. "Jerk," he muttered, without any real heat.

"You know I'm just messing with you." Nate gave him a friendly pat on the back. "I'm glad to see you rejoining the ranks of the living, my man."

"I'd be happier about it if the uniforms had actually caught the guy who broke into her apartment."

"What happened? Did she arrive home to find a mess?"

"No, she was there." Owen filled in the details for his partner, but he didn't talk about Hannah's lab accident. That felt personal somehow, and he didn't want to break the trust she'd placed in him.

"Do you think this is related to our case?"

Owen shrugged. "I'm not sure. On the surface, I'd say no. But I can't shake the feeling that this wasn't a coincidence." He paused, fatigue and a lack of caffeine clouding his mind like heavy fog. "Think about it—hours after we involve her in our case, an intruder breaks in and methodically destroys her things. That doesn't seem random to me."

"I agree. But I don't see a connection to our victims."

"That's what bothers me about it, too."

They were silent as they climbed into the car. By unspoken agreement, Owen headed for the precinct. There was paperwork to take care of, and there might be some preliminary reports from the scene. It would be enough to distract him while he waited for Hannah's call.

His phone buzzed in his pocket. He glanced at the display before answering but didn't recognize the number. "Hello?"

"Good morning, Detective," a woman purred.

"Who is this?" It came out a little harsher than he meant, but he wasn't in the mood for games.

"Marcia Foley," she said, her voice losing a bit of its warmth.

Great. He was going to have to play nice, at least until he figured out if she was useful to his investigation. "Ms. Foley, I didn't recognize your number. How are you today?"

"Just fine," she replied, slipping back into temptress mode. "I got tired of waiting for you to call, so I decided to take the bull by the horns."

"And what can I do for you?"

"It's really more what I can do for you, Detective."

Owen's curiosity perked up at that. Did she have information for him? Or was she playing him? He caught Nate's eye. *Marcia Foley*, he mouthed, then put her on speaker.

"You have my attention, Ms. Foley."

"I have some information that I think might be helpful to you. Perhaps we could meet somewhere to discuss it? Over lunch?"

He glanced at the clock. It would be several hours

before Hannah was done. He could probably fit in a quick meeting with Marcia before heading back to the morgue. "That sounds nice. What'd you have in mind?"

"How does Brasserie 19 sound?"

Nate whistled softly. The French restaurant was known for its romantic atmosphere, rich food and prices to match. Not exactly a casual dining spot.

"Uh," Owen began, but Marcia cut him off.

"My treat, of course."

Owen glanced at his partner, who offered him a shrug. *Why not?*

"That sounds nice," he hedged. "But I don't think we'll be able to get a table at such late notice."

"Nonsense," she said. "I know the maître d'. Just say the word, and I'll make a reservation."

He clenched his jaw, trying to muster up the energy to deal with Marcia Foley. He wanted so badly to hang up on her, but if she really did have information that was pertinent to the case, he couldn't afford to make her angry. Best to play along until things got too ridiculous.

"How does eleven sound? I know it's early, but I've been up since three working."

"Oh, you poor thing," she clucked sympathetically. "Eleven it is. I'll see you there."

She hung up before he had a chance to respond. "She sounds like a piece of work," Nate said as Owen pocketed his phone.

"Believe me, she is. And I'm really not in the mood to deal with her today."

"Oh, I don't know. She might be a good distraction for you. Keep your mind off other women."

Owen glared at him, and Nate held his hands up, laughing. "At least you'll get a decent meal out of it."

"I suppose," he muttered. But even the promise of good food didn't make the thought of lunch with Marcia Foley any more appealing.

"I'd go in your place," Nate offered, "but it sounds to me like she's hoping for more than just a professional lunch."

"You could come with me," Owen said hopefully.

Nate shook his head, not bothering to hide his smile. "Nope. This is all you. Besides, I've got a couple of leads of my own to chase down."

"I thought partners were supposed to look out for each other. What could be more important than protecting my virtue?"

"I've got to finish tracking down some of the clinic employees," Nate said.

"Fair enough," Owen replied. He parked at the precinct and tried to ignore the heat as he climbed out of the car. It was still fairly early in the day, but it already felt like an oven outside. Nate eyed him up and down as they walked into the building. "You're gonna have to change," he remarked.

"What?" Owen looked down to see what his partner was talking about. He was wearing the clothes he'd pulled on last night, after the message from Hannah: dark sweatpants, gray T-shirt, boots. Damn. Nate was right—he looked like a homeless man, not a respectable detective.

"I don't have time for this," he said, exasperation bleeding into his voice.

"Dude, relax. I have a spare pair of slacks in my locker. We're about the same size."

"Yeah? You don't mind if I borrow them?"

"Wouldn't have mentioned it if I did."

"Thanks," Owen said, feeling absurdly touched by the offer. It was the kind of thing his old partner, John, would have done.

"No problem," Nate replied. "I'm sure we can find you a clean shirt somewhere, too."

"One-stop shopping at the precinct," Owen said, shaking his head at the absurdity of it.

"Nothing better," Nate agreed. He pushed open the door to the squad room and threw a wicked grin over his shoulder. "C'mon, Cinderella," he announced loudly. "Let's get you ready for the big ball."

The call came just after Marcia sat down, her back to the wall of wine bottles that served as both decorative statement piece and functional storage in the otherwise-white color palette of Brasserie 19. The number on her phone display made her stomach clench, but she pasted on a smile as she lifted the phone to her ear. It wouldn't do for her to look anything other than composed while in public.

"Hannah Baker is at the city morgue."

Marcia's heart sank, and her hands grew cold. "Won't that make the detective suspicious?"

"She's not dead. Not yet, anyway."

Relief made her light-headed. It wasn't too late to warn Hannah of the danger she was in. "How do you know where she is? Are you following her?"

"Nothing so obvious. Although she escaped, last night was not a total loss. My associate managed to attach a tracking device to her purse before he had to leave her apartment."

"Why are you calling me now?"

"You need to stake out the morgue and make sure the next time she enters the building, it's in a body bag."

"I can't," Marcia replied, trying to stay calm. "I'm meeting the detective in a few minutes for lunch."

Dave Carlson made a low, dissatisfied sound. "You told me to distract him," Marcia pointed out.

"Very well. Keep him there as long as possible."

"What are you going to do?" She glanced around, checking out the other diners. No one seemed to be paying her any special attention, but it made her nervous to have this conversation in public.

"I'm going to take care of the problem. Make sure you do your part to help." He hung up, leaving the subtle threat in the air.

Marcia returned the phone to her purse, then wiped her sweaty palms on the folds of the pristine white tablecloth in her lap. Detective Randall was due any minute, which meant she had only a few minutes to regain her composure. She picked up her water glass and took a sip, pleased to see her hand was shaking only a little.

Was there time to warn Hannah Baker? Could she even risk it? She ran her fingertip across the smooth surface of her phone, considering. If Dave had planted a tracking device in Hannah's purse, how could she be sure he wasn't keeping tabs on her as well? Marcia never left her phone unattended, but Dave could easily tap into her phone records to see who she was calling. If she did warn Hannah, it wouldn't take long for Dave to connect the dots back to her.

She could tell Detective Randall. Surely he had the resources and know-how to keep Hannah safe. But the timing gave her pause. Dave now knew she was meeting the detective for lunch. If the detective ran straight to Hannah and whisked her away to safety, it would be obvious who had told him about the danger.

The risk was just too great. She couldn't afford to do anything but wait.

She glanced out the wall of windows, catching sight of Detective Randall as he approached the restaurant. With his easy, long-legged stride, he moved with an unconscious grace that was appealing, projecting confidence with every step. More than one female head turned to watch him go by, but if he noticed, he didn't show it. He had the look of a man who was in complete control, both of himself and his surroundings.

And she was going to lie to him.

Marcia rose as he entered the restaurant. He pulled down his sunglasses and glanced around, then offered her a smile when he caught sight of her. She smiled back, her heart threatening to beat out of her chest when he started walking toward her.

Showtime.

Dave Carlson slipped the phone back into his pocket with one hand and reached for the stress ball sitting on his desk with the other. It would be much more relaxing to squeeze the life out of Marcia Foley, but this would have to do for now.

The woman was more of a liability than ever.

In the beginning, she'd seemed like the smart choice. Cold, calculating and willing to do almost anything to advance her career. She had no friends and no problem stabbing coworkers in the back to promote her own interests. It was how she'd gotten her position in the first place. But somewhere along the way, she'd grown a conscience. Not a real one—even now, she was more worried about the consequences to herself than to others. But her concern was enough to make her sloppy.

He was too close to wrapping up this project to have her wreck things now.

His investors were quite pleased with the progress that had been made thus far. He'd identified a collection of toxic compounds, each one showing more damage than the last. The test subjects had all responded as expected, and the team had been happy to move things into the next phase of testing. It was only a matter of time until they delivered the remaining half of his fee and he could retire to some tropical island, to spend the rest of his days working on his tan and sipping cold drinks on the beach.

He knew they wanted to weaponize the compounds, but he didn't care. As long as their checks cleared, Carlson had no problem with doing as they asked. Nor did he have any interest in digging deeper, to find out who exactly was behind this project. Some things were better left unknown, and since he wanted to live to enjoy his retirement, he was content to let the identity of his investors remain a mystery.

He'd thought it would take longer for the police to identify the compounds found in the victims. That had been the plan, at least. But he would just have to adjust accordingly. If Marcia did her job and kept the detective distracted, there would still be time to finish their work.

But that left Hannah Baker as a loose end, which was something he couldn't tolerate. If she had just stayed out of it… But no. She was at the morgue, probably helping the medical examiner nail down the chemical structure. She always had been a meddlesome woman, poking her nose into different projects, offering advice or suggestions on things she had no business discussing. It was no surprise that she hadn't changed.

But what did shock him was the way she'd managed to escape death not once, but twice.

Hannah Baker must have been born under a lucky star to survive not only the lab explosion, but last night's attack as well. The man he'd hired had been instructed to kill her and ransack her apartment so that it looked like a random burglary gone bad. Unfortunately, the idiot had reversed the order of those two events, giving Hannah warning and time to escape.

He couldn't afford for her to escape again.

Her death would raise suspicions, but hopefully the detective would be so distracted by trying to find her killer, it would give them time to finish up the study and leave town. They only needed a few more days at the most.

He sighed, resenting these complications. For a second, he debated calling his investors and warning them. But he knew how they'd respond, and he didn't want to give them any ammunition against him. It was better for him to take care of things himself, to give no appearance of any trouble.

First, he'd deal with Hannah Baker. Then he'd handle Marcia Foley.

Hannah pushed her hair out of her face, trying to ignore the way her hand shook. Owen had been right—seeing an autopsy was nothing like dissecting a lab animal.

She'd thought she'd been prepared. After Gabby had called her, Hannah had spent the intervening time mentally preparing herself for what she would see in the morgue, trying to build up layers of detachment. She'd never seen a dead body before, and had no idea what to expect.

Gabby had tried to help. "It's not a person anymore, it's a shell," she said on the elevator ride down.

Hannah nodded, trying to ignore the uncomfortable squirming of her stomach. Intellectually, she knew that the body she was about to see belonged to someone who was long gone. But it was hard to shake the nervous anticipation that plagued her.

They stepped off the elevator and walked down a nondescript hall toward a plain brown door marked Suite 1. Gabby stopped and turned to face Hannah. "There's one more thing," she said, her expression almost apologetic. "There was extensive…trauma to the body after death."

A chill swept over Hannah. "What do you mean?"

Gabby winced. "Whoever did this is trying to make it harder for the police to do their job. So they mutilated the body to obscure evidence."

Hannah shuddered. "Why are you telling me this?"

Gabby held her gaze. "Because I want you to know that what you're going to see isn't pretty. But believe me when I say that this person didn't feel any of it."

Hannah fought the urge to take a step back. "There's a reason I didn't go to medical school," she said, trying to keep her voice light.

"I know." Gabby's eyes were warm with sympathy. "And if you want to back out now, I understand."

It was tempting, so tempting to back out. When

Gabby had asked for her help, Hannah had accepted immediately and without reservation. But now that she was about to enter the room, to see a body that had been desecrated, helping Gabby was no longer an abstract concept. This was real. She was about to see things that would stay with her forever, disturbing images she'd never be able to forget. Was she really ready for that?

Gabby watched her quietly, with no trace of impatience or frustration. Hannah realized that her friend was giving her the opportunity to back out, to spare herself the unpleasant, unnatural experience of watching a body being cut open. But if she chose to walk away, would she be able to live with the consequences of that decision?

Gabby hadn't asked her here on a lark, or because she was lonely. She'd done it because she thought Hannah could help. And Hannah trusted her friend's judgment. While she wasn't looking forward to experiencing what lay beyond that door, she'd feel worse if she walked away now, before she'd even tried.

Taking a deep breath, Hannah attempted to smile. "I want to help. Let's do this."

Gabby grinned at her. "There's my girl." She reached up to tug at the bouffant cap Hannah wore, pulling it farther down her head. "You're going to do great."

Now, standing on the sidewalk outside the building, Hannah wasn't so sure.

Gabby hadn't lied about the condition of the body. Hannah couldn't close her eyes without seeing flashes of the bruised, broken skin, the angry red slashes that covered the woman like a horrific road map. Even knowing the damage was all done postmortem didn't diminish the impact.

She took a deep breath of hot, humid air, trying to clear her sinuses. According to Gabby, since the body had been discovered that morning it was fairly "fresh," which she claimed cut down on the smell of decay and rot. But Hannah could still detect a faint stink of death that no amount of bleach or disinfectant could cover up.

Her phone buzzed in her hand, and she glanced down. Almost there. The knowledge that Owen would arrive soon brought a measure of comfort, and for a moment she imagined herself wrapped in his arms again. It would feel so good to sink into his embrace, to let him surround her with his warmth and strength. Part of her was shocked at her ready and eager acceptance of this man in her life. After all, there was no guarantee that he had any interest in sticking around after she had played her part in solving his case. But she ignored that voice of doubt, choosing instead to focus on the here and now. Maybe he would walk away later, when all was said and done. Maybe they didn't really have a future. But she refused to let her fears and what-ifs stand in the way of enjoying the time she had with him now.

Last night's encounter had shaken her in ways she was still trying to understand. Owen's enthusiastic exploration of her body and her scars had been an unexpected surprise, one that had made her feel alive again. She wanted to see him now, not just to help her forget the sights and smells of the autopsy, but to discover if he still made her tingle with awareness. Had last night's magic been due to adrenaline and nerves, or was it an indication of something real between them?

She shivered, still feeling cold from her time in the autopsy room. The green scrubs she'd worn had been a thin barrier against the industrial air-conditioning that kept the morgue a constant temperature in the Houston heat. A bright patch of sun lit the asphalt just past the curb, and she headed for it, shaking her head as she moved. It felt strange to be seeking out a sunny spot—usually, she couldn't wait to get inside and out of the heat.

Warmth settled over her like a blanket, and her limbs started to thaw. Hannah closed her eyes and turned her face up to the sky, enjoying the bright glow against her eyelids as the rays sank into her skin. Much better.

The rev of an engine reached her ears, but she didn't open her eyes. A busy street ran near the building, making traffic noise an inevitable nuisance. But then an escalating roar broke her reverie, and she glanced down, horrified to see a large black sedan barreling toward her.

Her heart leaped into her throat, and Hannah threw herself backward, trying to reach the relative safety of the sidewalk. She made it, but the car seemed to follow her, angling after her like a heat-seeking missile. In a moment of horrible clarity, she realized the car was actually *aiming* for her. *This is not an accident!* She scrambled to her feet and managed to dodge to the side, but it wasn't enough. The car hit her right side with terrific force, knocking the breath from her lungs and throwing her across the sidewalk. Her head spun as she sailed through the air, and then she came to a sudden, shocking stop against the ground.

Too stunned to move, Hannah stared up at the sky, blinking hard against the too-bright rays of sunlight. She tried to breathe, but she felt like an elephant was sitting on her chest. She couldn't get her rib cage to expand, couldn't pull in air. Her heart thumped out a panicked rhythm, but before she could try to draw another breath, a sickening pain hit her all at once, like someone had flipped a switch in her body. Everything hurt, a hot, incendiary agony that she couldn't control and couldn't escape.

I'm burning alive, she thought, feeling the flames of pain race along her limbs. She tried to move, to roll out of the fire, but her body ignored her commands. Tears leaked from the corners of her eyes as her vision narrowed, until finally, the fire consumed her.

Chapter 9

Owen grudgingly pressed his foot on the brake pedal, sighing as the car rolled to a stop. He wanted nothing more than to run the light, but as a police officer in an unmarked sedan, he couldn't very well break traffic laws just because he was anxious to get back to Hannah.

Lunch with Marcia had been a special kind of torture. She hadn't had any useful information for him at all, but had spent the time feeding him office gossip and insinuations that had nothing to do with his case. And the way she kept touching him… He shuddered, remembering her hands on his arm, his hand, his knee. He'd done everything he could think of to discourage her, even going so far as to tell her flat out that he wasn't interested in anything but a professional interaction. But she'd merely smiled like the Cheshire cat, as if she knew a secret he didn't.

He'd nearly yelped in triumph when Hannah's text had come through. Not only was he curious to know if she and the doctor had found anything during the exam, but he wanted to be near her again. If only he had enough time to swing by his place for a shower first—being around Marcia had made him feel dirty somehow.

The phone buzzed in his lap, and he glanced down, hoping it was another message from Hannah. He'd told her he was almost there, but perhaps she had gotten tired of waiting for him. He had just picked up his phone when the light changed, triggering a short honk from the guy behind him.

"I'm moving, I'm moving," he muttered. "Hold your horses."

He completed the turn before eyeing his phone again, only to frown when he saw the message wasn't from Hannah, after all, but from Marcia. Didn't the woman ever give up?

Enjoyed our lunch. Let's do it again soon.—M

Owen snorted. Not likely.

Tires squealed ahead, distracting him from the phone. He jerked his head up in time to see a boxy, black sedan pulling back onto the street after hopping the curb. The driver peeled out, smoke rising from the back tires as they spun against the hot asphalt. Before Owen could get a plate number, the car turned onto Old Spanish Trail and zoomed off, disappearing into traffic.

Owen reached for his radio, deciding to call it in. People shouldn't drive so recklessly—

His hand stalled as he approached the morgue.

There was a small cluster of people gathered on the sidewalk, all circled around something on the ground. He slammed on the brakes and threw the car into Park, his heart dropping as he took in the scene. People only gathered like that when something was wrong, and given the odd behavior of the sedan, maybe someone had been hit. This hunch was confirmed when he saw a pair of shoes sticking out of the circle of onlookers, a breach in the wall of pedestrians.

Moving quickly, he radioed in for an ambulance and relayed the last-known location of the car, along with a description. It was a long shot, but maybe a patrol car was nearby and could stop the driver.

He jumped from the car and approached the crowd, noting the drops of blood splattered on the pavement. He needed to get control of this scene now, before the well-meaning bystanders ruined evidence. "Make room, folks. I'm a police officer."

One woman turned to face him, her eyes wide with shock. "He just came up on the curb after her—like he was aiming for her! I was in the lobby, and I saw the whole thing!"

Owen nodded and pointed to a shady spot. "That's good. I'm going to need to ask you a few questions, but in the meantime, please stand over there for me."

The remaining crowd formed a tight cluster around the body on the ground, keeping him from seeing anything. He raised his voice. "People, I need you to back up. Give me some room. An ambulance is on the way."

He forced his way into the circle, noting with disgust that a number of people had their cell phones out and appeared to be recording video of the victim.

"Put those away," he snapped. "Don't you have any decency?"

There was a man kneeling on the ground next to the injured person. "I need a bandage!" he cried out.

Owen crouched next to him while a woman in the circle passed down a wad of paper towels. "Is she still alive?" The victim lay motionless on her back, her face obscured by a swath of hair.

The man didn't bother to spare him a glance. "For now. She has a compound fracture of her right upper arm, and I think she may have a head injury."

"Are you a doctor?"

"A pathologist. I usually deal with dead people."

"Well, you're doing great. Help is on the way."

Owen reached out to push the hair off the woman's face. It didn't seem right for her to be lying there with her features covered in a dirty, bloody mass of tangles. Moving gently, he brushed his fingers over strands that had once been light brown. Time seemed to stop as he looked at her face, his brain screaming with recognition while his heart cried out in denial.

Hannah.

His blood froze in his veins, making him cold all over.

"Hannah." Her name came out husky and raw, little more than a strangled sound pulled free from his impossibly tight throat. "Oh, please, no."

He was dimly aware that the pathologist was staring at him. "Do you know her?"

"Hannah, please. Wake up. Please just open your eyes." Not again. He couldn't stand to lose another person he cared about. He was barely holding it together after John's death. Losing Hannah would put him over the edge.

His vision wavered as he stared down at her broken body. Memories flooded him, making it hard to tell what was real and what was in the past. Hannah's face on John's body. John's blood on the ground near Hannah's shoes. Was she bleeding from the chest? When had John broken his arm? The lingering smell of burned rubber became the tang of cordite, and Owen put a hand on his gun, tensing to defend himself. Had there been a shot fired? From what direction?

"Hey, you doing okay there?"

The pathologist's voice cut through his fugue. Owen shook his head and scrubbed at his eyes, trying to make sense of it all. When he opened them again, there was only Hannah, flat on her back on the sidewalk, her arm bent at an unnatural angle.

Guilt swamped him. This was his fault. If he hadn't gone to her office, if he hadn't taken her with him to ChemCure Industries, none of this would have happened. His actions had made her a target. He had done this to her, as surely as if he'd been the driver of the car.

"I should have gotten here sooner," he muttered, hating himself. Just like with John. Once again, his delay had cost someone else dearly.

But Hannah wasn't dead. Not yet.

Moving on instinct, Owen grabbed her shoulders, needing to gather her into his arms and protect her from further harm. But his fingers were numb, and he couldn't do more than grip her shirt.

"Hey," the pathologist said, raising his hand to stop Owen. "You can't move her. Not until we know what kind of injuries she has."

"I need to help her!"

The man gripped his arm. "The best thing you can do for her right now is to leave her alone. The paramedics will probably be here soon."

It wasn't enough. Panic clawed at his chest, demanding he do something. If he didn't act, he was going to shatter into a million tiny pieces.

His desperation must have been clear. The man eased his grip and regarded Owen with a sympathetic expression. "Why don't you talk to her," he suggested.

"Can she hear me?"

The man shrugged. "Can't hurt."

Owen bent down and placed his mouth right next to her ear. "C'mon, Hannah, wake up for me," he urged in a low voice. "I need you to open your eyes. I'm here now. I'm so sorry I wasn't before."

Her eyelids fluttered, and his heart leaped into his throat at the sight. He reached down and grabbed her hand, squeezing hard. "That's it, baby. Open those eyes. Look at me, please."

Slowly, so slowly, she blinked. "Owen?" Her voice was a raspy whisper, but it was the sweetest sound he'd ever heard.

"It's me. I'm here."

"Hurts." She winced, trying to shift. He held her down gently, remembering the pathologist's earlier words. "Burning. So hot."

He glanced at the pathologist, wondering if this was normal. The man shook his head, her words not making sense to him, either.

Hannah grew more agitated under his hands. "The fire—put it out! Get it away from me!"

Was she having a flashback? "There's no fire," he said soothingly. "You're safe."

"No—too hot!"

She jerked, making Owen's grip on her shoulder slip. His palm connected with the pavement, and he drew back with a hiss. The sun had turned the sidewalk into a frying pan.

"The ground is like an oven," he told the pathologist. "No wonder she feels like she's on fire."

"I should have realized that," the man replied. "I wasn't thinking."

Owen's reply was drowned out by the wail of the approaching ambulance. The vehicle pulled up a few yards away, and the men hopped out, circling round to the back.

He turned his attention back to Hannah, who was grimacing and shifting. Small moans escaped her throat with each movement, but he didn't dare try to hold her down now that he knew how hot the ground underneath her was.

The paramedics arrived, and he reluctantly stepped away to give them room to work. They moved quickly and carefully, assessing her injuries and rolling her onto a gurney. Owen stood there feeling lost, knowing he should be interviewing witnesses and controlling the scene but unable to leave Hannah's side when she was so vulnerable.

A black-and-white patrol car, its lights flashing, pulled up behind his own vehicle. He walked over to meet the officers, badge in hand. After giving them a brief overview of what he knew, Owen tossed the guy on the left his keys. "Can you please park that for me? I'm riding with her."

The officer narrowed his eyes. "You John Prescott's old partner?"

Owen nodded, his throat too tight to speak. Did this officer blame him for John's death, too?

"Played ball with him a couple of times. Good man."

"The best."

The officer glanced from Owen to the ambulance and back again. "Don't worry about your car. I'll take it back to the precinct for you."

Owen blinked hard, touched by the offer and the knowledge that he wasn't the only one who missed John. "Thanks. I really appreciate it."

"Better get going. They're loading up now."

Owen turned and jogged over to the ambulance, climbing in after the paramedic. The man's brows shot up, but Owen flashed his badge. "I'm her friend."

"Works for me," he muttered.

"Owen?" Hannah's voice was faint but unmistakable.

"I'm here." He grabbed her hand, squeezing gently. The ambulance rocked as they set off for the hospital, triggering a whimper of pain from Hannah that cut through him like a knife.

"Can't you give her anything?"

The paramedic nodded slowly, absorbed in the process of starting an IV. He fiddled with some tubes, then pulled out a syringe and injected a clear liquid into one of the lines.

"She's getting a dose of morphine now. Can't do more until she gets to the hospital."

Owen bit back a scream of frustration. The man was only doing his job. Yelling at him wasn't going to make Hannah's pain go away. He settled for leaning down and pressing a kiss to the back of her hand. "Almost there, honey."

Just hang on.

"Wake up, sleepyhead. You can't stay here all day."

Hannah surfaced slowly, rising from dark depths into a world of white. A dark shape hovered over her, close to her face. She blinked a few times, and the shape resolved into a woman's head.

"There she is," the lady said encouragingly. "Time to wake up now."

She struggled to obey, her senses slowly coming back online. A collection of sounds beat against her ears: quiet voices, the squeak of shoes against the floor and nearby moans. "Where am I?" Hannah struggled to sit up but found she lacked the energy to rise.

"The recovery room. They had to put your arm back together."

She remembered then, the memories buffeting her like ocean tides, relentless and overwhelming. Standing in the sun. The roar of the car. The disturbing weightlessness followed by a sudden, jarring stop. And the pain, hot and searing along her body.

"Where is Owen?" He'd been with her in the ambulance and later, in the emergency room. The nurses had tried to get him to leave but he'd refused. "I'm staying with her," he'd said, showing them his badge and effectively ending the conversation. He'd stayed close right up until they'd wheeled her through the doors to the operating room.

"I'll be here when you're done, Hannah," he'd said, his voice carrying over the squeaky wheel of the gurney and the mechanical whir of the automatic-door hinges.

"Don't know any Owen," the nurse said. "Is he in the waiting room?"

"I think so." *Please, let him still be there.* She didn't want to be in the hospital alone. Not again.

"I'll check for you."

Hannah took a deep breath as the nurse walked away, trying to grab hold of her emotions before they got out of control. Her body reacted instinctively to the sickeningly familiar smells of hospital antiseptic, making her heart pound and her chest heavy. She wanted desperately to leave, to climb out of bed and crawl away if she had to, anything to escape this place where the walls were starting to close in.

Don't look, she told herself. Maybe if she didn't see the room, didn't have to look at the equipment and beige blanket and white sheets, she could control the panic starting to rise inside, moving from her stomach to the back of her throat with gravity-defying speed.

She squinched her eyes shut, but the lack of visual stimuli left her mind free to wander down memory lane. The hushed rustle of fabric, the pained groans of someone nearby, the smell—God, the smell!—it all combined to take her back to those first hours after her accident. The pain had been overwhelming, but she knew now, with the horrible benefit of hindsight, that the initial pain had been nothing compared to what she'd experienced during her burn treatment.

Her muscles tensed in memory and anticipation, the past and present swirling together and impossible to separate. She shifted on the bed, sending a fresh spike of agony down her arm. That was new…

She focused on the pain, examining it with almost clinical detachment. It was a bright, white-hot thing, like molten metal grafted to her upper arm. When did that happen?

Thick, choking smoke...
Burned rubber...
Shattered glass...
Squealing tires...
Owen...
Owen!
Owen?

A hand touched hers, and Hannah snapped out of her memories with a gasp, her heart pounding in a fierce rhythm against her breastbone. The woman was back. "I found your friend," she said, regarding her with a frown. "Are you all right?"

Her tongue was heavy, making speech difficult. Still, Hannah realized on a subconscious level that if she didn't speak now the nurse would take Owen away. Just the thought made her want to cry, so she nodded and managed to get out a soft "Yes."

The nurse raised a brow, looking as if she didn't believe her. Hannah offered her a smile, hoping to appear normal. Apparently it worked. There was a soft rustling as the nurse stepped back, and then Owen's face filled her vision.

"Owen!" She reached up with her unbandaged arm and he caught her hand, folding it in his large, warm grasp. His touch was like a balm, soothing her and calming her riotous emotions. Now that he was here, shielding her from the assault of her memories, she could start to think again.

Don't let go, she thought. *Don't ever let me go.*

"Are you okay?"

He huffed out a laugh, shaking his head. "You're the one who just got out of surgery, and you're worried about me?"

"You look tired." It was true. Maybe it was the aftereffects of the anesthesia, but Owen's face seemed haggard, with dark circles under his eyes and his brows drawn together in a seemingly permanent frown.

"I'm fine." He traced the back of her hand with a fingertip, sending a shiver up her arm. Then he squeezed gently. "I am so sorry I wasn't there." When he looked up and met her gaze, his eyes were shiny. "If I had arrived just a few minutes sooner, none of this would have happened."

"You can't know that," she said, her heart aching for him. "Whoever hit me meant to do it—this wasn't an accident."

"But if I had come faster, you wouldn't have been standing there by yourself!"

Hannah gave him a small smile. "So he would have come back another time, when I was alone." She tried to inject a teasing note into her voice. "After all, it's not like you're with me every minute of the day."

"Maybe I should be," he muttered.

Hannah's heartbeat picked up, causing the steady, quiet beep of the monitor to accelerate as well. Owen glanced at it, his mouth turning down at the corners. "What's this really about?" she asked, trying to distract him.

That dark blue gaze settled on her again. "What do you mean?" There was a wariness in his tone she hadn't heard before, confirming her suspicion that something else was bothering him.

Hannah closed her eyes, trying to gather her thoughts. She was feeling more awake by the minute, but she wanted to make sure she chose the right words to say to Owen. His uncharacteristic evasiveness told her she had to tread carefully or he would withdraw even further.

"You're feeling awfully guilty over something that isn't your fault. It makes me think there's a deeper issue here." He looked away, focusing on her hand again. She gave him a minute then tugged, drawing his attention back to her. "Talk to me," she said softly.

He glanced around, as if checking to make sure no one was nearby to hear him. Another puzzle piece clicked into place as Hannah watched him. Either he had secret information about the case, or he was about to tell her something deeply personal. And though his reluctance to talk was obvious, the fierce hope in his eyes made it just as clear that he needed to share.

Hannah could relate. Telling Owen about her accident, letting him feel her scars, was one of the hardest things she'd done in recent memory. But somehow, it had felt *right*. Now that he knew, she felt so much lighter, as if she'd been relieved of a burden she wasn't aware of carrying. She couldn't explain it, but in the short time she'd known him, Owen had quickly scaled her defensive walls and made it into her inner circle.

Had it been the same for him? From everything she knew of Owen, he was a very private person. When she had shared her story, he had listened without jumping in to take over or redirect the conversation, the way so many people did. At the time, she had appreciated his attention, but looking back on it now, she realized that he hadn't volunteered any information about himself.

Was it because he wasn't interested in sharing with her? Or because he didn't know how?

As she watched, a kaleidoscope of emotions flickered across his face. Anger, fear, pain, grief, yearning—each expression took over his features for a split second before morphing into the next, the emotions vying for dominance but none appearing to gain control. She'd never seen him so vulnerable before, and in a sudden, chilling instant, Hannah realized that if she didn't get him to talk to her now, he never would. He'd find a way to recapture the demons plaguing him, to bottle them back up and reinforce the mental chains holding them in place. But at what cost? Hannah knew from experience that every time the fear took hold, every time the pain gained the upper hand, it was harder and harder to beat back into submission. And as she watched the struggle play out across Owen's face, she knew that this time the price he would pay for one more victory would be steep.

"Did you know," she began, striving for a conversational tone, "you're the first person to touch my scars?"

He tilted his head, listening.

"Well, that isn't quite true," she amended. "I should say that you're the first nonmedical person to touch my scars. The first in my private life."

When he didn't respond, she squeezed his hand. "Whatever you have to say, it can't be worse than my scars. You can talk to me. I won't judge."

"You say that now..." He trailed off, shaking his head.

"I know what it's like to have people look at you and recoil in horror. If that's what you think I'm going to do, you're wrong. You've already helped me so much. Let me do this for you."

After a long moment that seemed to go on forever, he let out a deep sigh and nodded. "All right." He sat on the edge of the bed, still holding her hand in his lap. Hannah felt a surge of warmth at the realization that he hadn't let go of it the entire time he'd been by her side.

"Six months ago, my partner was killed in the line of duty."

Hannah sucked in a breath, taken aback by his matter-of-fact statement. His voice was calm, but she could see the storm of emotions raging behind his eyes. "It was my fault," he went on.

"Did you shoot him?" She probably should have stayed quiet, but she'd bet almost anything that Owen was blaming himself for something that was not his fault. The sooner she forced him to see that, the better.

He gave her an odd look. "Of course not."

"Then how could you think it was your fault?"

"We were working a case—a teenager had been shot, and we thought he might have some drug ties. John and I had a list of suspects to talk to, but we had taken a break. I was having dinner with my girlfriend when he called, said he wanted me to meet him at an apartment complex in Sunnyside. I told him to wait for me, but after I hung up, I didn't leave right away."

He shook his head, the corners of his mouth turning down. "Jessica and I had been fighting a lot at the time. She felt I put the job first, that I loved my job more than I loved her. So I stayed to finish dinner, trying to show her that she was a priority to me. I left about fifteen minutes after John's call."

A shudder shook his broad shoulders. "By the time

I got there, it was all over. I found John lying in a pool of blood on the sidewalk outside the building. The suspect had seen him through a second-story window and panicked. He fired what he thought was a warning shot, but it struck John in the shoulder and nicked his heart on the way out."

Hannah gave his hand a squeeze, unable to come up with the words to comfort him.

"The worst part was, he was still awake when I found him. It took him several minutes to bleed out, and he was aware of it the whole time."

His eyes lost focus, and Hannah knew he was reliving the memory. Her heart clenched as his hand drifted up to rest over his heart, an echo of the gesture he must have made when he found his partner dying on the ground.

"I'm so sorry," she whispered.

After a moment he blinked, coming back to the present. "If I had left right after he called, if I had gotten there a few minutes earlier, John would still be alive."

"You can't know that." When he didn't respond, Hannah gripped his hand tightly. "That man may still have shot John, even if you were with him."

"But I could have called an ambulance faster, stopped the bleeding somehow."

She shook her head. "You know it doesn't work that way."

"I would have seen the gun! I could have warned him."

It was a good thing Hannah's right arm was bandaged and immobile, because she had the urge to grab his shoulders and shake him. "Listen to me. It was evening. You're telling me you would have seen a gun aimed from a second-story window in the twilight? No one's that good, Owen. Not even you."

"You don't understand." He sounded almost sullen, and she could sense his withdrawal.

Not wanting to lose him, she softened her voice. "What happened after?"

He paused, and for a long moment, she feared he wasn't going to talk anymore. Then the breath gusted out of him as resignation took over his features. "I took a leave of absence from the job. I couldn't handle it."

There was a twinge of embarrassment in his voice, as if he thought this was the part of the story she'd find most repellent. "There's no shame in taking the time to grieve," she said gently.

His mouth twisted in a grimace. "Jessica didn't think so."

"Your girlfriend didn't support you?" What kind of woman let the man she loved go through hell alone?

"No. At first, she was sympathetic. But after a week, she thought I needed to go back to work. 'Get back on the horse' she said over and over again. Like I was some kind of damn jockey. When that didn't work, she decided that my grief over John was proof that I loved him more than I did her." He shook his head. "What was I supposed to say to that?"

"There's nothing to say. She had already made up her mind. That was just her excuse to leave."

A strangled sound that might have been a laugh escaped his throat. "I realized that. Eventually."

Hannah threaded her fingers through Owen's. "Sounds like we both got dumped in our time of need." She struggled to keep her voice light, angry on his behalf. She knew all too well what it was like to be abandoned by the person who claimed to love you, and she hated that he'd had to experience it.

"Sucks, doesn't it?" he asked. She could tell he was trying to be casual about it, but the pain in his eyes was unmistakable.

"Try to see the silver lining," Hannah replied, only half joking. "At least we're not stuck with the wrong people. Now we each have a chance to find that special someone."

Owen looked down at their joined hands. His thumb traced abstract patterns across her skin, and she focused on the sensation, enjoying the tingling awareness spreading up her arm. "We do," he murmured.

His gaze shifted, becoming warm and sensuous in the space between heartbeats. It was the same expression he'd worn last night as he'd touched her, kissed her. Caressed her. Hannah fought the urge to shiver as the memory triggered a wave of sensation, and she couldn't stop looking at his mouth, wanting—*needing*—to feel it against her skin again. She began to reach for him, only to catch herself just before her hand made contact with his neck. She blinked, trying to shake off the sudden arousal. Did she really want to pick up where they had left off in the middle of the hospital recovery room?

She glanced up at him, hoping he hadn't noticed her inner struggle for control. No such luck. His mouth quirked up in a sexy, satisfied grin that told her he knew exactly what was going on.

"Uh, sorry," she stammered, feeling her face heat. "I guess the drugs are affecting me more than I thought."

"No apology needed. Feel free to reach for me anytime."

Hannah nodded, at a loss for words. At least her embarrassment had brought a smile back to his face and lightened the shadows in his eyes.

"Okay, time to get you out of here," the nurse announced as she walked up. She was accompanied by a man in light green scrubs. "This is Austin, and he's going to take you to your room."

"When can I go home?" Why were they keeping her overnight? Were her injuries more extensive than a broken arm?

Owen noticed the expression on her face and placed his hand on her blanket-covered foot. His touch muted her anxiety, but it was still there, simmering under the surface.

The nurse shrugged and helped arrange the bed for transport. "That's a question for your doctor. You should see him tonight."

Hannah frowned, but it was clear the nurse didn't know any more than that. "Thanks."

The woman gave her a sympathetic smile. "Get well soon."

Austin gave a steady push to get the bed rolling. Owen walked beside her, his presence a comfort she no longer questioned. She closed her eyes, letting the gentle motion lull her into relaxation. When she got to the room, there would be time to talk, to ask Owen if he'd made any progress on the case and to tell him what she and Gabby had found. Until then, though, she was going to rest her eyes…

Owen had a hard time keeping his eyes off Hannah as the orderly wheeled her through the halls of the hospital. She looked so fragile lying there, her skin pale against the white sheets. But he knew that appearances were deceiving. Hannah had taken every hit life had thrown at her and had come back for more. He admired the strength and determination it took to get up off the mat and keep going. After John's death, he'd wanted to stay down, to give up and surrender to the pain. It was easier that way. But something had made him get back up and get back in the game. Stubbornness? Force of will? Survival instinct? Maybe all three. But although he couldn't identify what drove him, he knew Hannah had the same hunger inside her, as well.

She didn't realize it though, he mused, smiling to himself as her eyes drifted shut. She carried herself so carefully, her every move deliberate. He knew now it was because of her scars. The accident had damaged more than just her body, and she was still paying the psychological toll. He wanted so badly to help heal her, but was it possible?

And was he even capable of helping her? After all, he wasn't exactly in great shape himself. Telling her about John's death had been the right thing to do, but even now, his stomach quivered with the aftereffects of nerves. She didn't seem to think it was his fault, but maybe the drugs had affected her comprehension. She might change her mind after she had some time to think about what he'd told her.

A small, weak part of him hoped she would forget all about their conversation, that the drugs in her system would dull her memory. It was a long shot, he knew, and he recognized it was the coward's way out. But now that he'd told her, a nagging voice in the back of his mind kept wondering how long it would take for her to push him away. After all, it hadn't taken Jessica very long to issue her ultimatum, forcing him to choose between the memory of his best friend and a future with her.

He didn't regret his decision to let her go. Hannah was right—Jessica wasn't the person for him, but her actions had still hurt.

Would Hannah do the same? Would she soon grow tired of his lingering grief over John and issue her own decree?

Logically, he knew that one day his grief would lessen. That's what all the books said, anyway. It made sense—after all, wasn't time supposed to heal all wounds? The trouble was, he couldn't imagine a day when he didn't wake up with a heavy heart. Couldn't see a time when the world was more than muted shades of gray. Was it fair to ask Hannah to walk that road by his side, or should he let her go and try to find her again when he felt normal?

But what if he never felt normal again? The thought wasn't new, but it still sent a chill down his spine. What if this was his new normal? Could he really expect Hannah to stay, knowing things would never get better?

He should let her go. But the idea of walking away and never seeing her again made his heart clench. It was wrong of him to stay, but she'd made him feel warm for the first time in months. He'd been so cold since John's death, but being near Hannah gave him a measure of relief, like sitting by a roaring fire on a snowy night. And though it was selfish of him, he wasn't ready to give that up just yet.

The orderly wheeled the gurney into a small room, arranging the bed with practiced ease before leaving quietly, sidestepping an incoming nurse on his way out the door. Hannah opened her eyes as the woman walked over to the bed.

"My name is Grace, and I'll be taking care of you for the next few hours. Can you give me an idea of your pain level?"

A calculating expression moved across Hannah's face. "I'm actually feeling okay."

Owen spoke up. "They're not going to let you go home if you tell them you don't have any pain."

Hannah glanced at the nurse as if to verify the truth of his words. At the woman's nod, she sighed. "Okay, it hurts. About a five on a ten-point scale."

"Let's get that under control." The woman turned to leave, flashing him a grateful smile.

He pulled a chair over to the side of the bed. "You need to be honest. I know you want to get out of here, but I don't want you going home before you're healed."

Hannah shifted, wincing as she moved. "I know. I'm just not crazy about hospitals."

"Because of your accident?"

She nodded. "I was there for weeks. Do you have any idea how long it took to get the smell out of my sinuses?"

He laid his hand on her knee. "You won't be here that long. Besides, I'm going to keep you company now."

"That is an improvement over the last time," she muttered. "But can you really stay with me? Don't you need to work on the case?"

Just the mention of the investigation made him feel as if a heavy weight had been dropped on his shoulders. Over the past few hours, he'd pushed all work-related thoughts to the side, his worry for Hannah taking front and center in his mind. But now that he knew for certain that she was going to be okay, he needed to turn his attention back to the case. He owed it to the victims, and to Hannah, to get to the bottom of this disturbing mystery.

He didn't want to say anything just yet, but he was becoming more and more convinced that there was a connection between the deaths and Hannah. Was the killer he was looking for the same person who was targeting Hannah?

Owen frowned as his thoughts turned in a darker direction. What if Hannah had been a target for far longer than he'd thought? What if the explosion in her lab hadn't been an accident after all? A lab accident was a convenient excuse for offing a scientist, a tragic event that wouldn't automatically trigger a police investigation. The company could blame her death on a careless mistake, and no one would be the wiser.

But if that was the case, why hadn't they tried to finish her off when the accident failed to kill her? He hated to even think along those lines, but if someone wanted Hannah dead, they wouldn't have left her alone after she survived the accident. Her injuries would have provided the perfect cover for murder, and her death likely wouldn't have triggered any alarms. People died of burn injuries all the time, and it was easy to make a death look accidental, especially when dealing with someone who was injured to begin with.

"What's wrong?"

The simple question pulled him out of his thoughts. Owen blinked, and turned to find Hannah watching him from the bed. "What makes you think something is wrong?" He wasn't quite ready to tell her his suspicions yet—she'd already been through enough today, and he didn't want to make her worry about something that might not even be true.

Hannah tilted her head and gave him a droll stare. "You look like someone kicked your puppy."

He shook his head. "I was just thinking."

"Care to share?"

Should he? It was still just a half-formed theory right now, with no real evidence to support or refute his idea. It didn't feel right to dump everything on her. But perhaps he could ask her about her time at ChemCure Industries without causing too much stress.

"I'm just trying to figure out who attacked you today."

She frowned. "I wish I knew."

Owen paused, searching for the right words. "Can you tell me what it was like at ChemCure just before the accident?"

Hannah's expression turned guarded. "What do you want to know?"

"Do you recall anyone acting strangely? Any confrontations with your coworkers?"

She was quiet for a moment, and her eyes lost focus as she concentrated. Finally, she shook her head slowly. "No, nothing like that happened." Owen's heart dropped. It had been a long shot, but still…

"It's just…." She paused, then shook her head.

"What?" He held his breath, hardly daring to hope.

"It's probably nothing, but the day before the accident, I got into an argument with Marcia and her boss, Dave."

"About what?"

"They were unhappy with me because my team

hadn't identified any promising compounds in several months. I told them the data weren't there, that the chemicals we'd been testing were too toxic to move forward in the pipeline. But Dave wanted me to push some through, just so we could show the bigwigs the project had momentum."

"What did you say?"

She stiffened, her chest puffing out like an angry bird's. He almost smiled but caught himself just in time. "I said no, of course! I wasn't going to rubber-stamp something I knew wasn't working, just to meet some artificial company benchmark."

"Weren't you afraid they'd pull you off the project?"

Hannah snorted and rolled her eyes. "Hardly. There was no one else to run the project."

Interesting. That meant the pool of people who had the know-how to work with the chemicals was small. She had told him as much the other day in the car, but it was good to have it confirmed. "How did Dave and Marcia react?"

The corner of her mouth curved up, and he realized she had enjoyed defending her work. "They weren't thrilled with me, but in the end, they accepted my reasoning. After all, I didn't give them much choice in the matter."

"Did you have this type of discussion with them often?"

She held up her hand and tilted it back and forth. "We didn't talk about it all the time, but it was a fairly regular discussion."

The nurse walked back into the room, carrying a handful of supplies. Owen watched silently as she tended to Hannah, his mind whirring as he arranged the puzzle pieces of what he knew, trying to make sense of it all. A larger picture was starting to emerge, triggering a rush that was equal parts excitement and determination. While the nurse finished up, he retrieved his phone and stepped into the hallway.

"Where have you been?" Nate said, forgoing any kind of greeting. "I need to talk to you."

"Same here. I'm at the hospital—can you meet me here?"

"Hospital? What the hell is going on? Are you okay?" It was petty of him, but the concern in his partner's voice made Owen feel good, as though he belonged. Nate wasn't anything like John had been, but he was still a good man, and Owen enjoyed working with him. It was nice to have a partner once more.

"I'm fine. Hannah was attacked again, and this time, she wasn't so lucky." He rattled off her room number. "Can you get here soon?"

"Give me ten minutes. I've been busy, too, and I think you're going to like what I've got."

Owen ended the call and slipped his phone back into his pocket just as the nurse was leaving Hannah's room.

"Are you going to stay with her tonight?" she asked.

"Yes," he replied without hesitation.

She nodded, as if she'd expected that answer. "I'll get a spare set of sheets for you. The chair folds out into a single bed. It's not the most comfortable thing in the world, but it's better than the floor."

"Thanks."

He paused before heading back into the room. Would Hannah be okay with him staying the night? He hadn't even thought to ask her; he'd just answered reflexively, without any conscious debate. There was no way he could leave her alone and unguarded, not after there had been two attempts on her life in the past day alone. He wasn't going to take a chance that whoever was behind this would stop by to finish her off while she lay vulnerable in her bed.

But what if she didn't want him in the room? It was possible. She may want her privacy, especially since nurses and doctors would be stopping by regularly to poke and prod her. She was probably feeling especially exposed since she was naked under the thin hospital gown. Given her reluctance to let him touch her last night, the gentlemanly thing to do would be to stand outside her room so he didn't catch a glimpse and embarrass her.

Too bad he wasn't a gentleman.

No, he decided. He was going to stay with her tonight. Something told him that if he stepped back and gave her privacy, she'd use the space to rebuild her defenses. If he stayed, if he forced her to remember the intimacy of last night, she wouldn't have a chance. And while he knew that in the long term it would be better for him to leave her alone, his selfish side was in charge and calling the shots. If that meant Hannah had to spend the night feeling a tiny bit unsettled by his presence, so be it. He wanted her to get used to him, to need him as much as he was coming to need her. And forget that old adage about absence making the heart grow fonder—in this case, absence would only allow her to forget about him.

It wasn't a risk he was willing to take.

Chapter 10

When Owen came back into the room, there was something different about him. Gone was the earlier sadness that had clung to him when he'd told her about his former partner. In its place was an aura of fierce determination, as though he'd made up his mind about something and he was going to see it through, regardless of any objections.

Hannah used her feet and her good arm to push herself up on the bed. Owen looked as if he had something to say, and she didn't want to hear it lying down.

"I'm staying here tonight. With you."

She blinked, taken aback by his announcement. "Uh, don't you have work to do?"

"I can take care of it from here. I'm not leaving you alone."

A rush of relief swept through her, followed swiftly by the sharp bite of annoyance. "Don't I get a say in the matter?" Truth be told, she had been worried about being alone tonight. Even though the chances of her assailant coming back to attack her in the hospital were vanishingly small, she'd rest better knowing she wasn't alone. But Owen could at least pretend he was asking her permission before announcing his decision as if it was the law. She hadn't slept with a man in the same room in…well, longer than she cared to think about. And even though he wouldn't be sharing her bed, it still felt very personal.

His gaze narrowed as he stepped closer. "What's this about? You didn't mind spending time with me last night. Why the sudden change of heart?" His voice was steady, but as he approached, she saw a flicker of uncertainty in his eyes. It disappeared almost instantly, but that brief, unguarded reaction made it clear that her resistance had hurt him.

"It's not like that," she began, but he cut her off.

"I can assure you, I'm not expecting a repeat of last night."

Now, *that* stung. Even though she had no desire to get frisky in a hospital room, his knee-jerk rejection of the attraction they shared made her feel very small and alone. "I didn't think you were," she replied, hoping he couldn't tell she was upset.

"Then what's going on? A few minutes ago, you didn't want me to leave you alone in the hospital. Now you're trying to get me to run off to work." He ran a hand through his hair and lowered his head. "I'm not making that mistake again," he said softly.

"I want you to stay with me because it's what you *want* to do, not because it's something you feel you *have* to do," Hannah snapped. "I won't be anyone's obligation."

"Is that what you think?" Owen's eyes widened, his surprise plain. "Do you really believe I see you as some sort of obligation?" His indignation was almost palpable, and only served to make Hannah feel even worse. How had she bungled this so badly?

"No." She paused, looking around the room so she wouldn't have to meet that intense blue stare. "Maybe." From the corner of her eye she saw his brows shoot up, and she hastened to add, "I don't know! Okay? I don't know what to think."

He was still a moment, so still she didn't think he was even breathing. Then he moved, slowly and carefully, as if his very bones hurt. But as he neared the bed, Hannah realized her mistake—he wasn't in pain, he was angry. A fury like she'd never seen before glowed behind his eyes, and his muscles were rigid, tense with leashed emotion that he refused to express. His jaw was clenched so tightly she could practically *hear* his teeth grinding together, and as she watched, his hands curled into fists at his sides. He looked like a man on the verge of violence, and an instinctive burst of fear filled her, followed quickly by fascination. The two emotions swirled together, creating a potent combination in Hannah's system that made her chest feel tight and her palms go damp.

His anger caught her completely by surprise. In her experience, people only got upset to that degree if they cared about someone. While she knew they shared an attraction, she hadn't realized she had the power to ignite his temper. It was a heady sensation, the ability to push his buttons and cause this normally unflappable and composed man to lose his cool.

Her fear burned away quickly, leaving only curiosity in its wake as she watched him move. He was a big man to begin with, but since she was lying in a hospital bed, his legs seemed longer, his shoulders broader. Anger made his movements even more precise than usual, a clear signal that Owen was totally in control of himself and his emotions. Still, Hannah knew that even if he wasn't, even if he needed an outlet for his fury, she would never be the target. No matter what she did or said, Owen was not the kind of man to take his rage out on a woman.

He lowered himself to sit on the edge of her bed, then laid a hand on her thigh. His touch was warm, the heat of him burning through the thin hospital blankets. A wave of goose bumps broke out along her skin, radiating from the heavy weight of his palm, and Hannah struggled to contain a shiver.

"You," he said so softly she had to strain to hear, "are not an obligation." He punctuated his words with a gentle squeeze that made Hannah's skin tingle. "When I'm with you, it's because I want to be, not because I feel like I have to be."

She nodded, her eyes locked on that big hand of his. It had felt so good to be touched by him last night, skin to skin, their breaths mingling along with the sounds of sighs and soft moans. Her body, willfully oblivious to the tension between them, rejoiced in feeling him again. Her stomach fluttered in anticipation and her skin seemed to shrink, tightening and growing ever more sensitive. *Just a little higher*, she urged silently.

Slip that hand under the blanket and touch me like you did last night.

"Hannah." His deep voice brought her back to the room, to herself. "Look at me."

She didn't respond right away, earning another soft squeeze from his hand. She was tempted to keep her eyes down, wanting to feel that gentle pressure again, but she forced herself to look up.

"I care about you," he said, his gaze taking on a sensual heat she recognized. "I enjoy spending time with you. And I think you feel the same about me." He paused and she nodded, dropping her eyes to the sexy curve of his mouth. He rewarded her with a small smile and leaned closer. "Good. So make no mistake about it—I'm here because I want to be."

Hannah felt herself leaning forward as well, unconsciously straining toward him like one magnet seeking another. Just before their lips met, he drew back a little. "If you want me to go, I will. I don't want you to feel uncomfortable around me. But I will make sure another officer is here so you're not alone tonight."

She shook her head. "No. I do want you to stay. Please."

He nodded, then closed the distance between them. She sighed into his mouth, relaxing into the kiss and surrendering to her body's responses. He was better than any drug, she decided, the pain in her head and shoulder disappearing as endorphins flooded her system. The scientist in her knew she was merely experiencing a biochemical reaction to contact, but the woman in her recognized that it was the man kissing her that made her feel so good.

He drew back slowly, too soon for her liking. She

let him go reluctantly, her good hand still gripping his shirt as he eased away. He smiled, that sexy grin he seemed to reserve only for her. "I'm glad we got that straightened out," he murmured.

"Me, too," she said, giving his shirt an experimental tug.

He laughed softly. "You need to recover."

"I can recover much faster if you're distracting me from the pain."

Owen's reply was drowned out by the sound of an exaggerated cough from the doorway. Hannah turned to find Nate standing just inside the room, his cheeks as red as a fire truck.

"Uh, I can come back if this isn't a good time."

Owen straightened and ran a hand down the front of his shirt to smooth out the wrinkled evidence of her grip. "No, you're fine. Come on in." He stood and gestured for Nate to sit in the nearby chair.

Nate shot her an apologetic glance as he moved into the room. "What happened to you?"

"I picked a fight with a car and lost," she replied. It was a lame attempt at humor, but she hoped it would lighten the awkward mood. Nate laughed weakly, shaking his head.

"Do you know who did it?" His eyes cut to Owen, who shook his head.

"I came on the scene just after it happened. Called in the make and model, didn't get any plates."

"Damn," Nate muttered. "I don't suppose you got a look at the driver?"

It was Hannah's turn to shake her head. "No. There was too much glare on the windshield—I couldn't see inside the car."

Nate merely nodded, as if he'd expected that answer. Then he turned to Owen. "Same guy?"

"Hell of a coincidence," Owen replied.

"And you don't like coincidences," Nate finished.

With growing amusement, Hannah watched the two of them continue to talk. Did they even realize their conversation was all but indecipherable to an outsider? She could follow because the events had happened to her, but if she had just walked into the room, she'd be lost. *Must be a cop thing*, she decided. *No*, she amended after another moment. *Must be a partner thing.*

"I haven't even told you the best part yet," Nate said, digging in his pocket for his phone. His finger tapped the screen, then he flipped the phone around to show Owen. "Check it out."

Owen's brows drew together as he stared at the image on the screen. "What is this?"

"It's a flyer I found at the free clinic advertising an asthma study. Notice how there's just a strip of phone numbers at the bottom?"

"Sure."

"I compared it to all the other medical-study advertisements at the clinic, and talked to some of the clinic staff. Apparently, medical studies have to be approved by an advisory board, and that approval has to be displayed prominently on the advertising, along with information about the hospital or university conducting the study."

"I don't see anything like that here."

"Exactly!" Nate's excitement was contagious. Hannah caught herself leaning forward, and had to remind herself to breathe. Apparently, Nate didn't have that problem, since he barreled ahead without pause. "Which means it can't be an official study."

Owen nodded slowly. "It's worth checking out. Do we have anything to tie this to our victims?"

"I thought you'd never ask." Nate took the phone and scrolled to another photo. "Remember the first victim? The one found wearing jeans?"

"Yeah. But we didn't find any ID on him."

"We didn't, but Forensics retrieved a scrap of paper from his front pocket. A scrap of paper that just happens to be the same size as the phone-number strips at the bottom of this ad."

Owen's head jerked up, his eyes growing bright. "Tell me they're working on a match right now."

Nate grinned. "They are indeed."

"How long until we'll know?"

"I asked the guys to call as soon as they knew something. Maybe another hour or so?"

"We've got to find out who answers this number."

"It's a cell phone. Waiting on a warrant." Nate ran a hand through his hair, letting out a deep sigh.

Owen shook his head. "That'll take too long. We need to move on this before they figure out we're looking at them."

"What do you propose?"

A sly smile took over Owen's mouth, making him look positively mischievous. Hannah felt her stomach clench at the sight, and realized in that instant she wasn't going to like what he said next.

"Done any undercover work lately?"

Marcia stared out the windowed wall of her office, the impressive view of Houston's skyline failing to hold her attention. Lunch with the detective had gone fairly well, but he seemed to be the determined type, and it was highly unlikely a few hours of distraction would be enough to redirect his focus, especially when she hadn't had any decent red herrings to throw in his path.

"Dammit, Dave," she muttered. He wanted her to control the situation, but he refused to give her the resources she needed to do a good job. Was that because he wanted her to fail? If she couldn't handle this situation, would that give him the ammunition he needed to hang her out to dry?

A spike of pain pierced her stomach, making her reach for the antacids. Her hands shook as she fumbled with the top, but she managed to shake out a few tablets. She chewed slowly, then took a sip of water to wash everything down.

What were her options? Dave was like a wild animal. She expected him to turn on her at any second. And what had she done to protect herself? Not enough. Oh, she'd made notes of their phone conversations, but he was too smart to commit anything to writing. She still had the debris from the lab explosion in her desk drawer—perhaps the police could get prints off the threatening note that was still attached. But something told her they wouldn't find anything.

Her best bet would be to outmaneuver Dave. If she went to the police first, it would be her story they listened to, and Dave would be put on the defensive. She didn't have a ton of evidence against him, but the one thing she did have in her favor was the fact that he didn't expect her to betray him. He thought she was totally under his control, a good little soldier who carried out his orders without question. If she did throw him under the bus, it would come as a shock, which meant he was more likely to make a damaging mistake as he scrambled to control the fallout.

She didn't try to stop the smile curving her lips as she imagined the look on his face when he learned of her defection. What she wouldn't give to see him get the news in person! She took a moment to enjoy the thought, then shook her head. As much fun as it would be to gloat over Dave's fall, it wouldn't be safe. He probably had any number of safeguards in place, complete with patsies set up to take the fall for him. If Dave managed to get away, it wouldn't take long for him to seek revenge.

A chill skittered down her back on spidery legs. The thought of Dave's retribution had been enough to keep her from going to the police before. But now, with the bodies of innocent victims piling up, she couldn't keep silent any longer. Even the fear of going to jail herself wasn't going to stop her this time. Things had gone far enough.

She turned to face her desk and took a deep breath for courage. Then she reached for her phone and started to dial before she could change her mind.

Chapter 11

It took a few hours and some fast talking, but Owen managed to convince his captain that they couldn't just go in, guns blazing.

"As soon as these guys get a clue, they're gone. Besides, we don't know if they have a victim with them now. If we bust down their door, it could turn into a hostage situation."

"Assuming they have their next target," Captain Rogers pointed out. "They might be alone."

Owen nodded, conceding his point. "It's possible. But consider the timing of the bodies we do have. The interval between discoveries is shrinking not growing. That makes me think they've entered a new phase and are picking up victims more frequently. It stands to reason they've already got their next one."

Captain Rogers was quiet a moment. Owen resisted the urge to keep talking, knowing he needed to let the other man think. The captain was an analytical man who liked to consider a situation from all angles. Pressing him for a decision would only backfire.

After a moment, the other man let out a long sigh that crackled over the line. "What do you want to do?"

Owen sketched out his plan, making sure to include the latest updates from the forensics team. Nate had gotten the call about half an hour ago—the paper found in the first victim's pocket was a match to the flyer from the clinic. While it wasn't quite a smoking gun, the match did make for a compelling piece of evidence.

He finished up and held his breath, waiting for his boss to make the final call. If the captain didn't agree with him, it was back to the drawing board, something he didn't have the patience for at this moment.

After an endless second, Captain Rogers made a thoughtful sound. "Seems like a solid plan. But we need a few hours to get things set up. I don't want you running in alone."

"But we need to move on this. The longer we wait, the more time they have to kill someone else or pack up and move on. We can't miss this opportunity!"

"No buts," the captain replied firmly. "We're not going to half-ass this. We do it right or not at all. That means waiting for the pieces to assemble."

"Captain—"

"I want you on board, Owen. This has been your case from the beginning, and I want you there when it closes. But if you push it, I won't hesitate to go forward without you. Are we clear?"

"Yes, sir."

"Good. You'll make the call in the morning."

"Yes, sir." Owen disconnected and swallowed hard,

pushing down the lump of disappointment rising in his throat. He had wanted to get started right away, but logically, he knew his boss was right. Better to wait for everything to get set up than to go in unprepared. After all, that was how John had gotten killed...

Gray clouds of grief rolled in at the memory of his old partner, and Owen shook his head to dispel them before they dominated his thoughts. He didn't have time to indulge, not when he had to stay sharp for tomorrow's plan.

With a sigh, he tucked his phone back into his pocket and stepped into Hannah's hospital room. She'd dozed off and on over the past few hours, and he and Nate had been careful to speak quietly, not wanting to wake her. She was awake now, and both she and Nate turned to face him with curious expressions.

"We're on for the morning," he said, unable to keep a note of pride from creeping into his voice. The fact that the captain had not only agreed to Owen's plan but was letting him run the show went a long way to restoring his shaky confidence. Now he just had to pull it off.

Nate grinned, his enthusiasm clear. "Good to hear. Was it a hard sell?"

Owen shrugged. "Would have been a lot harder without the forensic evidence. That was a great find."

The tips of Nate's ears turned pink. "Just got lucky."

"It was more than luck," Owen replied. "It was good detective work."

Nate stood, clearly uncomfortable with the praise. "Well. I'd better head out. Get ready for the big show tomorrow."

"Call me if anything comes up."

"Will do." Nate offered Hannah a smile. "Get some rest, okay?"

She nodded. "I'll try."

As soon as Nate had cleared the door, Hannah turned to rest her gaze on Owen. He could tell by the look on her face she was going to argue with him about tomorrow, but he wasn't quite ready to hear it yet. He'd already defended his ideas to his captain—he didn't want to have to defend them to her as well.

He busied himself by walking over to the table beside her bed and picking up her water jug. He gave it an experimental shake and was rewarded with the sound of sloshing. "Want me to get you a refill?"

"No, thanks."

"What about more ice? It's all melted now."

"That's okay."

He put the jug down, straightened the box of tissues. "How's your shoulder?"

"It's fine. Are you done stalling?"

The question made him pause. "What makes you think I'm stalling?"

"I'm a professor. I see this kind of thing all the time from students trying to delay the inevitable. I'm a pro at recognizing it." There was no mistaking the amusement in her tone, and some of his worry lifted at hearing it. Perhaps she wasn't upset after all.

He sat down and faced her. The chair was still unsettlingly warm from Nate, but he ignored the discomfort and focused on Hannah's face. "Is there something you want to talk about?"

"I'm just wondering if this is really the best approach."

"You don't think the plan will work?" The insecurities he'd thought were under control came screaming back into his mind. She didn't believe in his idea. Did she doubt him as well?

She shook her head. "That's just it. I don't know what will happen."

"No one does."

"I don't like uncertainty. Especially not when your safety is at stake."

Relief hit him like a strong gust of wind, making him feel curiously light. He gaped at her for a second, then threw his head back and laughed.

She stared at him as if he'd grown an extra head. "What's so funny?"

He held up his hand, unable to stop. It felt so good, as though all the stress, worry and grief of the past few months was pouring out of him with each full exhalation.

What a fool he'd been! Hannah didn't doubt him, after all—she was simply worried about him. He'd been so paranoid, so quick to see the negative, that he'd never even considered the fact that she was reluctant about tomorrow because she cared about him. The thought made his heart swell, and he put a hand on his chest, half expecting to feel the bulge of it behind his breastbone.

How long had it been since someone cared enough to worry about him? John had, of course. And Jessica—at least in the beginning of their relationship. By the end, he was pretty sure she only thought of him if he was standing right in front of her. The guys at work worried, but in that low-level kind of way that extended to everyone on the force. They certainly weren't losing sleep over the thought of him in danger.

Even though he hated the idea he was a bother to Hannah, he was perversely pleased at her reaction. She liked him enough to worry about him, which made him feel more confident that his feelings for her were not misplaced, and she wasn't going to just walk away when this was over. A question loomed large in his mind though: Did she care enough to give their budding relationship a chance? More important, did he have the patience to find out, or was he going to blow it by pushing for too much too quickly?

"Sorry," he said, his laughter drying up. "I'm not laughing at you. It's just…well, I'm not used to having people worry about me. It feels nice."

Before Hannah could reply, his phone buzzed in his pocket. "Just a sec," he said. When he saw the now-familiar numbers on the display, he frowned. He really wasn't in the mood to talk to Marcia again, especially so soon after their completely wasted lunch. Besides, he only had a handful of hours before tomorrow's takedown, and he wanted to spend them talking to Hannah, not wasting his time with a woman who couldn't take a hint and was of no help to his investigation.

He sent the call to voice mail and slipped the phone back into his pocket. "Sorry."

"No problem." Hannah's gaze was direct, but he could see the fatigue in her eyes. "You don't need to take that?"

"Nope. They can leave a message if they need to talk to me that badly."

She nodded, then broke into a huge yawn. Owen fought the urge to do likewise and smiled at her when she opened her eyes again.

"Sorry," she said, her cheeks flushing a pretty pink. "That was rude."

"Not at all," he assured her. "Why don't you get a little sleep."

"What will you do? I'd hate for you to just sit here staring at me. Talk about boring."

On the contrary. Watching her sleep would be a pleasure. He wanted nothing more than to look on while she sank into oblivion, her body going limp in relaxation, her breathing growing deeper as she began to dream. Would those dreams show on her face? Was she a quiet sleeper, or did she make soft little sounds? He found he had a burning desire to find out.

"I'll be fine," he said. "I'm going to run down to the cafeteria and grab a sandwich. I'll be back in a few minutes, so why don't you just close your eyes and rest?"

She nodded, her eyelids already starting to droop. "Just for a little bit," she mumbled.

He stood there for a moment, mesmerized. She was so beautiful. Her delicate features should have made her look vulnerable, but he knew too much about her to see her in that light. To him, she was a warrior, a woman who kept going no matter the obstacles in her path. It was inspiring for him to be around someone like that. He wanted nothing more than to stay and watch her, but his stomach growled, a reminder that he had planned to get food.

The nurses' station was a few feet away, and beyond that, a security guard sat in the small waiting area, idly thumbing through a magazine. Perfect.

The man glanced up as Owen approached. "Can I help you?"

"I hope so." Owen showed the guard his badge. "There's a woman down the hall who I don't want to leave alone. I'm just going to duck down to the cafeteria and grab a sandwich. Would you make sure no one enters her room?"

The guard's face brightened at the request, as if he was relieved to finally have something to do. "No problem. Take as long as you need."

"Thanks." Owen shook the man's hand before turning to leave. Even though he wouldn't be gone long, he felt better knowing Hannah would be watched over in his absence. He pulled his phone from his pocket while he walked. Better to make his calls now so he didn't risk waking Hannah when he returned. He didn't want any distractions to interrupt his time with her.

Hannah woke to a dark room, her back tingling insistently. She wriggled against the bed, but the movement did nothing to relieve the itching of her scars.

"Everything okay?" Owen's voice was like a soft caress and she closed her eyes, allowing herself a moment to enjoy the low, rumbling sound as it rolled over her.

"I'm fine," she replied automatically. She forced herself to remain still, hoping the itching would go away. But it didn't.

She moved again, pressing her back hard against the sheets. The added friction provided some relief, but the underlying irritation didn't ease.

"You don't seem fine." Why did he have to be so observant? Why couldn't he just nod off like any normal person so she could figure out how to scratch her back in peace?

"What is it? Are you in pain again?" Now he sounded

concerned. Hannah heaved a mental sigh, knowing he wasn't going to drop the subject until she gave him an explanation.

"It's my back. My scars itch."

"Oh." He was quiet for a moment. "Is there anything I can do?"

"You can get a nurse. I need to put some lotion on my back. I usually do it myself before going to bed, but that obviously didn't happen today."

More silence. Then he spoke, his voice so husky she had to strain to hear. "I could do it for you."

She sucked in a breath, the suggestion hanging between them. Her body flared to life, skin warming at the thought of Owen's hands on her again. Hadn't she been fantasizing about that very thing only a few hours ago?

The word *yes* was on the tip of her tongue, but she couldn't bring herself to say it. She wanted Owen to see her as desirable, attractive. Having him slather lotion on her scars would only serve to remind him that she was damaged, something she couldn't bear right now.

As if sensing her hesitation, Owen leaned forward and laid his hand on her bed. "Please." It was said so softly, empty of any pressure or insistence. Just a simple, heartfelt request.

That one word broke through her defenses more effectively than any long-winded argument. He sounded so sincere she couldn't help but nod slowly, her heart in her throat.

He gave her a sweet smile that struck her square in the heart. She took a deep breath when he turned to fetch the travel-sized lotion from the toiletries the hospital had provided. She felt as if she was standing on the edge of a cliff, about to jump into the abyss. And all because of the man before her.

Did he feel the same? Did he know how he affected her? Probably not. After all, she couldn't even explain it to herself.

He turned back, his face in the shadows. "Can you lean forward?"

She nodded, even though he probably couldn't see her that well. Using her uninjured arm, she grabbed onto the bed rail and pulled herself up until she was sitting on the bed. "Scoot up a bit," he instructed, moving to stand next to her. She complied, bending her legs at the knee and inching toward the foot of the bed. Before she could ask why, Owen slid into the space behind her, his long legs coming to rest on either side of her body.

His breath was a warm weight on the nape of her neck. Seconds later, she felt his fingers playing with the strings that held her gown closed. "I'm going to have to untie this knot." A thrill shot through her system at the dark promise in his words. One firm tug, and the thin fabric of the hospital gown would fall, exposing her nakedness. The prospect left her both excited and scared. Even though the room was dim, Owen was sitting close enough to see the full extent of her scars. He would know, without a doubt, how disfigured she really was. What if she disgusted him? After all, it had happened before…

Hannah held her breath, knowing this was her last chance to go back. She could refuse, ask for a nurse. He'd get up from the bed and give her back her personal space, and they could both pretend this moment had never happened. It was the rational, safe thing to do.

But she was tired of playing it safe.

She nodded, not trusting herself to speak past the lump in her throat. His fingers started to move and she slammed her eyes shut, struck by the foolish notion that if she couldn't see him, he couldn't see her. After what seemed like an eternity, the fabric slid slowly, gently off her shoulders, skimming down her arms to pool softly in her lap.

She should have felt cold, sitting in the chilly room with only her legs covered by the thin blankets. But Owen was putting off so much heat, she felt as if she were sitting in front of a roaring fire. It was a comforting sensation, and she wanted nothing more than to lean back and sink into his warmth, to completely relax and let go of all her fears and worries. The idea made for a nice fantasy, but she realized with a growing sense of dread that's all it would ever be.

Owen hadn't spoken a word since asking her to move down. Now that she was sitting with her scars in full view, his silence was distressing. Hannah's muscles tightened as despair clawed at her throat. Of course he was repulsed by her injuries. Why had she thought he'd react any differently from Jake?

Her eyes burned with unshed tears and she fisted her hands in the gown, ready to pull it back over her body and cover her destroyed skin. But before she could make a move, something soft brushed across the back of her neck.

She stilled, focusing hard. It happened again, a gentle, teasing caress, this time accompanied with a huff of warm, humid air.

Shock flooded her system as Hannah realized that Owen was kissing her. Those were his lips, moving with exquisite care down her neck, over her shoulders and beyond. "So beautiful," he murmured, humming softly as he drifted across her back. "So lovely."

Hannah's breath left her body on a shuddering sigh, and a fine tremor shook her limbs. Tears ran down to drip off the end of her nose, landing on her hands and soaking into her gown. Owen's reaction had caught her completely off guard. Never in a million years would she have imagined a man could not only accept her scars but find them beautiful.

He continued to move down her back, exploring the terrain with kisses, licks, nuzzles. And through it all, he whispered almost reverent words of affection, words that made her feel beautiful and desirable. It had been a long time since she'd felt wanted by a man—so long, she thought she'd forgotten how to respond. But her body remembered, and it warmed under his hands, his mouth. She felt like a flower, turning her face to the sun after a long, cold winter.

Her muscles softened, growing languid and liquid until holding her head up was a chore. She slumped forward a bit until her forehead rested against her knees, and let out a long sigh. "Owen," she murmured.

"Hmm?" He paused but didn't move away.

She shook her head weakly, unable to form the words to tell him how much his response meant to her. For the first time in years, she felt *normal* again.

Owen's touch left her back and she whimpered, missing his warmth. "Patience," he chided, a note of amusement in his voice. She heard the snap of a plastic lid, then the light, slightly floral scent of lotion filled the air. She expected him to start applying the lotion right away, but he didn't, surprising her once again. He hesitated for a few seconds, then touched her, laying his palms flat against her back. With sure, smooth strokes, he began to spread the now-warm lotion across her back.

A groan of pleasure rose up her throat. The itchy irritation that had plagued her burn scars vanished under his skilled attention, relief spreading in its wake. She couldn't decide if it was his hands or the lotion that was the true balm, but as the pleasure spread across her skin, she realized it didn't matter.

He moved slowly, teasing her with light then firm strokes, his fingers lingering on the curve of her shoulder, the slope of her back. His touch was everywhere at once, drowning her in sensation. Her head reeled, her thoughts fragmenting and reassembling shards of stained glass. She couldn't focus, couldn't piece together a coherent sentence. Finally, she gave up trying to think and embraced the overwhelming storm of physical stimuli, letting it carry her away to another plane of consciousness.

Gradually, she became aware that the quality of Owen's movements had changed. The interval between his touches grew longer, and she had the fuzzy realization that he was going to stop. "No," she protested weakly. She didn't want him to stop touching her—as long as he kept his hands on her, she could pretend the rest of the world didn't exist, that it was just the two of them, here in the dark.

"I'm out of lotion," he said, his voice deep and soothing.

"Don't care," she mumbled.

He chuckled, a low rumble that she felt as much as heard. "Aren't you a greedy one."

"Mmm-hmm."

He ran his hands from the top of her shoulders to her waist, then reached around to grab the fabric of her hospital gown. He pulled it up her body and tied the strings back into place. Her modesty thus restored, he laid his hands lightly on her shoulders and gently pulled her back to rest against his chest.

"Feel better?"

Hannah tried to respond, but all that came out was a contented sigh. His mouth moved against her ear, curving into a smile. "Me, too."

She shifted, snuggling closer to him. It was then she realized that Owen wasn't as relaxed as she was—or at least, part of him wasn't relaxed. Wanting to give him the same pleasure he'd given her, she ran her hand up the outside of his thigh, making an inquiring noise in her throat. His hand covered hers, squeezing gently.

"Rest now," he said softly, the words warm in her ear. "Just rest."

She nodded, releasing her loose grasp on consciousness. As she surrendered to the seductive pull of sleep, she could have sworn Owen spoke again. "Thank you, sweet Hannah." Before she could puzzle over his word choice, she slipped under, her dreams punctuated by the steady, reassuring beat of his heart against her ear.

Chapter 12

"We're ready here."

Owen acknowledged the tech guy with a nod. "Everyone else set?"

There was a small chorus of affirmative responses, and Owen felt a surge of pride. He really did work with the best guys on the force, and their willingness to step up and support his plan of action both humbled and energized him. "Let's do this."

Nate held out a piece of paper with a phone number. Owen picked up the handset and dialed.

After an endless moment, someone picked up. "Clinical Associates." It was a woman, and something about her voice sounded vaguely familiar to him… He caught a movement out of the corner of his eye, and turned to look at Hannah. She was frowning, and had stepped forward as if she was trying to hear better. Did she recognize the voice?

The woman repeated her greeting, an edge to her voice. "Uh, yeah," he stammered. *Get back in the game!* "I'm a patient at the Thomas Street clinic, and I saw your flyer on the bulletin board. My asthma's pretty bad, and I was wondering if I could enroll in your trial?"

"How old are you?"

"Thirty."

"That's perfect!" The woman sounded pleased now, as if he'd said something particularly clever. "We'd love to have you come in for an initial evaluation."

He glanced at Nate, who gave him a thumbs-up. "When can you see me?"

"Let me see…" She paused, and he heard the *click* of computer keys. "We actually have an opening today at two. Can you make that?"

The tactical guy nodded his approval. "Sure can. Where is the office?"

She rattled off an address, and one of the tech guys quickly pulled it up on a map. The place was about six blocks away from the clinic. "Okay," Owen said, knowing he needed to wrap up the call. "Do I need to bring any money?"

"Oh, no, nothing like that." She laughed, and that prickle of awareness intensified, making the fine hairs on the back of his neck stand on end. He *knew* this woman somehow. "The first visit is just an evaluation, to see if you're a good fit for our study."

That didn't sound promising. He needed to find out if this so-called clinical trial was the real deal or just one more roadblock keeping him from finding the killers. "But my symptoms are pretty bad," he hedged. "I was hoping to get help right away."

"That's not a problem," the woman informed him. "If you're enrolled in the trial, you'll get your first dose of medication today."

Owen nodded, relaxing a bit. Good. That meant they had the chemicals on-site, which would strengthen his case against them. "That's a relief," he said. "This spring has just been brutal for me."

She laughed again. "We get that a lot. Hopefully we'll be able to help you."

"I guess I'll find out at two," he said.

"See you then." She hung up, and Owen looked to the tech guy. The man nodded. "She's using a cell phone, but I was able to narrow down her location. She's not anywhere near the address she gave you."

"Where is she?"

The man frowned at the monitor. "Near the junction of I-10 and 610. In the northwestern part of the city."

Owen leaned forward to look at the screen, hardly daring to breathe. Could it be…? Satisfaction flooded his system as his eyes confirmed what he already knew to be true. There on the screen, near the intersection of I-10 and 610, sat a large complex of buildings.

ChemCure Industries.

He looked for Hannah, wondering if she'd made the connection herself. If her pale face and shocked expression were any indication, she had. He reached for her, and she moved to stand next to him, gripping his hand like a lifeline.

"I don't think it's a coincidence," he murmured.

She shook her head. "Probably not."

"Did that woman's voice sound familiar to you? I felt like I'd heard her before, but I couldn't place where."

Hannah nodded, her shoulders sagging. "I think you may be right. It sounded just like Shelly Newman."

The pieces snapped into place. "Yes! That woman we met in the hall at ChemCure Industries." He turned to find Nate. "Run a check on Shelly Newman, see if she's got any outstanding debts, medical bills, bad mortgage. The usual stuff."

Nate nodded. "Got it."

The tactical officer spoke up. "We've got a preliminary plan in place. We're going to deploy now, scout out the area. I'll be in touch soon."

Hannah's grip on his hand tightened, so he squeezed back, hoping she'd find the gesture reassuring. "Sounds good."

"I just can't believe it," she murmured, shaking her head. "I thought I knew her. We ate lunch together. She baked me a cake every year for my birthday. She's not the kind of person to get mixed up in something like this." She looked up at him, her eyes shiny with unshed tears. "There must be some mistake. I'm sure the woman who answered the phone just sounds like Shelly. It can't really be her." There was a pleading note in her voice, as if she wanted Owen to confirm that this was a simple misunderstanding.

Sympathy tugged at Owen's heart. He'd give almost anything to spare Hannah the pain of realizing her former friend was involved in the murders of several innocent people. But he couldn't lie to her. And as much as this was going to hurt her, she needed to accept the truth.

He gave her hand a tug, pulling her away from the group and into the small break room that housed the coffeemaker and vending machines that kept the squad running. He pulled out a chair for her, and she slumped into it, cradling her injured arm. She looked dazed, and he wished he had time to hold her while she absorbed the bad news. Unfortunately, that wasn't an option.

He took a cautious sniff of the dark brew in the coffeepot. It smelled fairly fresh, but more important, it was hot. Moving quickly, he poured a cup and doctored it with some cream and sugar packets. He couldn't tell if her lack of color was due to residual stress from her accident or the shock of realizing Shelly wasn't who she seemed to be. Either way, he didn't want to take a chance that Hannah would faint on him.

"Here you go." He pressed the cup into her unresisting hands. She folded her fingers around the plastic, but didn't take a sip.

He settled into the chair across from her. "Are you okay?"

She shook her head. "I don't know anymore."

"Fair enough." He didn't press her, knowing it wouldn't help. She needed to process things at her own speed, and his interference would only make it worse.

"It's just…I thought I knew Shelly. But now I'm questioning everything. Everyone I ever worked with, all of my time spent at ChemCure Industries. Did I misjudge everyone so completely? And if so, what kind of an idiot does that make me?"

"First of all, you don't know for sure that Shelly is involved. It's possible the woman on the phone wasn't her."

Hannah shot him a skeptical look. "We both know that's not the case."

He lifted one shoulder, refusing to abandon the point. "Until it's confirmed, we have to assume it could be someone else. But let's pretend it was Shelly. You don't know how long she's been involved. We've only been working this case a few weeks, after the first victims showed up. That means it's possible Shelly's involvement doesn't go back very far. And if that's the case, it's very likely her hands were clean when she worked with you."

"Maybe." Hannah didn't sound convinced. "But I still can't understand why she'd get involved in the first place. It's so clearly wrong!"

"You're assuming she knows the full scope of what's happening. I don't think that's actually the case. An operation like this doesn't stay secret if all the players know exactly what's going on. I think she might only know what they're telling her, and they only tell her enough to keep her from getting suspicious."

Hannah tilted her head to the side, regarding him as if he were some kind of exotic puzzle. "Why are you defending her? I figured you'd be excited about this new lead."

"I am," he assured her. "But I have to keep an open mind. If I go in thinking I have everything figured out, I run the risk of missing an important clue."

"I guess that was my problem," she said, dropping her head. Her finger moved idly across the surface of the table, tracing the scratches and grooves that had been etched into the wood over the years. "I never thought the people I worked with were anything other than what I saw every day."

"Why would you?" He leaned forward and captured her wandering hand with his own, entwining their fingers. "You're not a paranoid person, Hannah.

It isn't in your nature to suspect everyone around you of wrongdoing."

She shrugged, wincing as the movement pulled her injured arm.

"Time for another dose of pain meds?"

"Not yet."

A sigh built in his chest. Why was she being so stubborn? "Remember what the nurse said—you need to take the medication regularly, or it won't work properly. If you wait until you're in too much pain, it's too late."

She glanced up then, a flash of anger in her eyes. "I'm fine, thank you," she said tightly.

His brows shot up at her reaction. "Okay," he said, leaning back to give her some space. "I'm just worried about you, that's all. I don't like for you to be in pain."

A quiet breath escaped her, and she seemed to deflate a little before his eyes. "I'm sorry," she said softly. "I didn't mean to bite your head off. I'm just having a little trouble processing everything, you know?"

Owen nodded, but as she wasn't looking at him, she didn't see his response.

"What if…" She paused, then shook herself. When she spoke again, her voice was so quiet he had to lean forward to catch the words. "What if my accident all those years ago wasn't really an accident?"

So she shared his suspicions. He felt a brief flash of relief, knowing that he wouldn't have to be the one to plant *that* particular seed in her mind. Still, best to let her explore the idea without pressure from him. Even though the thought of someone deliberately hurting her made his blood boil, he had to focus on the case at hand. There would be time later to make sure that the people responsible for the lab explosion were brought to justice.

"Is that what you think?"

"If you'd asked me that ten minutes ago, my answer would have been no. But now, after hearing Shelly's voice answering a phone number that's linked to the deaths of innocent people? I can't shake the feeling that the corruption at ChemCure Industries goes back years."

Owen said nothing, but he silently agreed with her. He'd had a bad feeling about the company since his first conversation with Marcia Foley. There was something off about her, and the way she kept trying to insinuate herself into his investigation. Most people wanted nothing to do with the police, and they were always eager for him to leave. But not Marcia. She was a little too happy to talk to him, and the lunch she'd insisted on the other day had been a complete waste of time.

He couldn't tell if she was actively trying to obstruct his investigation, or if she was just really bad at conveying a romantic interest. Either way, her behavior was suspicious.

And why had she called him again last night? She hadn't left a message, and he hadn't bothered trying to reach her. But should he? What if she had finally decided to be honest with him? Could he afford to ignore her now?

"Do you think I'm off base?"

Hannah's question pulled him out of his head. She was watching him, her eyes shiny but focused. *Her world is imploding*, he reminded himself. The least he could do was pay attention to their conversation, rather than drifting off on mental tangents.

"No," he replied, trying to put all the conviction he felt into his voice. "You're not. You're a scientist, which makes you a logical person. You're just looking at the evidence in a new way."

"Yeah, well. I don't like feeling this way."

"I don't blame you." He gave her hand a gentle squeeze, and she rewarded him with a small smile. "It's going to be okay."

"How can you be sure?" Her vulnerability bruised his heart, but he knew she wouldn't respond to empty promises or casual reassurances.

"I'm not," he said honestly. "But I can't dwell on the alternative." He was surprised to find it was the truth. After so many months of seeing only the dark, only the gray, in life, was he really looking for the light? Was he really seeking out the positive? It was what John would want, he knew. In his mind's eye, he could see his old partner wearing his "I told you so" expression, one brow arched in amusement and arms crossed.

"I'm glad to hear you say that," Hannah replied. "I have to confess, you had me worried yesterday."

Before he could figure out what exactly she meant by that, Nate stuck his head in the room. "Owen? We're ready to move."

He stood, excitement bubbling in his stomach. Time to get these guys, to put an end to the damage and destruction they were causing.

He was halfway to the door before he realized Hannah hadn't moved. "Aren't you coming?"

She looked up, confusion in her eyes. "What do you mean? I thought I was supposed to stay here."

"No, you're not."

Nate cleared his throat. "I'll just wait outside. Why don't you find me when you're ready."

Owen glanced at him. "Don't go far. This won't take long."

Hannah's brows shot up. "I didn't think you'd want me to tag along."

"And why is that?"

She gestured toward her right arm, cradled in the heavy cloth sling the hospital had provided for her. "I'm not exactly in fighting form."

He fought back a smile. "Good thing you won't be fighting, then."

"What exactly will I be doing?" She kept her voice casual, but there was an underlying thread of worry in her tone.

"You'll be staying with the paramedics," he explained. "The ambulance will be a few blocks away, just in case anything happens."

Some of the color drained out of her face, and her eyes widened. "You think something will happen?"

"No," he replied automatically, his assurance echoed by Nate, who spoke a split second later. Hannah looked from him to the doorway, her fear morphing into amusement.

"Well, I guess that settles things," she said drily. "Am I supposed to do anything, or shall I just sit there and twiddle my thumbs?"

He started to nod in agreement, but the sudden gleam in her eyes made him feel uneasy. "That's the general idea," he tried.

"I don't think so," she responded. "If you're dragging me along, I want to be useful."

A strangled noise that sounded suspiciously like a smothered laugh drifted in from the hall. Owen heaved a mental sigh. Damn Nate! Why couldn't his partner back him up on this?

"What do you think you could do that would be useful to this operation?"

That seemed to give her pause. She rocked back on her heels and bit her bottom lip, the pressure from her teeth making the soft pink flesh go pale. His gaze zeroed in on her mouth, and he had the sudden, intense urge to kiss her until her lips were red and swollen. He shook himself, dismissing the thought.

"I'm not sure," she said, starting to sound doubtful. "But I don't want to be a burden."

"You're not," he said.

She narrowed her eyes at him. "I also don't need a babysitter."

That was a little harder to refute, as his motivation for leaving her with the paramedics was to make sure someone was with her at all times. No way was he going to leave her alone again, not when there was an unknown assailant trying to hurt her. He cast about for something benign to say and was saved when Nate stuck his head back into the room.

"We need you in the ambulance because you've worked with these chemicals before, and you'll know how to neutralize them in case someone is exposed."

Owen glanced at his partner, trying to hide his surprise. As excuses went, it was a good one. How had he come up with that so quickly?

Hannah turned her thoughtful gaze on Nate, and Owen felt a bit of relief at no longer being in the hot seat. "I see," she said, the words practically dripping with doubt. It was clear she saw the lie for what it was, but he couldn't tell if she was going to challenge it or let it slide.

He held his breath while Hannah looked from him to Nate and then back again. Her expression communicated volumes, but after a moment, she merely nodded. "Well, then," she said, stepping forward to give Owen's shoulder a friendly pat as she moved to the door. "Let's go. We're wasting time."

Owen released his breath on a sigh, surprised to hear the same sound coming from Nate. He cocked a brow at the other man, and Nate raised his hands defensively. "What? She kind of scares me."

"That was a nice save," he muttered, careful to keep his voice low so Hannah wouldn't overhear.

"I have my moments," Nate replied. "But I have to admit, I'm surprised you wanted her to come along. I figured you'd want her to stay here."

Owen shook his head. "Nope. I want her as close to me as possible." He didn't elaborate. He knew his growing dependence on Hannah was probably a sign of weakness, but he didn't care. After losing John, he felt an almost uncontrollable need to know where she was, to make sure she was safe. He wasn't going to lose her the way he had his friend, and the only way he knew to keep her safe was to keep her by him. Her proximity guaranteed his peace of mind, something he wasn't willing to risk today.

Nate stopped, a speculative light entering his eyes as he regarded Owen. "Is it serious?"

Wasn't *that* a loaded question? And how exactly was he going to answer it?

At this point, Owen figured he had two options. He

could deny Nate's suspicions, which would only make his partner press harder. Or he could come clean and admit that he did have feelings for Hannah. It was probably best for him to be honest. Besides, Nate had walked in on them practically kissing in her hospital room. It would be an insult to the man's intelligence to pretend he hadn't seen anything. Still, that didn't mean he had to confess that his feelings for Hannah went well beyond a fling.

In the end, he settled for honesty. It was the easiest thing, and he didn't want to lie to his partner. They were still getting to know each other, but if Owen started lying to Nate now, their partnership was doomed before it ever really got going.

"I care about her," Owen responded. "A lot more than I probably should."

Nate studied him for a moment, his expression morphing from teasing to serious. "Nothing wrong with caring about a person," he said simply.

Owen jerked up one shoulder in a shrug, acknowledging the point.

"For what it's worth, I'm glad to hear it." Nate clapped a hand on Owen's shoulder, giving him a friendly squeeze. "I'm happy to see you're coming out of your shell a bit, at least where women are concerned."

"Thanks. I think." Feeling suddenly self-conscious, Owen nodded toward the room at large. "Let's get to it, shall we?"

"Lead the way. You're the man with the plan."

Owen nodded and kept his head up as he walked through the squad room, trying to project an air of absolute confidence despite the fact that he felt as if he'd just chugged a bottle of champagne. Nerves were a normal part of any operation. Besides, he was working with the best guys on the force.

What could possibly go wrong?

Hannah walked a few steps behind Owen, her eyes glued to his back. She couldn't look away—she was hungry for the sight of him, as if it had been weeks or even months since she'd last seen him. Part of it was her growing attachment to him, but there was a small, morbid part of her that worried this might be the last time she saw him.

He'll be fine, she told herself sternly. *He knows what he's doing.*

It was the truth, but her fears would not be put to rest so easily. Even the most careful plan couldn't account for all possible variables. What if he was hit by a stray bullet? Or someone bashed him over the head as he walked in the door? Her imagination kicked into overdrive, spinning increasingly disturbing fantasies that all shared the same outcome: Owen, bleeding or dead, and her powerless to help him.

She couldn't lose him now. Not when she had let down her walls, let him inside her heart.

It was silly, she knew. After all, they'd only known each other for a few days. But in that short amount of time, she'd been able to see what kind of man he was. Proud. Determined. Honorable. And kind.

He'd been so gentle with her last night. So achingly tender. Just the memory of his hands, his lips against her skin made her shiver, and a rash of goose bumps broke out across her arms.

Owen had given her a precious gift. Intellectually,

she had recognized that she would one day sleep with a man again, perhaps even have some kind of lasting relationship. But she had always envisioned this mystery man as ignoring her scars, or at best, merely tolerating them. She certainly hadn't expected anyone to lavish attention on them.

But Owen had blasted through those low expectations, and in the process had shown her what was really possible. He celebrated her body, all of it. The scars hadn't affected his touch or muted his words. Neither had they dulled his own excitement. Her cheeks warmed as she recalled the feel of his arousal against her lower back. He had wanted her, scars and all. And she had reveled in it.

Even though they hadn't had sex, Hannah still felt closer to him than to any other man. Even Jake, her former fiancé, hadn't compared. Sure, she and Jake had been physically involved, but on an emotional level, Owen made her realize that what she'd had with Jake had been superficial and immature. And having experienced something so profound, Hannah wasn't willing to settle for anything less. How could she? Owen had made her realize that she not only deserved more, but also that she could have it. It was a lesson that had taken her a long time to learn, and she refused to go back to the way things used to be.

Owen came to a stop and pushed open a door, holding it for her to follow him. She stepped through and gave in to the temptation to lean in close as she passed him, trying to be subtle as she inhaled. His scent filled her senses, that unique combination of detergent, soap and the warm musk of his skin. She'd woken with his smell on her this morning, feeling safe for the first time in days. She'd hated having to bathe, as it made her feel as if she was washing away part of her memories of last night. But she'd been covered in iodine, dried blood and the sticky remnants of tape and bandages, so despite her desire to hold on to the magic of the night before, the bath had been a necessity.

Owen met her eyes as she passed, and for the briefest second, she saw a flare of heat in his dark blue eyes. So he was remembering, too. The realization made her skin feel warm and tingly, as if she'd just stepped out of a hot bath. They hadn't had time to talk this morning—everything had moved so quickly, and they couldn't very well have a discussion about their fledgling relationship in front of all his coworkers. But she needed to speak to him. There were so many emotions and feelings swirling around inside her that she felt volatile, as if the slightest provocation would set her off. She wanted to laugh, to cry, to hold Owen tight and never let go. But at the same time, she wanted to run away and hide, to take some time to herself to figure out just how her world had transformed over the course of a few short hours.

Did Owen feel the same? Was he as affected by her as she was by him? It was hard to tell. He'd been tense and removed today, wearing a demeanor of professional detachment like a suit of armor. But as she'd watched him, as she'd cataloged the various ways he interacted with his colleagues and his boss, she'd realized he was nervous. He hid it well. No one could tell by looking at him. But she'd studied him closely and had seen the way his expressions shifted and his body moved. The way his mouth turned down in a small frown when he thought no one was paying attention, or his habit of rubbing his thumb down his index finger in a repetitive motion that was oddly soothing to watch.

She reached for his hand now, giving it a quick squeeze as she walked by. Even though they couldn't talk, she needed to touch him, to reassure him that she was here, that he wasn't alone. Her heart jumped a bit when he lifted his hand, but he paused just before he touched her, his gaze flicking over to encompass the other officers before returning to hers. She nodded subtly, ignoring the small sting that accompanied his refusal. Of course he couldn't acknowledge her in that way, not in front of the guys. Their relationship was still new, still fragile, and she couldn't expect him to go shouting it from the rooftops. Especially not when the case that had brought them together was still active.

Maybe he read her thoughts, or maybe he just shared them. But as Owen released the door, he leaned forward, his lips almost brushing her ear. "Soon," he whispered, trailing a finger down the center of her back, the light touch tracing the valley of her spine. Hannah didn't try to suppress the delicious shiver of anticipation that thrummed through her body. Was it wrong that she still felt such a strong, elemental pull toward Owen in the midst of this stressful situation? What did that say about her, that she was focused on her physical desires, when he was getting set to walk into danger in an effort to prevent the deaths of more innocent people?

Guilt descended swiftly, but she pushed it away. She wasn't going to waste any more time feeling like a second-class citizen in her own life. As Owen had said earlier, she was going to focus on the positive and hope it worked out.

"I'll see you after," he said, pulling her to a stop

with a gentle tug. She raised her face to his, tracing his features with her gaze, committing them to memory, just in case.

"Be careful."

His lips curved in a crooked smile that made her toes curl. "Yes, ma'am."

"I mean it." She poked his chest gently and he grabbed her hand, holding it against his heart for a fleeting moment.

"I know," he said softly. "And believe me, I want nothing more than to find you when this is over so we can finish what we started."

"I'd like that," she said, her body warming at the promise in his words.

"So it's a date?"

She smiled up at him, their surroundings fading into obscurity. In this moment, they were the only two people in the world. "It's a date," she confirmed. His dark blue gaze brightened and a wide smile stole over his face, making him look like a kid on Christmas morning. His anticipation was contagious, and Hannah's stomach gave an answering flutter.

"I'll pick you up at the ambulance," he said with a wink. Then he turned on his heel and walked away, leaving her standing there with her heart in her throat.

Chapter 13

The office was just another storefront at the end of a strip-mall shopping center. There was nothing special about it, no signs or posters to make it stand out from its neighbors. Floor-length windows made up the front of the place, tinted dark as defense against the punishing Houston sun.

Owen eased the car into a parking spot, scanning the area. There was a nail salon next to the office, but he didn't see any customers inside. A woman glanced up as the sun glinted off his windshield, but she returned her focus to her magazine when she realized he wasn't a potential customer.

"Ready?"

"You are go for entry" came the reply.

"Roger that." He climbed out and made a show of locking his car, using the opportunity to get a better look around. There were a few cars at the other end of the strip mall, likely belonging to people who were shopping at the stationery store on the other corner. There wasn't much traffic at this end of the complex, and he began to wonder if there would be anyone here to arrest. Had they picked up and moved already? Had someone warned them?

Owen pushed on the door, half expecting it to be locked. It swung inward, and he stepped into a wall of air so cold it made goose bumps pop up on his skin. A subtle chime announced his arrival, but there was no one in the lobby to greet him. The place had an empty, desolate feel, and the furnishings were so nondescript as to be almost invisible. Several padded folding chairs were grouped around small ply-board tables in a classic waiting-room configuration. A drooping plant stood in one corner, its leaves coated with a fine layer of dust. It was the kind of room that could be set up and broken down in a matter of minutes, and the temporary feel only served to strengthen his confidence that this was the place.

At the far end of the room, a cubical wall prevented him from seeing the rest of the office space. A desk sat before the wall, and as he approached, a woman stepped around the wall. *There must be a hall, or some rooms back there*, he mused.

"Oh, hey," he said. "I didn't see you back there behind the wall." He hoped the team heard him so they had a better understanding of what they'd be facing when they stormed in. The wall was an obstacle that would conceal the escape of any suspects. Or provide nice cover for an armed defender. He didn't want his team walking into a hail of bullets because they hadn't known what to expect.

"You must be our two o'clock appointment," the woman replied. She smiled, but it didn't reach her eyes.

Owen nodded. "I'm so glad you guys could see me today. I've been feeling awful." He punctuated this with a wheezing cough, hoping it sounded convincing.

"I think we can help you with that. Why don't you follow me." She beckoned him to come forward, that fake smile still in place.

"Don't I need to fill out some paperwork or something?"

"We'll take care of that in the exam room."

Interesting. After Nate had shown him the flyer, he'd done a little research on clinical trials. From what he'd been able to find, any legitimate medical trial was accompanied by reams of paper—consent forms, study descriptions, warnings—a veritable forest of forms that had to be navigated before the patient was even seen by a doctor. Funny how they seemed to be skipping such an important step.

She stepped back around the cubical wall and beckoned him to follow her. He did, slightly surprised to find the office proper extended down a short hall lined with doors. As he walked, he heard the sound of muffled voices behind one of the doors. There was a higher, likely feminine, speaker, her voice growing louder as he approached. She was abruptly cut off by a deeper voice. Their discussion was animated, and he could tell by the rhythm of the conversation that whoever was behind the door was arguing. Trouble in paradise?

The receptionist paused beside an open door farther down the hall and was waiting for him to catch up. Wanting to hear more of the muffled conversation, Owen dropped his keys. "Whoops," he said, offering the woman a sheepish smile. He knelt down to gather them, straining to hear more of the conversation. He caught tantalizing snatches "come too far for that now" and "I want out"—but the receptionist was watching him closely, and he could tell by the look on her face that she found his behavior odd. He needed to be careful here. If she grew suspicious, she might warn the arguing couple that he was not what he seemed.

Reluctantly, he rose to his feet. As he did, the door to the office flew open and a woman stormed out, drawing up short just before she ran into him.

"Pardon me," he said automatically.

"Sorry," she muttered. Then she glanced up, and his heart stopped in his chest.

Marcia Foley sucked in a breath when she met his eyes. "What are *you* doing here?"

"Do you know this man?" Owen glanced to the doorway to find a tall, dark-haired man staring at him with narrowed eyes.

"I've never seen her before," Owen said, stepping back to put some distance between himself and Marcia. He looked back at her, concerned to see that her face had lost all color. She looked like a marble statue, standing stock-still in the middle of the hall. He cursed silently. "I've never met you before, ma'am," he said, nodding at her in the hopes she'd nod back. It took her a second, but she finally responded. Her movements had the mechanical quality of a puppet on a string, completely unnatural and stilted. *Dammit.*

"My mistake," she said haltingly.

Owen kept one eye on the other man, who was still

frowning. He was standing half in, half out of the office, which meant Owen couldn't see one of his hands. The guy could be doing anything, hiding anything. "Guess I just have one of those faces," he said, trying to salvage the situation.

"Is that true, Marcia?"

Marcia gave another unconvincing nod, but at least she was facing away from the man so he couldn't see her face. One look at her stricken expression, and he'd know she was lying.

"Who are you?" the man asked, turning his attention back to Owen.

"I'm your two o'clock patient," he replied, trying to sound casual.

"Very good," the man replied. "I'll be in to see you in just a moment. Marcia, would you do me a favor and get this gentleman started on his paperwork?" The man's tone made it clear that while he had phrased the request as a question, it was more of an order.

Apparently Marcia realized it, too. Her shoulders stiffened, and she cast a panicked glance in Owen's direction. *Hold it together just a little longer*, he urged silently. He lifted his arm, gesturing for her to precede him. "After you," he said.

She hesitated, so he took a step to prod her into motion. He moved to stand between her and the mystery man, hoping his body would shield her face from view. He tried to be casual about it, but he could feel the man's gaze on him as he walked down the hall.

The receptionist gave them another false smile as they walked past her. She shut the door behind them, leaving them alone in a small, windowless room.

He rounded on Marcia as soon as they were alone. "What are you doing here?" he whispered fiercely.

She stared up at him with round, wide eyes. "I tried to call you. Why didn't you pick up?" She sounded dull and lifeless, like a prisoner who had just surrendered.

"I was busy. What the hell is going on here?"

"I told him I wasn't going to do this any longer. That I was done. It's all too much—things have gone too far."

"What things?" He held up a hand. "Wait—there's no time. Just tell me who that guy is, and what this place is used for."

"Dave Carlson. He's my boss at ChemCure Industries. He's been using this place to illegally test chemicals on human subjects."

He felt a brief flare of satisfaction at the news that his suspicions were correct. "The same chemicals Hannah worked with?"

She nodded, her expression miserable. "He's also the one behind the lab explosion that almost killed her."

A wall of anger slammed down on him so hard and fast he forgot to breathe. His vision went dark as he imagined getting his hands on the man in the hall. Violent fantasies flooded his mind, each one more extreme than the last. The rage built inside him, the pressure increasing and fighting for release. He curled his hands into fists, his muscles shaking with the effort to stay in control.

Marcia took a step back, fear flashing across her face. Her reaction broke through the haze clouding his vision and he took a deep breath, tightening his grip on the reins of his self-control.

"Do you have proof of his involvement in the lab explosion?"

"There's a piece of shrapnel in my desk drawer. It probably has his fingerprints on it."

Owen frowned, trying not to let his disappointment show. It wasn't quite the smoking gun he was hoping for, but it was a start.

There was a soft sound from the hall, as if someone was moving and trying to be quiet about it. Owen held his finger up to his lips and walked to the door, leaning close to pick up any stray noise.

Marcia emitted a strangled gasp behind him and he turned to find her backing away from the door, her face a mask of horror. "What's wrong?" he hissed, his attention split between the noises coming from the hall and the increasingly unstable woman in the room with him.

She pointed at the floor, shaking her head back and forth as if she couldn't believe what she was seeing. He glanced down, blinking in disbelief at the dense, light brown vapor oozing into the room.

He took an instinctive step back, wanting to avoid contact with the viscous smoke. It had an oily, slick quality that made it seem sinister as it rolled along the floor with an eerie, mesmerizing grace.

"It's the mustard compound," Marcia said, her voice hoarse with panic. "Oh, God, he's killing us!"

He smelled it then, a faint tinge of garlic that was oddly appealing. His nose started to drip, and he quickly pulled his shirt up over his nose and mouth. It was poor protection against the poison, but it was better than nothing.

He grabbed the door handle and twisted it savagely, but it didn't turn in his hand. Locked. "Football,

football, football!" he yelled, using the danger signal
that would incite the team to storm the office. "We're
locked in a room with chemicals pouring in." He kicked
savagely at the door, but it remained stubbornly solid
under the blows. Giving up, he backed away from the
door, trying to keep out of the spreading cloud. It was
growing larger by the second, and the vapor had started
to climb the walls at the corners. Marcia grabbed at his
collar and pulled, urging him up to stand on a chair
next to her.

"I'm sorry," she said, her eyes blurry with tears.
He couldn't tell if the gas was making her eyes water
or if she was crying. Probably a bit of both. "I should
have come to you from the beginning. I'm so sorry I
let it get this far."

He grabbed her hand and gave it a squeeze. "You
have a chance to make it right. They're coming for us,
and you can help us fix this."

She didn't acknowledge his words, and he wondered
if she'd even heard him. She was withdrawing, but he
couldn't bring himself to care. He was focused on the
world outside this room, straining to hear the sounds of
his team coming to the rescue. *Hurry, please hurry...*

The garlic odor was getting stronger and had gone
from pleasantly familiar to acrid and stinging. His eyes
and throat burned, a painful, raw sensation that made
it hard to breathe. He coughed, trying to expel the
gas from his throat, but it merely forced him to take
a deeper breath.

They had to get out of here—that much was clear.
But there was no window, and the only door was
locked. He glanced up and felt a surge of hope when
he noticed the ceiling tiles. Maybe they could crawl out

that way. But a quick upward push crushed that idea. A chill raced down his spine as he realized the tiles had been glued down, almost as if this room had been specially modified to keep people inside.

How had he let this happen? No wonder some people questioned his fitness after John's death. He'd let himself get so distracted he'd walked right into a trap, as trusting and unquestioning as a lamb being led to slaughter.

He thought of Hannah, waiting in the ambulance with the EMTs. Had he really been that naive, thinking she'd be safe there? It was just one more aspect of the operation he'd misjudged. *She can't see me like this*, he thought frantically. He didn't want her to view the evidence of his failure. She'd realize he really wasn't able to keep her safe, that she'd be better off without him.

A loud bang shook the building, causing a fine shower of dust to rain down from the ceiling. *What the hell—*

"Oh, my God!" Marcia cried. "He's blowing up the building!"

Owen grabbed her arm and squeezed tightly, shushing her. He couldn't focus with her screaming in his ear, and he needed to hear.

Had his team just walked into a booby trap? It was clear Dave had rigged some kind of charge to prevent them from gaining access to the building. But had it been a diversion, or something more serious? Were his teammates lying dead at the entrance? Was anyone coming?

Marcia let out a wail of distress, and her body shook as spasmodic coughs racked her slender frame. An answering tremor went through him as his own lungs fought for air. "Hold on," he said, no longer sure if he was trying to reassure Marcia or himself.

One thing was clear—his team was occupied, and if he was going to get out of this mess, he'd have to do it himself.

He took a deep gulp of tainted air and jumped down from the chair. Grabbing it by the legs, he heaved the chair against the wall just next to the door. If he couldn't get through the door, maybe he could break through the wall...

He managed to land a few blows before his vision started to flicker. The chair had made a nice dent in the wall, but it remained stubbornly intact. Still, he couldn't just give up.

He stepped on the nozzle, hoping to stem the flow of gas into the room. The damn thing was metal though, and resistant to the pressure of his foot. He kicked at it, trying to shove it back under the door, but to no avail. Carlson had made sure to rig it in such a way that Owen couldn't disable it from inside the room.

Black spots danced in front of his eyes, but Owen kept trying. He couldn't just lie down and give up, not when Hannah was still out there. Carlson would go after her next, and Owen had to protect her. He wouldn't fail her like he'd failed John.

His head pounded viciously, and he felt like his brain was using a pile-driver to escape his skull. Still, he picked up the chair again and swung drunkenly at the wall. He missed, and the momentum carried him forward, sending him to his knees. Grabbing the door handle, Owen tried to pull himself up, but his arms and legs wouldn't respond to his commands. The world went black, but he still reached out, trying to connect with something, anything he could use to get out.

His hand landed on the floor and his arm gave out, unable to support his weight. He fell hard and lay there, too stunned to move. A woman's high-pitched scream broke through the blackness, and then he heard nothing.

Hannah sat in the passenger seat of the ambulance, trying not to show how worried she was. She hated not knowing where exactly Owen was or what he was doing. Had he found what he needed to close the case? Or had he walked into an empty office, the bad guys long gone? More important, why hadn't he checked in?

There was a burst of static from the radio, and she jumped, her heart flying into her throat. A woman spoke, a jumble of codes and acronyms spilling into the cab of the ambulance.

The paramedic gave her an apologetic smile as he reached for the radio. "Sorry about that—let me turn it down a bit."

"Is someone trying to contact you?"

He shook his head. "That's just Dispatch calling for another unit."

"Oh." She fell silent, her nerves still jangling. When was he going to check in? He'd been in there for twenty minutes already—how long could this take?

"Can I ask you a question?" the medic asked.

She shrugged. Why not? It might be a nice distraction. "Sure."

"What's a lady like you doing here? You're not a cop or anything, so why did they bring you along?"

It was a legitimate question, but one that she couldn't

answer. There simply wasn't enough time to explain the details of Owen's case and the way she'd gotten involved. Or the fact that she'd somehow become a target and would be in danger until Owen and the police figured out who was behind the attacks. Furthermore, she didn't really want to talk about those things with a stranger. He was a nice man, to be sure, but he was still a stranger and she couldn't bring herself to share everything with someone she'd only just met.

She let out a quiet sigh. "There's a chance that some hazardous chemicals are in the office building. The police think that I may be able to help them if anyone is accidentally exposed."

The man glanced at her injured arm. "I see," he said, sounding unconvinced.

His doubt rankled, but she didn't have the energy to refute it. The conversation died after that, which suited her just fine. She was so focused on Owen and what might be going on with him that she couldn't muster up the energy for small talk.

After a moment, the radio crackled again. "Unit one, please respond. Unit one, respond."

She thought it was just another update, but the medic started the ignition and stomped on the gas. The truck shot forward, the force of it pushing her back in the seat. "What's going on?" Her voice wavered, barely audible over the wail of the siren. "Is someone hurt?" *Please, don't let it be Owen!*

"Not sure," the EMT replied. "But we've been called in, so it's safe to say something is going on."

He turned hard to exit the parking lot, throwing her against the door. She braced herself, trying to keep her mounting panic under control. Just because the police had called for the ambulance didn't mean Owen was hurt. Maybe one of the suspects had tried to run and tripped. Or maybe they just called for the EMTs as a matter of routine. She clung to these mundane excuses with the desperation of a drowning woman grabbing a life jacket. If she didn't acknowledge the possibility that Owen was hurt, then he had to be fine. Right?

The short trip took an eternity. Now that they were on the street, the driver was agonizingly careful, a fact that Hannah would have appreciated under normal circumstances. But her worry for Owen overrode her natural caution, and she had a wild, desperate urge to lean over and press on the gas.

Finally, they pulled into the parking lot of a strip mall. The place was mostly empty, but there was a swarm of activity at one end that made it clear something unusual was going on. The driver pulled in front of the door and jumped out, heading to the back of the ambulance to help his partner. Hannah climbed down as well, but once her feet hit the pavement she found she couldn't move. She stood frozen in place, watching the men streaming in and out of the building. The squawk of radios and the boom of shouted orders was almost overwhelming, and the strobe of siren lights only added to the chaos. *Where is Owen?*

She rose to her tiptoes, straining to see over shoulders and between bodies. The front of the building looked burned, and the doors were hanging off their hinges like some terrible force had blown through. She caught a glimpse of a tangled mass of folding chairs and cheap office furniture, but she couldn't see if anyone was still inside. Then the wind changed direction, and the faint scent of garlic drifted over. *Oh, no.* She recognized that smell. Mustard compounds.

Had Owen been exposed? Was he all right? Her mind screamed at her to move, to find him, but her body refused to obey. Bile rose in her throat, hot and burning, and it took all her willpower to keep from throwing up on the sidewalk.

It's fine, she told herself. Even if Owen had been exposed, once they got him into fresh air and hosed him off he'd be fine. That was the standard treatment for exposure to these chemicals. There was no reason to think this time would be any different.

Unless the chemicals had been modified to be more lethal...

Hannah's knees threatened to give out at the thought, so she leaned back against the ambulance for support, ignoring the heat pouring off the engine. It was entirely possible, likely even, that the toxins had been altered, making them even more dangerous. It would certainly explain the autopsy findings. She closed her eyes and was immediately assaulted with memories of the latest victim's lungs, the damaged, degraded tissue that had practically dissolved away.

"Make a hole!" The shout came from within the office, and Hannah opened her eyes to see two officers holding up a third man between them, half carrying him out into the afternoon sun. It was Owen, his head hanging down as his feet fumbled to keep up with his rescuers.

Relief flooded her at the sight of him, followed quickly by alarm. As they drew closer, she could hear him coughing, a wet, tearing sound that made her throat ache in sympathy. The paramedics met the trio with a gurney, and the men quickly arranged Owen on the bed. The EMTs slipped a mask over his nose and mouth, but he continued to cough.

Hannah wasn't aware of moving, but suddenly she was standing beside Owen, looking down on him. His face was wet with tears, an uncontrollable reaction to the caustic chemical. As she leaned over him, she caught another strong whiff of garlic. The chemical must have saturated the fabric of his clothes.

"You have to cut his clothes off," she instructed, blinking hard as her eyes began to water. "Get them away from his body, and rinse him off with water if you can."

Owen's eyes popped open at the sound of her voice, and he started to shake his head. "Don't argue with me," she said, her strong words undermined by the quaver in her voice. "This is why you brought me along." She tried to smile but couldn't quite pull it off.

He made a shooing motion with his hand, as if he wanted her to go away. Was he worried about exposing her to the chemical, or did he just not want her to see him like this?

She shoved the questions to the back of her mind. There would be time to ponder them later. Now she had to make sure Owen was getting the care he needed. "I'm not going anywhere," she told him, tugging at his shirt with her free hand to lift it off his skin. One of the EMTs had been called away to help another victim, but the remaining man was working quickly, slicing through Owen's pants with practiced ease. Inch by inch his skin was exposed, and she studied all of it, looking for telltale blisters or any other signs of irritation. The skin that had been directly exposed to the chemical was pink—his forehead, his forearms and a strip along his torso, right above the waistband of his pants. She frowned at that, but then realized with a jolt that he had likely pressed the hem of his shirt to his face, sacrificing his stomach in an attempt to keep from breathing in the noxious fumes. His skin hadn't blistered yet, but that could take hours to develop.

The medic dumped the scraps of Owen's clothes on the ground, then dashed back to the ambulance, returning a few seconds later with two large bottles of water. "It's all I have," he said apologetically, twisting the cap off one and passing it to Hannah.

"Better than nothing," she replied. She turned back to face Owen. "Close your eyes—I'm going to pour this over your head."

His eyes widened, but when she lifted her arm and tilted the bottle above his head, he realized she wasn't kidding. He scrunched his eyes shut a split second before she tipped her wrist and doused him with the water. She poured a steady stream over his head, letting the liquid sluice down his face and neck. Satisfied she had gotten the chemical residue off his face, she turned her attention to his arms, pouring the rest of the bottle down his biceps and over his hands. The EMT followed suit, starting at Owen's feet and working his way up until they met in the area of his belly button. Owen squirmed at the treatment, but she didn't relent. Once the bottles were empty, she wiped the water off his eyelids so he could look around again.

He opened his eyes, the lashes spiky from his impromptu shower. She met his gaze, suppressing a crazy urge to laugh. He looked so pitiful lying on the gurney with his hair plastered against his head and soggy socks hanging off his feet. Tenderness swelled in her chest, leaving a lump in her throat that made it hard to swallow. For the first time, he looked vulnerable. Even though she hadn't known him long, she'd grown used to Owen seeming larger than life, standing tall and taking up space with his broad shoulders and confident movements. Now, lying on a wet bed with his features obscured by an oxygen mask, he looked small and almost fragile.

It scared her a little, this apparent role reversal. But she pasted on her best attempt at a brave smile. "You're going to be fine," she said, hoping it was true. Despite working with chemicals for years, she'd never had the type of exposure Owen had just experienced. Although she and the EMT had taken the proper steps to initially treat him, all the warning labels that accompanied a chemical advised those who were exposed to Seek Immediate Medical Attention. Four simple words, and yet they gave no indication of what to expect for those people who were unlucky enough to require said attention.

Worry gnawed at her stomach, but she ignored it. She didn't want Owen to see her fear. His dark blue eyes were trained on her face, and she knew he'd pick up even the smallest sign of her distress.

He lifted his hand, but rather than gesture for her to leave, he reached out for her. She grabbed him, savoring the contact, wishing she could communicate all her affection and concern for him through the simple touch. It was a bit early for her to entertain the idea of love, but she didn't bother to deny she was heading in that direction, and fast.

He squeezed her hand, as if to say, *I'm still here*. His coughs had subsided, and he seemed to be breathing easier. The redness of his skin had begun to fade, as well. Maybe he wouldn't get blisters after all.

Apparently satisfied with Owen's condition, the medic stepped over to help his partner. The two men leaned over a prone figure, but their bodies blocked Hannah's view of the second victim's face. She managed to catch a glimpse of pale blond hair and a slender wrist, and she frowned, craning her neck to try to get a better look. There was something about the hair that tugged at her memory. Where had she seen that color before?

Owen tugged on her hand, breaking her concentration. She turned back to face him, refocusing her attention on the man before her. "Everything okay?"

He nodded, reaching up to pull on the oxygen mask. "Oh, no, you don't," she said, intercepting his fingers. "You need to leave that on."

His eyes narrowed and he shook his head. "I'm fine," he said, his voice rough and faint behind the mask.

"Humor me," she replied.

The paramedic returned and gave Owen a once-over. "Ready to go?"

"Where are you taking him?" Hannah asked. Would they let her come along, or did she need to find another way to the hospital?

"Herman Memorial," the man replied.

Owen shook his head violently. "No," he said, his voice much stronger this time. He disentangled his fingers from Hannah's grasp and succeeded in pulling the oxygen mask down. "I'm not going to the hospital."

"But you have to go!"

He met her eyes. "No, I don't."

She turned to face the paramedic. "Tell him he has to go."

The man stepped back, hands up. "He's right, ma'am. I can't force him to go to the hospital. Although," he said, turning back to Owen, "I do strongly recommend that you get checked out, just to make sure you're okay."

One of the officers chose this moment to join him. He was an older man, tall, with short hair that was more gray than brown. Hannah recognized him from the police station but didn't recall his name. He stepped up to Owen's side and put a hand on his shoulder. "How you doing, son?"

"I'm fine, sir. Ready to get back to work."

"He's refusing to go to the hospital," Hannah interjected. It was petty of her, she knew, but maybe this man could talk some sense into Owen.

The officer glanced up at her, then back at Owen. "That true?"

Owen shot her a quick glare. "I'm fine. Ready to get back to work," he repeated stubbornly.

"I'm sure that's the case," the man said. "But do me a favor and get checked out. It won't take long." He looked to the paramedic for confirmation, and the man nodded. "In and out," he said.

Owen clenched his jaw, his mouth pressing into a thin line. He was clearly unhappy, but he gave a single nod of assent.

The officer nodded, satisfied. "Very good," he said, stepping back. "I'll see you in a few hours."

The EMT fiddled with the gurney and then gave it a push. Hannah walked alongside, feeling uncertain. Would Owen want her to come along after she'd embarrassed him into going to the hospital? She glanced down at him, trying to read his expression. He stared straight ahead, the mask back on his face. But then he held out his hand, clearly seeking hers.

A tingle of awareness shot up her arm when she slipped her hand into his, and her anxiety melted away. This felt right. It took a few seconds to get him into the ambulance, but she didn't hesitate to climb in after him. She slid along the bench and sat next to his head, then leaned down so she could whisper in his ear. "Thank you."

His eyes flickered over to meet hers, then he returned his gaze to the paramedic climbing into the ambulance bay. He didn't speak but reached for her hand again.

The EMT made sure Owen was settled, then headed back out to help his partner with the second patient. Hannah pulled Owen's hand into her lap and leaned back against the wall, relaxing for the first time since the ambulance had been called in. Even though things hadn't gone to plan, Owen was here, they were both safe and they were together.

It was enough for now.

Chapter 14

"You need a lawyer."

Marcia Foley shook her head, her normally sleek blond hair hanging in tangled strands around her face. "No."

Owen exchanged a loaded glance with Nate. The other man raised one shoulder in a shrug, the gesture reflecting his own thoughts.

He tried again. "You do realize that the information you provide to us will be held against you?"

"I know." She looked down. "But I'm tired of the lies. What I did was wrong, and I want to make it right. This is my chance."

"Are you absolutely certain?" Nate tried.

She lifted her head, gifting them with a thin smile. "Detectives. I appreciate what you're trying to do here. But I want to talk to you, and I wish to do it without legal counsel present. I understand the repercussions of my decision."

Owen glanced at Nate again, seeing his own confusion reflected in his partner's eyes. From all accounts, Marcia Foley was an intelligent woman. Why, then, was she so willing to talk to them without a lawyer present? She was practically guaranteeing a prison sentence, and yet she didn't seem the least bit troubled by it.

"One moment, please," Owen said. He stepped into the small anteroom attached to the interrogation room, where Captain Rogers watched the proceedings behind the one-way glass.

"Have you ever seen a suspect so willing to incriminate herself?" he asked.

The older man shook his head. "No. But she's been Mirandized, and she clearly stated three times that she doesn't want counsel. I'd say we're covered on that front."

Owen nodded. "All right. I'll get back to it, then."

"Tread carefully," Rogers said. "She may have refused an attorney, but that doesn't mean she's being truly honest. I'd be surprised if she's not playing some kind of game."

"Agreed." He glanced through the one-way glass, taking a moment to watch Marcia. She was completely still, unmoving except to blink. If it weren't for her disheveled hair and borrowed hospital scrubs, he could have easily mistaken her for a woman sitting in a boring meeting rather than a police interrogation room. In his experience, people tended to fidget when sitting in those uncomfortable metal chairs. Guilty or not, no one liked to be formally questioned. But if Marcia felt nervous about her situation, she didn't show it. Either she had the most overdeveloped sense of self-possession he'd ever encountered, or she suffered from an almost sociopathic detachment.

Given what she'd started to tell him back in the office, he was leaning toward the latter.

He reached for the doorknob but turned back just before giving it a twist. "Do me a favor, Captain?"

At the other man's nod, he went on. "Check on Hannah for me? Make sure she's holding up okay?" She'd been very quiet at the hospital, spending most of the time watching him with wide round eyes. He couldn't tell if he had scared her with his exposure, or if she was worried because he hadn't managed to find the people responsible for hurting her. He certainly deserved her scorn on that front, and truth be told, his failure embarrassed him.

As soon as the doctor had cleared him, he and Hannah had come back to the station. Neither one of them had spoken much, and although her silence worried him, he didn't know what to say to make her feel better. He'd left her sitting at his desk, guilt and shame tying his tongue as effectively as a gag. Although he wanted to check on her, he figured that at this point, his presence would make things worse not better.

The captain's gray eyes warmed a bit, as if he understood the true motivation behind Owen's request. "Don't worry about her. I'll make sure she's fine. You just keep your head in the game." He angled his head toward the glass before turning to leave.

"Right," Owen muttered to himself. He took a deep breath, steeling himself against the upcoming conversation. What the captain didn't know—what even Nate didn't know—was the depth of Owen's anger toward Marcia. She had known the explosion in Hannah's lab had been no accident. Had she been a part of it herself? For her sake, he hoped that wasn't the case. He didn't think he'd be able to control himself if he found out Marcia had played a direct role in Hannah's attempted murder.

Still, even if she hadn't had a hand in the explosion, she wasn't an innocent. She had clearly been playing a part in these homicides—at the very least, she was guilty of obstruction, the way she'd tried to distract and mislead him during the investigation. But was that her only sin? What else did she know?

It was time for him to find out.

How much longer was this going to take?

Hannah toyed with her empty coffee cup, debating the wisdom of a refill. She already felt jittery and on edge, but drinking more would at least give her something to do.

She'd been waiting for Owen for what felt like forever. And even though she hated being kept in the dark, she wasn't sure she wanted to see him right now.

There was something different about him today. She'd noticed it in the ambulance ride and then at the hospital. He'd pulled away from her, and she felt as if he was holding part of himself in reserve. Try as she might, she didn't understand why. Had she done something to upset him? Was he angry with her for using his captain to force him to go to the hospital?

She shook her head at the thought. If that was the case, then he could just stay mad. She wasn't going to apologize for making sure he was okay, not after what had happened at that office. He'd been adamant about getting right back to work, but she knew too much about chemicals to be so casual about his health after such an extensive exposure. Forcing him to get checked out had been the right thing to do, even if it had been a blow to his ego.

But was that the only explanation for his withdrawal? Owen didn't seem like the kind of man to pout over something like that, especially when the ER doctor had explained that he wasn't out of the woods just yet. There was still a chance that he would have problems in a few hours or even days, as tissue damage became evident. The doctor had given him some breathing treatments, hopefully to stave off any issues, but he'd made it clear that Owen needed to take it easy for the next few days.

Yeah, right. Like that was going to happen. Owen had nodded dutifully, but Hannah could tell by the look in his eyes that there was no way he was going to sit back and relax, not until he'd closed his case.

The office site had been nothing but chaos, making it hard for Hannah to determine what, exactly, had happened. Owen had been tight-lipped about it, but from what she could tell, he hadn't found what he'd been looking for.

Marcia's presence at the office had been a depressing confirmation of Hannah's suspicions. She wanted to pretend she was shocked that her former boss was somehow involved in all this, but she couldn't muster the energy to fake it. Hearing Shelly's voice answering the phone had been a surprise, but she'd quickly accepted the idea that the people she had worked with had crossed a line. Seeing Marcia at the test site had only served to confirm it.

Part of her was desperate to know what had transpired between Owen and Marcia in that office. What had she told him? What was she telling him now? Was she protesting her innocence, shifting the blame to others? Or had she cracked and admitted to her part in all of this?

Hannah shook her head. It was hard to believe Marcia would come clean so easily. She'd always been so controlled, so tightly wound. Hannah had trouble picturing the other woman in a confessional mood. Besides, one thing she did know for certain was that Marcia Foley was a survivor. She'd do anything in the name of self-preservation. If she was talking, it was because she thought it was in her best interest to do so.

Suppressing a sigh, Hannah stood and stretched. It felt good to move after sitting for so long. Her muscles were stiff from lack of activity, and her arm ached something fierce. She glanced at her watch—time for another pain pill to take the edge off.

She walked over to the coffeemaker, but then thought better of it and filled her cup at the watercooler. She was tired of waiting. Owen had said he'd take her home when he was done questioning Marcia, but why did she have to wait here while he did it? Her apartment was in terrible shape, and she needed to start putting things back together. Classes started up again in a few days, and she wouldn't have time to take care of it then.

Even though her back was to the door, her body felt his presence before her mind really registered it. There was a change in the air, a fine charge that made the hairs on the back of her neck prickle. She froze, her stomach fluttering under the weight of his gaze. What had he discovered? And did she really want to know?

The seconds ticked by, but she didn't move. If she stayed in place, if she ignored his presence, she could pretend for just a moment more that everything was okay. That her time at ChemCure Industries wasn't built on lies, that her work hadn't been corrupted and used to murder innocent people. It was cowardly of her, she knew, but she wanted to hold on to her denial a little bit longer.

He seemed to sense her mood. He moved quietly, stepping into the room and gently shutting the door behind him. Her heart sank. It couldn't be good news then. He wouldn't give her privacy if he had something positive to tell her.

Gathering up her courage, she turned to face him. He sat at the table, his eyes on her. His expression was serious but still guarded, and she clenched her jaw in sudden irritation. What was his problem?

"Are you okay?"

"Fine," she replied.

He nodded, but it was clear he didn't believe her. "Okay. But you look a little upset."

Damn him! Why could he read her so easily? "Are you going to tell me what's going on, or do I have to guess?"

He ran a hand through his hair and let out a long sigh, and she realized how tired he was. When was the last time he'd really slept? He couldn't have gotten much rest at the hospital last night, and before that, she was willing to bet he'd been putting in a lot of late nights working this case. Sympathy welled in her chest as she took in the dark circles under his eyes and his disheveled hair. Was it any wonder he'd been acting strangely today? He was exhausted, probably on the verge of collapse. And taking out her bad mood on him wasn't going to help.

"Are you okay?" she asked, coming to sit next to him.

He glanced up at her, surprise written all over his face. "I, uh...yeah." He cleared his throat, but his voice was still hoarse from the chemical exposure. "Yes, I'm fine. Thanks for asking."

"When was the last time you got some rest?"

He shook his head. "It's not important."

"You can't keep going like this."

"I have to. Besides," he added quickly, catching her frown, "it's not going to be much longer."

"You've solved the case?" Her voice rose in excitement, and she reached out to touch his arm. He glanced down at her hand and smiled briefly.

"Yes and no."

"What does that mean?" She tilted her head to the side, trying to read his expression.

"It means I know who is responsible for these deaths, but I don't know where he is."

"Oh." She slumped back in her chair and let her hand slip off his arm. A flicker of disappointment showed in his eyes, but it quickly disappeared.

"Hannah, we need to talk."

"No." She shook her head. "I don't want to know."

He shifted in his chair so that he turned to face her, and grabbed her hand, cradling it between his own. "I know this is hard for you. But you need to hear what I've learned today."

"Why?" she retorted. "Why is it so important that I

hear this? It's not going to change anything." She pulled her hand from his and gripped her empty cup again. "If it's all the same to you, I'd rather stay in the dark."

Owen stared at her for a moment, apparently shocked speechless. Then he shook his head slowly. "If I thought you really meant that, I'd walk away and not bother you again. But you're not the kind of woman who runs away from something, even though it causes you pain. I know you better than that."

He was right, of course. It was both annoying and thrilling in equal measures—he was one of only a handful of people who seemed to really get her, but that meant she couldn't hide from him. The realization left her feeling naked and exposed, and she let go of the cup to wrap her arms around her stomach.

Owen didn't push her, didn't insist she face the truth. He merely sat and watched her, his deep blue eyes patient and understanding.

It was his silence that touched her. He gave her the space she needed to make a decision, and she knew whatever she chose, he'd respect it. If she insisted he leave her alone, he would get up and walk out and not say another word. It was so different from the way Jake used to talk to her. If she disagreed with him or didn't want to do something, Jake would pester her until she changed her mind. He'd always said he was just being persuasive, but now that she saw how Owen behaved, she realized Jake's actions were born of a lack of self-confidence. He couldn't handle someone questioning him, and he always had to be right. But not Owen. Owen was secure enough in his own skin that he didn't mind if she challenged him, or if she had a different opinion. It was a refreshing change, one that continued to surprise her.

After a moment, she slowly nodded. Owen didn't speak. He continued to watch her, giving her a chance to change her mind. "All right," she said finally. "Tell me what you've learned."

His eyes warmed and she felt a quick surge of pleasure, almost as if she'd passed some kind of test. "That's my girl," he murmured. Then he cleared his throat and leaned forward, placing his hands on the table.

"Marcia was quite chatty this afternoon," he remarked. Hannah couldn't stop her snort of disbelief. Owen's brows shot up, and she waved away the interruption.

"Sorry. I just have a hard time believing she doesn't have an ulterior motive."

He nodded thoughtfully. "I'm sure she does. Regardless, she disclosed a lot of information, and we're busy verifying what we can now. It looks like she's telling the truth."

"What did she say?"

"She's implicated a man named Dave Carlson. Said he's the one behind all the deaths. You told me earlier that you spoke with him on occasion?"

"I did. He's Marcia's boss. I didn't interact with him much, but when I did, he was generally pressuring me to provide the results he wanted to see."

"That fits with what Marcia told us. Apparently, he took compounds from your old lab and used them in unauthorized human trials."

Hannah's stomach twisted, and revulsion rose to burn the back of her throat. "Why?"

Owen shrugged one shoulder. "Money. According to Marcia, Dave was looking at the most toxic compounds, the ones that did the most damage. He was testing them out on people to characterize the damage they caused and how long it took to work."

"That's despicable." Revulsion skittered along her skin, making her shudder. How could anyone be so cold, so calculating? How could a man who worked for a pharmaceutical company—a business that was devoted to developing medications to ease human suffering—have such a complete disregard for human life?

"Money is a powerful motivator," Owen said, sounding philosophical. "You'd be amazed at what some people will do for it."

"Apparently, Dave and Marcia would kill for it," she observed drily.

"Indeed." He took a deep breath, then continued. "But that's not all. Marcia implicated Dave in the explosion in your lab."

That made her sit back. "But that was years ago! How can she be sure it's connected?"

"A few months before the lab accident, Dave approached Marcia and asked her to keep him apprised of developments with your project."

Hannah frowned. "That's not terribly unusual."

Owen conceded the point with a nod. "Apparently, he wanted more than the usual updates. She became suspicious, started asking questions. Then you made it clear some of the compounds weren't suitable for further investigation. Marcia claims Dave decided to stage the explosion to get you out of the way and to send her a message."

Hannah regarded him dubiously. "That seems a little far-fetched. Are you buying this?"

"Under normal circumstances, I wouldn't. But she claims a piece of shrapnel from the explosion was sitting on her chair the next morning, along with a threatening note. I've got officers going to pick them up now."

She felt the color drain from her face at his words. It was one thing to hear that Marcia had made these fantastical claims. Hannah could dismiss her words as a last-ditch attempt to explain away her involvement in this crime. But if there was actual evidence to support her story...

Owen leaned forward and reached out to lay a hand on her shoulder. "Whoa. You okay?"

His touch steadied her, and for a moment she leaned into it, soaking up his strength. "I'm fine," she said, shaking her head. "It's just a lot to take in, you know?"

"Hannah..." He trailed off, clearly reluctant. "There's more."

A sense of inevitability settled over her, weighing her down. "What else could there be?"

"Dave is the one who orchestrated the recent attacks on you. He's gunning for you again."

"Me?" She shook her head, convinced she had misunderstood. When Owen didn't correct himself, her confusion turned to denial. "That doesn't make any sense! I'm not involved in that work anymore. Why would he still care about me?"

"Because you got away."

"That's ridiculous!" She pushed back from the table and stood, needing to move, needing to burn off the nervous energy that had been building inside ever since Owen had entered the room.

"Dave was at the office when I went in for my appointment."

She stopped, surprised by this news. "I didn't see him there. Did you arrest him?"

He shook his head and lowered his gaze, looking defeated for the first time today. "He managed to escape. He's the one who locked me and Marcia into a room and released the chemical to hurt us."

"Are you sure it was him?"

"Marcia confirmed it. And before I saw him, I heard them arguing behind a closed door. She claims it was about you. He's upset that you're still alive, and he's planning on doing something about it."

A chill slithered down her spine, and she resisted the urge to hunch her shoulders. Her mind whirred, the pieces clicking into place. But something wasn't adding up.

"Let me get this straight. Dave locked you and Marcia in a room and tried to off you both with a dangerous chemical, the same chemical he's been testing on innocent victims?"

Owen nodded encouragingly.

"That means he must know that you're a cop."

"Maybe. He became suspicious after he saw the way Marcia reacted when she saw me in the hall. He might not know I'm a cop, but he knows we're chasing him now."

"How did he escape, anyway? I thought you guys had the office covered."

Owen winced, as if the question pained him. "We did," he muttered. "But we didn't realize the air ducts ran through the entire building, rather than just the single office. He climbed into the vents and crawled all the way down to the store at the end of the building, then walked out as if nothing was wrong."

She raised a brow, and he had the grace to blush. "It wasn't our finest moment," he allowed.

Taking pity on him, she decided not to comment further. "Regardless, I think we can safely assume he knows the police are after him now."

"Most likely. We weren't exactly trying to hide today." He made an impatient gesture with his hand. "What's your point?"

"My point," she replied evenly, "is that he's probably focused on running right now rather than coming after me."

Owen gaped at her, disbelief written all over his face. "I can't believe you're not taking this seriously."

"What's to take seriously?" She held up her hand, ticking off her points as she spoke. "You have the words of a desperate woman who's probably trying to distract attention from her own involvement. You have a man on the run who is probably more concerned with saving his own skin than coming back for me, a person who hasn't been involved in this work for years. How, exactly, do you think I should respond?"

He stood and moved toward her, crowding into her personal space. She refused to back down, raising her head to meet his gaze. "We need to make sure you're protected in case he tries something again."

"Now who's being unreasonable? Do you realize how unlikely it is he's going to come after me? Are you really suggesting I change the way I live on the off chance I'm still in danger?"

"I'm not asking you to change your life," he told

her, running a hand through his hair. "I just think you need to be careful."

"And what does that entail, exactly? A bodyguard? Moving to a new place? Only going out at certain times, and to certain places?" She shook her head. "No, thank you."

"It doesn't have to be like that—"

"I'm not doing it," she said, cutting him off. "I've lived in fear before, lived with constant insecurity and worry. I'm not going to do it again." It had taken her a long time to find peace of mind after the accident, and she refused to sacrifice it now based on such thin evidence.

"I don't want you to be afraid," he replied, a definite edge to his voice. "But you need to recognize that you're still a target."

She opened her mouth to respond, but he cut her off. "You're right—Dave is probably too worried about getting caught to try something himself. But that doesn't mean he won't hire the job out."

That possibility was a little harder to dismiss, but she still wasn't ready to give in. "When do you think this attempt on my life will happen?"

Owen blinked, taken aback by the question. "I, uh—"

"Today? Tomorrow? Next week?"

"I don't know. I can't say for certain."

"Exactly." Hannah folded her arms across her chest, treating the right one gingerly. "You don't know. So how long am I supposed to take precautions? How long do I have to keep up my guard? And if he really is after me, don't you think he'll just wait until things settle down again? Strike when I least expect it?"

Owen's hands fisted at his sides. "Yes, dammit! Is that what you want to hear?"

He clenched his jaw so tightly it made a muscle on the side of his face stand out in relief. She had gotten under his skin, that much was clear. Now she needed to drive her point home. But could she do it without hurting him?

She touched his arm, which was as solid and unyielding as stone. "Owen," she said softly, waiting until he looked at her before continuing. "I just want you to see that there are no guarantees. Maybe he'll come after me, but most likely he won't. You can't expect me to turn my life upside down for such a small chance. Besides," she said, giving him a small smile, "I hardly think your captain will be willing to waste precious man-hours on a threat that may or may not materialize."

"My captain has nothing to do with this," he said stiffly. "I was going to take care of it myself."

Hannah closed her eyes for a second, kicking herself for having missed it. This wasn't just about keeping her safe; it was a point of pride for Owen, to be the one protecting her. No wonder he was so upset by her reaction. In his mind, her rejection of his suggestion was tantamount to rejecting him.

"I wouldn't be able to forgive myself if you wasted your time like that," she said, trying to make him feel better.

"I wouldn't consider it a waste," he said quietly.

She was silent for a moment, digesting that. Maybe she could bend a little, if it meant not hurting Owen. "What did you have in mind?"

"I'm still working on it," he admitted, his gaze faltering. "But I thought you could stay with me, at least for the time being."

"So much for my life staying the same," she muttered.

"Or I could move in with you," he amended hastily. "Either way, we'd be spending a lot of time together. But that's a good thing, right?"

The shock of his words hit her like a bucket of ice water. "You want us to live together?" she said numbly.

"Temporarily, at least until we get something worked out. But don't worry," he added, after seeing her expression. "I don't expect anything physical to happen between us—I wouldn't take advantage of you in any way."

And why was that a little disappointing? Before she could really consider it, he pushed ahead.

"It would just be until I was certain you were safe. That's all." He sounded so matter-of-fact, as if their living together was a business transaction and nothing more.

But it wasn't.

She couldn't imagine having such an impersonal living arrangement, especially with a man she cared about. And while part of her was thrilled at the prospect of spending more time with Owen, her pride couldn't accept the fact that he'd be there not because he wanted to spend time with her but because he was doing a job.

Maybe she was being selfish, but she deserved more than a man who saw her as an obligation. For a brief period of time, she'd thought Owen might be the guy for her. It was nothing short of miraculous, the way he'd broken through her defenses and installed himself in her heart. But it was clear that while she'd been falling in love with him, he'd seen her as part of his case.

She shook her head, kicking herself for having been so naive. Owen was a wounded soul, a man crushed by the death of his partner. He was convinced John's death was his fault, since he had arrived too late to save his friend. Of course he'd feel the same about her. She wasn't a woman he cared about, at least not in the way she cared about him. She was his chance at redemption. If he could keep her safe, maybe he'd stop blaming himself for John's murder.

The trouble was, she didn't want to be his savior. She wanted to be his partner, his lover, his friend. But she couldn't be responsible for his happiness. He had to discover that for himself.

"Owen," she said slowly, searching for the right words. "That's not going to work."

"Sure it will," he cajoled. "You won't even know I'm there."

"That's the problem. When I live with a man, it's going to be because we have a relationship. Not because he's on guard duty."

"Hannah—"

"No." She took a step back and swallowed hard, trying to push down the sudden lump in her throat. Her eyes prickled and she blinked hard, trying to hold back tears. "I like you, Owen. A lot. I was falling in love with you. But I'm not going to be an obligation. I'm not going to be a job to you."

"You're not! I promise you, you are not an obligation. Please, just hear me out." His pleading tone was hard to ignore, but she pushed on, needing to finish.

"I know you still blame yourself for John's death, even though it wasn't your fault."

His head jerked back as if she'd slapped him, the color draining from his face.

"I think you see me as a kind of second chance. That if you can keep me safe or save me from danger, you'll have earned forgiveness. But I can't be the one to offer you absolution. You have to figure this out for yourself, that you didn't do anything wrong. I'm not your salvation."

He stood frozen in place, staring at her as if she'd just taken him out at the knees. His reaction broke her heart, but she knew it was for the best. For both of them.

The silence stretched between them, growing cold and brittle. She wanted to say something, anything, to take back the hurt she'd caused him, but she didn't know the right words. And she refused to apologize. What she'd said was harsh, but it was also true and it was time they both acknowledged it.

She gave him a final smile, one that she hoped conveyed the affection she still held for him. Even though he didn't care for her the way she wanted, she still liked him, still wished him the best. "Let me know if there's anything I can do to help you wrap up your case," she said softly.

Then she walked past him and out the door, trying to ignore the wrenching pain in her heart.

Chapter 15

Three weeks later...

Owen sat at his desk, trying to focus on the paperwork he was supposed to be filling out. The forms were simple enough—just fill in the blanks—but his concentration had deserted him, leaving him staring blankly at a page that should have taken less than two minutes to complete.

It had been like this since Hannah had walked away, leaving him standing in the break room with a hole in his chest where his heart had been.

He wasn't sure why her leaving had hurt so much. After all, he'd figured she would. What kind of woman would want to stay with a man who couldn't protect her, who had let her assailant slip through his fingers, free to hunt her again? He didn't deserve her, but he couldn't stop thinking about her.

He'd spent the past few weeks chasing down every lead, every clue. Even though the FBI had been brought in, Owen hadn't stopped working on the case. He'd dug into Dave Carlson's background, searched the man's home and office, and talked to his friends and family. Owen had done everything possible to get inside the guy's head, and yet he still didn't know where he was and couldn't predict what he'd do next. From all accounts, Dave was a cool, methodical man who was highly organized and made sure all angles were covered before he acted. His friends and family had all agreed Dave was long gone, probably settling into a new life in a nonextradition country, far from the mess he'd left behind in Houston.

But Owen didn't buy it.

Because in addition to describing Dave as a cautious planner, people who knew him also talked about his long memory. And those who'd gotten on his bad side had shared tales of Dave's retribution. Apparently, Carlson was not big on forgiveness, and he didn't forget people who he thought had wronged him in any way. Even though months, or in some cases years, had gone by, Dave didn't miss an opportunity to retaliate.

So even though he was on the run, Owen figured Dave hadn't gone far. His pride wouldn't let him leave, not when Hannah was still alive. She had been the key to unraveling this whole mystery, and Carlson had to know it. She had bruised his ego, and a man as conceited as Carlson couldn't let that pass.

But as the days passed with no sign of him, Owen's patience had begun to wear thin. Captain Rogers was sympathetic and wanted Owen to keep pursuing the case, but the leads were growing cold, and they had new cases coming in. While the captain hadn't expressly told him to devote his efforts elsewhere, Owen knew it was just a matter of time before he'd be asked to put it aside and focus on the newer stuff.

Nate had been supportive, chasing down leads with him and never expressing doubt or insinuating that they were wasting their time. He hadn't asked about Hannah, but sometimes Owen would catch his partner watching him with a concerned expression on his face, the way he had back in the early days of their partnership. He'd been tempted to confide in Nate, but every time he thought about talking to him, the words froze on his tongue. Besides, what could he say? *Hannah thinks I see her as an obligation, as a way to make up for getting John killed. Do you agree with her?* Not really the kind of conversation he wanted to have with anyone, much less a man he had to work with every day. Better for Nate to suspect his inner turmoil than for him to spell it out in excruciating detail.

Besides, the only one who would really understand was Casey, John's widow. He'd been meaning to call her, to see how she was faring. Was she still raw with grief as he was? Part of him was afraid to find out, scared that he'd discover she had moved on and had adjusted to life without John. And if that was the case, did that mean something was wrong with him? If John's widow could recover, why couldn't his friend? He hoped he wasn't the only one who still felt jagged and gray, even though it pained him to think that way.

Get over yourself. It was high time he called and checked on her. He'd left her alone for too long. Granted, the last time they'd talked she'd told him never to call again, but that was her pain talking. He'd let his shame and grief blind him to Casey's own suffering, and he needed to reach out, to make sure she was okay. He owed John that much.

Paperwork forgotten, he reached for his phone and dialed automatically, the number coming back to him effortlessly. He held his breath while the phone rang, torn between hoping she would answer and hoping she wouldn't. It would be easier to leave a message, but there was no guarantee she'd call back, and he really wanted to hear her voice so he could gauge how she was feeling.

After a few endless seconds, someone picked up. "Hello?"

"Casey?" It came out rough, so he cleared his throat and tried again. "Casey? It's—"

"Owen!" She sounded genuinely pleased, and he felt a weight lift off his shoulders. "How are you?" she continued. "I've been meaning to call you."

She had? That was surprising. Where was her anger, her disgust with him over his part in John's death? "I'm fine," he replied, feeling a little out of sorts. "How are you?"

"Doing better." She punctuated this with a short laugh. "I have good days and bad days, as I'm sure you know."

"Yeah," he replied automatically. "I do."

"Say, are you free for a drink? I have some things to show you, and I'd love to buy you a cup of coffee."

"Uh, that sounds nice." He named a place not far from where he knew she lived. "Meet you there in half an hour?"

"Sounds great!"

Owen hung up and stared at his phone, questioning

whether that conversation had really taken place, or if it was just an elaborate fantasy he'd concocted to ease his mind. He checked the call log, verified that he really had dialed out and that the call had been received. Then he put the phone on his desk, shaking his head.

Strange. He'd been expecting her rage, pain and scorn. But she sounded good, as if she wasn't drowning in despair. He was glad to hear it, and it lit a spark of hope in the depths of his soul. If Casey was okay then maybe he could be, too. Maybe she'd even share her secret with him. He almost laughed at the thought—*A Police Widow's Twelve-Step Guide to Grief for Partners Left Behind.* It would be a bestseller for sure.

He'd felt almost normal again when he was with Hannah. Something about her made him feel as if he was going to be okay, that he could persevere and come out the other side relatively unscathed. She wasn't a magical cure-all for his grief, but she gave him a reason to keep pushing, keep moving forward. It hurt to know she thought he was using her to assuage his guilt over John's death. Nothing could be further from the truth, but how could he make her realize that? And should he even try? After all, she'd been the one to walk away. Chasing after her wasn't going to change her mind, and he did have his pride.

Scooping up his phone, he pushed back from his desk and stood. Nate glanced up, and he gave him a quick wave. "Just stepping out for a few minutes," he said.

Nate nodded. "Call me if you need me."

"Will do."

It was a short walk to his car, and for once, Houston traffic cooperated to make for an uneventful drive to the coffee shop. He found a close parking spot and sat for a moment, gathering his thoughts and composing himself. If Casey was doing as well as she sounded, he wanted to convince her that he was fine, as well. It wouldn't be right for him to lean on her, not when she was dealing with her own issues.

He stepped into the shop with his heart in his throat, glancing around to see if Casey had arrived first. The rich aroma of coffee enveloped him in a comforting embrace, but he resisted the temptation to order a drink. It would be too easy to hide behind a cup, and he needed to face this head-on.

Casey waved at him from a small corner table. He smiled and began to wend his way through the shop, stepping over bags and dodging chairs. She looked different, he noted as he approached. She no longer had dark circles under her eyes, and her face had lost that haunted look she'd worn in the days after John's death.

"Owen!" she said, standing to greet him. She moved around the table and pulled him into a tight hug. He sucked in a breath as the contact sent a fresh wave of pain across his skin. In the days after his chemical exposure, blisters had erupted along the skin that had been directly exposed to the gas. While they were mostly healed now, every once in a while he'd move the wrong way or brush up against something, and a spike of pain would remind him of their presence. Oblivious to his reaction, Casey gave him a squeeze before releasing him and sitting back down. "It's so good to see you!"

He took the empty chair across from her and simply drank in the sight of her, momentarily speechless while the pain faded. This reception was so different from the last time he'd seen her, when she'd screamed at him while tears streaked down her cheeks. It was good to see her doing well again.

"You look great," he offered, which made her smile widen.

"I'm trying," she confessed. She tilted her head, studying him with slightly narrowed eyes. "How are you, though?"

He debated how to respond for a moment, vacillating between lying and telling her the unvarnished truth. Ordinarily, he would hesitate to dump all his problems on someone else, but sitting here across from Casey he thought he could actually *feel* John's presence. It was silly, and probably just a trick of his imagination, but he liked to think John was looking down on them, smiling at the fact that they had gotten back in touch.

He opened his mouth, and the words came tumbling out. He told her about his case, Hannah, all of it. Even the way she'd walked away, confirming his worst fears.

To her credit, Casey didn't interrupt with superficial reassurances or comforting words. She simply listened, her expression rapt, as though he were the only person in the world.

When he finished, she sat there for a moment, absorbing what he'd said. Then she let out a long sigh. "I should have checked in on you," she said softly. "I'm so sorry I pushed you away and left you to deal with your grief on your own."

"You didn't," he said, blinking hard against the sudden sting of tears. "You were hurt. You needed time to heal."

She gave him a sad smile. "I wasn't the only one

who lost John. And it took me a while to realize it. I'm sorry I never called you."

"Don't be." He reached for her hand, gave it a gentle squeeze.

Casey let out a sigh, then pasted on a bright smile. "Well. Let's see what we can do about your lady friend."

Owen leaned back in his chair, the familiar sense of defeat stealing over him again. "I don't know that there is anything to do. She clearly doesn't want to be with me, and I'm not going to try to force the issue."

Casey gave him an exasperated look. "Owen, I always thought you were smarter than that. Of course she wants to be with you."

He frowned. "But she left…"

She held up a hand, dismissing the point. "She left because she thought you were using her to make up for John's death. She thought that you were trying to save her so that you could forgive yourself for losing John. What she wants is for you to be with her because of *her*."

He tried to speak but she shook her head, stalling him. "Tell me this," she continued. "Do you still blame yourself for John's death?"

The question hit him like a blow to the chest, pushing him back in his chair. "It was my fault," he said softly.

Casey's expression shifted into a blend of pity and sadness. "No, it wasn't," she said just as quietly. "Why can't you see that?"

"You don't understand—"

"Yes, I do," she said firmly. "I know exactly what happened that night, and I know you had nothing to do with it. When are you going to stop blaming yourself for something that isn't your fault?"

"I can't."

It was her turn to lean back, and she regarded him with a level stare across the small table. "You want to know what I think?" Without waiting for a response, she charged ahead. "I think you're afraid, and that's why you blame yourself. You've buried yourself under mounds of guilt so you don't have to face the reality that John is gone. Blaming yourself for his death gives you a way to hold on to him, and keeps you from moving on. From continuing to live."

Her words were like icy daggers, each one striking with a cold sting. His breath froze in his chest, and he couldn't come up with a response.

He wanted to dismiss her outright, to flat out reject what she was saying. But it made a strange kind of sense, and he had a sneaking suspicion she had a point. Hadn't Hannah also told him he wasn't to blame? His analytical skills switched on as he considered the odds that two women who'd never met each other would say the same thing. Highly unlikely.

And it was also unlikely they were just trying to make him feel better. Casey certainly had no reason to absolve him if he really was responsible. Her husband was gone, and she wasn't the forgiving type— not for something like that. So if she didn't blame him for John's death, maybe he really was being too hard on himself.

His guilt had become an integral part of his identity over the past few months, a thick, black hedge that blocked out the light with roots that ran deep into his soul. But as he considered Casey's words, some of the branches began to wither and fall away, creating cracks in the dark wall that surrounded him.

He felt a momentary flash of panic—what was on the other side? What would life be like if he really let go of his guilt and accepted the fact that John was gone? Would he lose what little he had left of his friend? How was he going to handle the world without this screen in place?

As if sensing his panic, Casey reached across the table and gripped his hand. "Let it go," she said, her voice kind. "I know how much it hurts, admitting he's really gone. But you can do it. And you have someone to help you through it."

He shook his head. "Who?"

"The woman you're in love with."

He didn't even bother to refute Casey's description of Hannah. *Love* was a loaded word, fraught with meaning, and yet it perfectly captured his feelings for her. Too bad she didn't reciprocate.

"Weren't you listening? She's gone."

"Go after her."

"Casey, I'm not going to chase after a woman who doesn't want me. I'm not a stalker."

She laughed at that, a full-throated, genuine sound that lightened his heart, even if she was laughing at him. "What's so funny?"

"You." Her eyes were shiny with tears, and she reached up to wipe them away. "You are such a man, Owen."

He frowned. "What's that supposed to mean?"

"Have you tried to contact her since she left?"

"Well, no."

"And I take it you haven't visited her?"

He shifted in his chair, suddenly feeling as if he was being interrogated. He wasn't used to being on this side of the table, and he didn't like it one bit. "Of course not," he said stiffly.

"She walked away because she's giving you a chance to figure out your feelings. She told you she didn't want you to see her as part of your work. And you don't. So now you need to tell her that."

Did women really do that? And if so, how was he supposed to figure that out?

"Why didn't she just say that?"

Casey gifted him with an indulgent smile, one that suggested he was acting like a puppy that had finally learned a new trick. "I'm sure she did, but not in those words."

"So you really think I should try to talk to her?"

She nodded emphatically. "The sooner the better. And if she gives you the brush-off again—which I doubt she will—then you'll know to give up. But don't quit right now. It's not over yet."

She sounded so confident about it that Owen felt his own doubts begin to fade. He trusted Casey and took her opinion seriously. If she really thought he should try to see Hannah again, then maybe that was the right thing to do.

The longer he thought about it, the sillier he felt. In all other aspects of his life, if he wanted something, he went after it without hesitation. But he was more cautious when it came to Hannah. Was it because she'd been hurt badly before, both physically and emotionally? He certainly didn't want to hurt her again, but he'd seen the core of strength she possessed, and he knew she wasn't some fragile beauty. Besides, it was better to talk to her again and find out exactly what she thought. He could live with a definite rejection, but he knew he'd regret walking away if there was still a chance she'd have him.

"I think you're right," he said slowly, his mind already racing ahead to work out the right words to say to Hannah when he saw her again. How could he convince her she wasn't a job to him or his second chance—that she meant so much more than that? He'd have one shot at this, and he had to make sure he did it right.

Casey nodded, her eyes brightening. "Does that mean you're going to talk to her?"

"Yes," he replied, his stomach starting to churn as nerves kicked in.

"Excellent! Get going, then." She made a shooing motion with her hand, urging him to stand. He pushed back from the table but then paused, wanting to make sure Casey was okay before he ran off.

"Thanks for this, Casey. It means a lot to me. Let's do it again soon."

She nodded once more. "You bet. I have to say, being with you today made me feel a little closer to John."

Goose bumps popped up along his arms, and the fine hairs on the back of his neck rose. He didn't believe in ghosts, but the fact that both he and Casey had felt John's presence was something he couldn't ignore. Was John really smiling down on them? Even though his logical side scoffed at the idea, the thought was comforting.

"Me, too," he said.

She smiled at him with perfect understanding and grabbed her purse. "Oh, wait! I almost forgot." The bag landed on the table with a solid thump, and she began digging through the contents with surprising speed. "I know I put it in here," she muttered. "There it is!" With a triumphant gesture, she pulled a piece of paper from her purse and handed it to him.

It was a photograph, he realized as he looked down. A picture of him and John in their formal uniforms on the day they received the department's Meritorious Service Award. They were grinning at the camera from above their official stamped certificates, both of them tickled at the recognition they'd received after successfully closing a particularly difficult case.

"I was so proud of him that day," Casey said, a smile in her voice. "He was thrilled to win that award, but even more excited by the fact that you'd won it, too. Honestly, I think he would have turned it down if you hadn't been included."

"Good thing they notified us at the same time," he said, swallowing down the lump in his throat. He studied the picture again. "That was such a great day," he said softly.

"Yes, it was," she agreed. "Anyway, I want you to have it. I know you already have the official picture, the one where you guys are looking appropriately serious, but this is the good one. You both let your hair down, and it's clear how much you enjoyed yourselves. That's the John I've been thinking about, and it's the one I want you to remember, too."

Owen ran his finger over one corner to smooth back the fold that testified to the photo's journey in Casey's purse. She saw the gesture and winced. "I didn't have time to frame it," she said apologetically.

"No, this is perfect," he assured her. And it was. Having the photo in his hands made it more immediate, more real, an effect that would be diminished if he put it behind glass and boxed it in with a frame. This was a picture that needed to be tacked to his refrigerator door, or pinned to the small corkboard next to his desk. Someplace where he'd see it often and be reminded of his friend as he was in life. Maybe someday, this memory would loom larger than his recollection of John lying on the sidewalk, growing colder by the second as the light faded from the sky.

"Thank you," he said, his voice husky. "I think I needed this, to remind myself of the way things were."

Casey nodded, looking satisfied, as if she'd expected him to say that. "I'm glad it helped. John wouldn't want you to punish yourself for his death. You know he'd want you to move on with your life."

"I suppose I owe him that much."

"Yes, you do." She rounded the table and gave him a quick hug. "Now, go get your girl!"

Owen carefully tucked the photograph in his back pocket and allowed his anticipation to bubble through him. He felt light and his head spun a bit, as if he were standing on the edge of a cliff looking down into the abyss. He took a deep breath and gave Casey a smile.

"I will."

Hannah shifted the stack of papers she carried, trying to free her hand so she could unlock her office door. It took a bit of juggling, but she managed to insert her key without dropping anything. She shoved the door open and stepped over to her desk just as the papers slipped out of her grasp. They landed on her keyboard and slipped to fan across her desk, but at least she hadn't spilled them on the floor.

Over the past few weeks, she'd become more adept at doing things one-handed, since her arm was still immobilized. The doctor told her it would be a few more weeks before the cast came off, and even then, she would need several appointments with a physical therapist to ease her arm back into service. She faced another long recovery, which was a little discouraging. She'd had enough of that to last a lifetime. Still, brooding about it wasn't going to change things, and she was ready to get started.

But first, she had to organize this mess.

She sat and began scooping the papers back into a pile. The students had moaned and groaned when she'd announced a pop quiz, but keeping them on their toes was the only way to ensure they studied regularly. What they didn't realize was that she disliked the quizzes almost as much as they did, since it increased her grading load—a task that had grown more difficult with her dominant arm in a cast.

It took a moment, but she managed to excavate her keyboard and arrange the papers into a loose pile. She grabbed her red pen and eyed the first quiz with distaste, then focused with a sigh. The sooner she started, the sooner she'd be done. Besides, grading kept her occupied so she didn't spend all her time mooning over Owen.

It was almost embarrassing, the way she pined for him. As if he was dead and gone instead of someone she'd voluntarily left.

I did the right thing, she told herself for the millionth time. And she had. She wanted a man who was a true partner, not one who saw her as an obligation. Owen's pain had nearly broken her heart, but she couldn't be the one to heal him. He had to do that himself. In truth, she'd walked away because she was scared. Scared that if she'd stayed, Owen would have grown to resent her when she proved unable to provide the redemption he seemed to need. So even though it hurt, even though she'd second-guessed herself every day since, she knew leaving had been for the best.

The grand irony of it all was that Owen had been the one to give her the courage to leave. Before knowing him, she would have taken the attentions of a man and been grateful for it. But he had shown her that she was worth so much more, that her scars didn't define her. He had made her realize that she could have a relationship, and now that she knew it to be true, she couldn't accept anything less.

And so she was alone. Again.

She shook her head with a sigh. Maybe she was destined to be single. It wasn't anything to be ashamed of—lots of women were, and it suited them just fine. She would get used to it again, like she had after Jake had left. Better to be alone than stuck with the wrong person.

The problem was, she didn't think Owen was the wrong person. He was a good, honorable man and she cared for him very much. And from what she could tell, he cared about her, too. But the timing was off. Maybe one day, after his case was closed, they could find their way back to each other. It would be nice to explore what was between them without the outside stress and pressure of his investigation weighing on them.

Assuming he was still interested. After all, she had been the one to walk away. And she'd said some things that may have hurt him. Things that may have caused him to retreat into his shell and continue to punish himself for John's death. Guilt slammed into her at the realization that while she had tried to be gentle, she may have inadvertently hurt him deeply.

She reached for the phone without thinking, her body taking the lead before her mind could catch up. She had started to dial his number before she realized what she was doing, and she hastily hung up before completing the call. If she had hurt him, she would be the last person he'd want to talk to. It had only been a few weeks, and the whole thing was still too fresh. She'd give him some time. If she didn't hear from him after a week or so, then she'd try to call.

Feeling somewhat satisfied with this approach, Hannah turned back to the papers. Enough stalling. Time to get back to work.

She uncapped her pen and started reading, but a soft knock on her door distracted her again. She glanced up, expecting to find a student with a question, or one of her coworkers stopping by for a conversation. But she was wrong on both counts. It was Owen.

He filled her doorway, his tall frame and broad shoulders making it impossible for her to see past him. Not that she wanted to. She ran her gaze over his body, drinking in the sight of him. Even though it hadn't been long since she'd seen him last, her memories of him were flat and dull compared to the real thing. Seeing him now, she realized anew how vibrant he was. His presence filled her small office, and she inhaled deeply, enjoying the familiar, warm scent of his soap.

"Hello," she said, feeling a little breathless.

"Hi," he replied. He gave her a shy smile. "Mind if I come in?"

"Yes." His face fell, and she realized her mistake. "I mean, no. I mean, come in. Please, have a seat." She gestured at the chair across from her desk, her pulse kicking up a notch when he stepped closer.

He lowered himself into the chair, moving a little gingerly. "Are you okay?" she asked, leaning forward in concern.

A rueful smile curved his mouth. "I'm fine. Just a little sore. I had a few blisters pop up after my exposure, and they ache a little."

She half rose from her seat, but he waved her back down. "I'm really okay."

"Have you seen a doctor?" She tried to keep the alarm out of her voice, but it was a losing battle.

Owen tilted his head and raised one brow. "Of course I have. I'm not an idiot."

Hannah's face grew warm. "I didn't say you were. It's just that in my experience, men don't voluntarily seek medical attention unless they're actively dying." She thought fleetingly of her uncle, who had been dragged, kicking and screaming, to the emergency room when he suddenly lost the ability to move his right side. He'd insisted the whole time that he was fine, and not even the news that he had experienced a stroke had been enough to convince him otherwise.

He chuckled softly. "Fair enough. But since I'd just been exposed to a chemical agent, I decided to play it a little safe."

"Do you have any permanent damage?" Her scars tingled at the thought, and she surreptitiously rubbed her back against her chair to ease the sensation. Would Owen have scars of his own now? Or perhaps internal damage that was invisible but just as troublesome? A lump of dread formed in her stomach as she considered the possibility.

He shook his head, and she relaxed a bit. "Doesn't look that way. The doctor is pretty happy with my lungs, and he said I shouldn't have any long-term damage to my skin."

"I'm glad to hear it," she said, feeling better. Even though she hadn't been the one to dose him with the chemical, she still felt somewhat responsible. If it hadn't been for her involvement, Dave might not have felt the need to escalate things so quickly.

"How's your arm?"

She wiggled it reflexively, ignoring the mild ache that started up anytime she forced her arm to do anything but rest. "Better. I get my cast off in a few weeks, and then it's back to physical therapy."

He nodded, and silence fell over them now that the pleasantries had been exchanged. Hannah shifted a bit in her chair, feeling a little awkward and not knowing what to say. Why was Owen here? Had he closed the case? Or was it something else?

"I'm glad you stopped by," she said, gathering up her courage.

His gaze warmed, and his cheeks grew flushed. "You are?" His voice held a hint of disbelief, as if he wasn't really convinced she was telling the truth.

"Yes. I want to apologize for the things I said to you back at the police station. I was out of line, and I'm sorry. I didn't mean to hurt you."

He looked down and shook his head, and she felt a stab of worry. Was he refusing to accept her apology? Had her behavior been worse than she'd thought?

"Don't apologize," he said, meeting her eyes once

more. "Everything you said was spot-on. In fact, that's why I came here today. To talk to you about it."

A nervous quiver twitched in her stomach. "Oh?"

"You were right. About me blaming myself for John's death. And it's taken me a while to understand that it wasn't really my fault." He looked down again, his gaze fixed on his hands. "I had a long talk with John's widow a few days ago, and she didn't pull any punches. She made me see that I was blaming myself as a way to hold on to John. To pretend he wasn't really gone." He lifted one shoulder in an elegant shrug. "I know it doesn't make sense, but in some twisted way, I thought my guilt kept John's memory fresh, kept me from forgetting him." Now he looked up, his dark blue eyes rueful. "But I realize that's not the case. And Casey helped me see that I wasn't just hurting myself, but I was hurting other people, too. Like you."

Hannah could only nod, hardly willing to believe her ears. Here he was, saying the words she'd been wanting to hear for weeks. Her heart rejoiced but her mind wasn't ready to celebrate just yet. Owen had been carrying around his guilt and sorrow for months. That wasn't something a person could easily cast aside, even one as strong-willed as Owen. If he truly believed what he was saying, he was going to have to overhaul his entire way of thinking about his partner's death, and while she hoped he was doing just that, her inner skeptic was having a hard time believing such a massive change had occurred in the few short weeks they'd been apart.

She swallowed hard, trying to keep her doubt from showing. "When did you figure all of this out?" she asked as delicately as she could manage.

"Honestly?" He gave a short laugh and ran a hand through his hair. "A few days ago."

"Ah." So her fears were true. He'd only just started to change his thinking. She was happy he was finally starting to forgive himself, happy he was on the right path. But she couldn't help but wonder if he had really changed for good, or if he was going to fall back into his old patterns once he faced an obstacle.

"I know what you're thinking," he said, shooting her a knowing glance. Hannah's face warmed as she realized he probably could read her thoughts, since she had a terrible poker face.

"Is that right?" she asked, trying to sound innocent.

He nodded. "Yep. You think my change in attitude isn't permanent, and that I'll go back to being the sad sack I was in a few days, after my newfound resolve wears off."

Hannah gave up trying to pretend and let her shoulders slump. "I wasn't thinking those exact words," she said lamely. "But can you blame me?"

"Not at all. Hell, even I'm not sure if this is going to last. But I'm determined to make a change. And with you as my motivation, I know I'll be able to do it."

"Me?" The word came out as a squeak, but she didn't bother trying to clear her throat.

Owen nodded, his expression as serious as she'd ever seen it. "I want to be with you, Hannah. But I want to be a man who deserves to be with you. That means I have to fix myself, and I'm willing to spend the rest of my life working on it, if you'll be patient with me."

The breath froze in her chest, and she couldn't speak. Was he saying what she thought he was saying? Was that even possible?

"I know we haven't known each other very long," he continued, once again reading her mind. "But I've felt drawn to you from the moment I met you. There's something about you that calls to me, and I feel my best when I'm around you. I know that's not a great motivation for you to be with me, but I'd like to think you feel something for me, too."

She nodded dumbly, at a complete loss for words. Cold shock had given way to a warm glow, one that was slowly spreading throughout her body. If he kept talking like this, she was certain she'd go up in flames.

"So I guess what I'm asking is for you to give me a chance. I know I messed up, making you think you were some kind of obligation. But you've never been one, and you never will be. You're someone I care about, very much. I want you to be a part of my life, and for me to be a part of yours. I don't know where we'll end up, but I think we owe it to ourselves to give it a shot." He leaned forward, reaching across the desk to take her free hand in his own. The hope in his eyes was shining so brightly, it almost hurt to look at him.

"So what do you say? Are you willing to try again? We can have a proper start this time, do things right."

A new start. One that didn't involve a murder case and ghosts from his past. A chance to wipe the slate clean and get to know each other without all the other drama of the past few weeks. The very idea filled her with a sense of contentment and peace.

She nodded, unable to stop the grin spreading across her face. Owen stared at her, his expression a mix of hope and disbelief. "Really?" he asked. "Are you sure?"

Hannah laughed at the question. Was he trying to change her mind? "Were you wanting a different response?" she teased.

"God, no!" he breathed. Keeping hold of her hand, he stood and rounded the desk, pulling her out of her chair with a gentle tug. As soon as she was on her feet, he pulled her close and wrapped his arms around her, cradling her against him as if she was the most precious thing in the world.

"I missed you so much," he murmured, the words muffled by her hair.

She turned her head to the side, nuzzling against his chest and fitting her nose in the hollow of his throat. He smelled so good—soap, warmth, *Owen.* "I missed you, too," she told him. The sling on her arm kept her from hugging him the way she wanted to, but it was still so good to be close to him. Satisfaction welled in her chest and bubbled up her throat, making her hum softly with the sheer pleasure of feeling Owen against her again.

"Hannah," he whispered. His hand cupped her jaw, and he tilted her face up to his. His dark blue eyes filled her vision, and the joy in his gaze nearly stole her breath.

He dipped his head, touched his mouth to hers. The kiss was soft, a gentle exploration that told her more than any words how much he cherished her. Her bones turned to liquid and she melted against him, trusting his strength to support her. He didn't disappoint.

She didn't know how long the kiss lasted. It could have gone on forever, and it wouldn't have been long enough to suit her. She was so focused on the man in front of her—his warm, familiar scent, his possessive hold, his intoxicating flavor—everything else faded into obscurity. Now that Owen was here, all her other worries and problems didn't matter so much anymore. Whatever the future held in store for her, she knew she could handle it with him by her side.

Slowly, he pulled back, breaking the kiss so he could draw a large breath. His chest inflated against her, pushing her back a little and making her smile. "I should let you get back to work," he said softly, a hint of regret in his tone.

Hannah sighed, knowing he was right but reluctant to see him leave. "My next class is over at five," she told him. "Can I see you after?"

He huffed out a laugh. "You couldn't get rid of me if you tried. I'm tempted to sit in the back of your class just so I can watch you."

Now it was her turn to laugh. "I don't think so," she told him. "Talk about a distraction!" Just the thought of his intense blue eyes following her every move made her shiver in delicious anticipation.

"All right," he acknowledged. "But I am coming back for you."

"That won't be necessary," said a voice from the doorway. "Since you're not going anywhere."

Owen stiffened against her, then turned to face the new speaker, maneuvering so he kept her behind him. She rose up on her toes to peer around his shoulder, and her heart froze in her chest.

Dave Carlson stepped into her office, closing the door behind him. His hand disappeared into his jacket and he withdrew a large, wicked-looking gun that he pointed at Owen. A thin, cold smile stretched across his face, giving him the look of a satisfied ghoul.

"How nice to see you both again," he said courteously. "Saves me an extra trip."

Chapter 16

Owen couldn't decide if Dave Carlson had the worst timing in the world, or if this was the opportunity of a lifetime.

Was it really just a moment ago he'd been kissing Hannah, feeling as if nothing could go wrong ever again? He'd come to see her, hardly daring to hope that she'd even give him the time of day.

But she had. And now that he knew she was giving him a second chance, he wasn't going to let some two-bit psycho interrupt one of the greatest moments of his life.

A curious calm fell over him, and his senses sharpened as adrenaline pumped through him. He watched as Dave stepped closer, noting the tension in his shoulders and the faint tremor in his arm as he held the gun. He obviously wasn't familiar with the weapon, a fact that Owen could use to his advantage.

Dave's forehead was shiny with a thin sheen of sweat, and for all his projected confidence, he reeked with the stale, metallic scent of fear. He was a desperate man, one driven to the edge. That made him unpredictable.

Under normal circumstances, Owen wouldn't hesitate to take whatever risk was needed to incapacitate Dave. But he was keenly aware of Hannah's warm presence behind him. No way could he take a chance when her safety was at stake.

"What's your plan, Dave? You do realize if you shoot, people are going to come running?"

Dave smirked at him, and Owen's finger's itched with the desire to punch the smug bastard in the face. "I know. That's why I have a silencer." He pulled a black tube from his jacket and fumbled to screw it on the end of his gun.

Owen's frustration mounted in the face of Dave's obvious unfamiliarity with the weapon. He'd be damned if he let some jerk who didn't know how to use a weapon get the better of him. The guys at the station would never let him live it down. But more importantly, Hannah might get hurt.

It took Dave a few minutes to install the suppressor, and as he struggled with it, Owen considered his next move. Dave still had the gun pointed at his chest, so any sudden movement would result in him getting shot. And if he went down, Hannah would be left unprotected.

His best bet was to distract Dave so that Hannah had a chance to get away. Keep him talking, maybe draw him farther into the room and away from the door, so Hannah would have a clear path out.

"It's not like in the movies," Owen informed him.

"The suppressor isn't going to fully mask the sound of the gun. Are you sure you really want to do this?"

Dave shot him a glare over the top of the gun. "Is this the part where you try to talk me out of it? Are you going to explain that if I tell you my side of the story, you'll talk to the DA and try to get the charges reduced?" He shook his head. "I don't think so. I'm not that stupid."

"You can talk all you want," Owen replied coolly. "It doesn't matter what you say. I've already got the story from the people who worked with you. Marcia, Shelly—they couldn't wait to tell me all about what you did. You're going to spend the rest of your life in jail." Hannah whimpered softly behind him, and she grabbed the fabric of his shirt, crumpling it in her fist. Unless he missed his guess, she was scared that Owen was going to taunt Dave into shooting them both. He wished he could offer her some kind of reassurance, but doing so would tip his hand. He settled for reaching back and giving the side of her leg a pat. It wasn't the most comforting gesture, but it was better than nothing.

"If there's no incentive for me to talk," Dave said, raising the gun to aim at Owen's head, "then there's no reason I shouldn't just shoot you now."

"Wait!" Hannah's voice was loud in the small room. Owen felt her shift behind him, and he moved to try to keep his body between her and Dave. He didn't want her exposed until she was closer to the door and had a clear path out.

She was too quick for him, though. With his back to her, he couldn't see which way she was moving, and she easily stepped around him. He cursed silently and tried to pull her back, but it was hard to maneuver around the furniture in the small room.

Hannah squared her shoulders and lifted her head as she stared at Dave. "I want to know why you tried to kill me by blowing up my lab. I never really spoke to you. Why did you hate me so much?"

Dave stared at her, his expression puzzled. "I didn't hate you," he said, sounding surprised that she would think so. "You were in my way."

"So because I disagreed with you, you wanted me dead?"

He shrugged. "I just wanted you gone. I knew firing you wouldn't work because you'd probably come back and sue, so I had to come up with another strategy."

Hannah stiffened, and Owen could tell Dave's explanation had shocked her. She was used to dealing with people who had a conscience, people who had a moral compass that guided their behavior. But Dave was a psycho who didn't understand why killing someone was wrong. He had hurt her not because he disliked her or wanted to make her suffer but because he saw her as an obstacle, and blowing up her lab seemed like the simplest way to remove her from his path.

Hannah shook her head and moved to the side, taking her farther away from Owen's reach. What was she doing? Why was she separating herself from him? He couldn't protect her if she was too far away, but she didn't seem to notice or care.

She started talking again, asking Dave questions, expressing her shock. It was then Owen noticed how Dave's attention had shifted. The other man was now totally focused on Hannah, studying her like a bug under a microscope. By moving away from Owen, Hannah had drawn Dave's focus and had given Owen a clear path to attack. Clever lady.

His worry melted into admiration for her bravery. She showed no regard for her own safety. She was simply trying to give Owen a chance to do his job, and doing her best to make it easier for him. He wanted to gather her into his arms and kiss her senseless for it, but that would have to wait.

She was still talking, and Dave seemed totally absorbed. Owen judged the distance between them. He had one chance to disarm Dave, and he couldn't botch it. He knew once Dave felt threatened he wouldn't hesitate to start shooting. Owen didn't want to draw his own gun in such a cramped space, and he wasn't about to risk a shot. Even though he was too close to miss, the bullet might pass right through Dave and slam into the hall or the next office.

No, he was going to have to do this the old-fashioned way. With his fists.

Hannah shifted just a bit more, and Owen saw his chance. He surged forward, hand outstretched for the gun. Dave caught the movement and turned, his eyes widening. He lifted the gun and pulled the trigger, and Owen felt the air move past his shoulder as the bullet whizzed by. Dave's expression shifted from disbelief to panicked fury when Owen kept moving forward, but Owen was on him before he could do anything more.

Owen grabbed the gun and wrenched it from Dave's hand with a savage twist. Dave let out a cry of pain, but Owen didn't stop. He grabbed the barrel and brought the handle down against Dave's temple in one fluid motion. Dave's body went limp and he sank to the floor, his eyes glazed. Owen tossed the gun to the side and drew out his cuffs, quickly anchoring Dave's hands behind his back. Satisfied the man was no longer a threat, he stood and turned to find Hannah.

She was wedged in the corner, taking in the scene with wide eyes. Her hand was pressed to her mouth, but he couldn't tell if that was out of reflex or if she was trying to stifle a scream. She hadn't made a sound while he had disarmed Dave, but maybe she was having a delayed reaction? Had she been shot? He was fairly sure the bullet had hit the wall behind him, but what if it had grazed Hannah?

"Are you okay?" He reached for her, forcing himself to move slowly so she saw him coming. She nodded and grabbed his hand.

"I'm fine."

"You didn't get hit?" He scanned her face, her arms, her legs, checking for a telltale darkening on her clothes. But she appeared fine.

She shook her head. "No. Did you?" Her eyes widened as she considered the possibility, and she completed her own scan of his body.

He pulled her close, needing to hold her. Even though she was safe now, his heart was still pounding over their close call.

"No, I'm okay."

"What happens now?" She gripped him tightly, apparently drawing her own comfort from their embrace.

"I'll call it in. But I just need to hold you for another minute. Okay?"

He felt her smile against his shoulder. "Absolutely."

It took several hours for the police to finish "processing the scene," as Owen called it. Hannah was content to stay on the sidelines, watching and waiting. She'd already given her statement, and the officers didn't need her while they gathered evidence and spoke to others. It seemed to go on forever, but they finally wrapped things up, leaving Owen and Hannah alone once more.

He gave her a crooked smile. "What a day, huh?"

"Definitely memorable."

He looked down for a moment and took a deep breath, as if he was gathering himself to say something difficult. Feeling uneasy, Hannah took a step forward, wanting to get closer to him.

When he looked up, she was shocked at the intensity of emotions swirling in his eyes. "I need to ask you a question," he said quietly.

"Okay." A lump formed in her stomach. He was clearly upset—what was wrong?

He took a step, closing the distance between them. "What the hell were you thinking today?"

Hannah leaned back, his worry and anger hitting her like a blow. "What do you mean?"

"I mean, what did you think you were doing, talking to Dave when he had a gun pointed at us? You could have been killed!"

Her own anger rose to the surface. "I could ask the same of you," she said, raising her chin to look him in the eyes. "You're the one who attacked him barehanded."

"Because I was trying to protect you!"

Her heart softened at his admission. He was such a good man, but he didn't seem to realize it. The fact that he was so ready to sacrifice himself for her safety made her want to cry, but she blinked hard, knowing he'd mistake her tears for sadness or pain.

"I couldn't stand there and do nothing. Maybe a few weeks ago I would have cowered behind you and let you handle the situation, but not now." She shook her head. "I've changed since I met you. I'm no longer satisfied to take a backseat in my own life. Being with you has reminded me of the strong person I once was." She reached out to lay a hand on his chest, needing to touch him He echoed her gesture, laying his hand on her cheek, and she leaned into his touch, drawing comfort from his warmth.

"I miss the woman I used to be," she continued. "And while I can't go back to being the exact same person, I'm going to try to be someone she'd be proud to know. That means no more hiding from life, and no more excuses."

He was quiet for a moment, digesting her words. Then he tugged her until she was pressed to his chest. "I guess we both have some habits to break," he said, wrapping his arms around her and holding her tight.

"We certainly do," she replied, her lips against his throat. "But as long as we stick together, I know we can do it."

"You know what?" He leaned back to press a soft kiss to her mouth. "I think you're right."

* * * * *

If you loved this novel, don't miss other
suspenseful titles by Lara Lacombe:
LETHAL LIES
FATAL FALLOUT
DEADLY CONTACT
Available now from Harlequin Romantic Suspense!

Available June 2, 2015

#1851 Colton Cowboy Protector

The Coltons of Oklahoma • by Beth Cornelison

Widow Tracy McCain wants to bond with her deceased cousin's son, despite the concerns of the child's attractive father. But when she becomes an assassin's target, the only man who can save them is the one cowboy who might break her heart.

#1852 Cowboy of Interest

Cowboys of Holiday Ranch • by Carla Cassidy

Nick Coleman's best friend is murdered, and the grieving rancher knows he's the number one suspect. Public relations maven Adrienne Bailey is positive that Nick murdered her sister. When sleuthing suggests Nick isn't the culprit, it puts them both in the real killer's crosshairs.

#1853 Course of Action: Crossfire

by Lindsay McKenna and Merline Lovelace

Set in exotic locales, these two stories feature military heroes who must overcome devastating odds if they are to survive long enough to pursue the extraordinary women they've fallen for. Thrills, passion and danger—romantic suspense at its best!

#1854 King's Ransom

Man on a Mission • by Amelia Autin

As king, Andre Alexei IV of Zakhar has everything he wants... except the one who got away. Actress Juliana Richardson is lured to his castle by a prominent role. When sinister plots for the throne unfold, will he be able to save her?

REQUEST YOUR FREE BOOKS!
2 FREE NOVELS PLUS 2 FREE GIFTS!

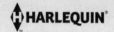

ROMANTIC suspense

Sparked by danger, fueled by passion

YES! Please send me 2 FREE Harlequin® Romantic Suspense novels and my 2 FREE gifts (gifts are worth about $10). After receiving them, if I don't wish to receive any more books, I can return the shipping statement marked "cancel." If I don't cancel, I will receive 4 brand-new novels every month and be billed just $4.74 per book in the U.S. or $5.49 per book in Canada. That's a savings of at least 12% off the cover price! It's quite a bargain! Shipping and handling is just 50¢ per book in the U.S. and 75¢ per book in Canada.* I understand that accepting the 2 free books and gifts places me under no obligation to buy anything. I can always return a shipment and cancel at any time. Even if I never buy another book, the two free books and gifts are mine to keep forever.

240/340 HDN GH3P

Name	(PLEASE PRINT)	
Address		Apt. #
City	State/Prov.	Zip/Postal Code

Signature (if under 18, a parent or guardian must sign)

Mail to the **Reader Service:**

IN U.S.A.: P.O. Box 1867, Buffalo, NY 14240-1867
IN CANADA: P.O. Box 609, Fort Erie, Ontario L2A 5X3

Want to try two free books from another line?
Call 1-800-873-8635 or visit www.ReaderService.com.

* Terms and prices subject to change without notice. Prices do not include applicable taxes. Sales tax applicable in N.Y. Canadian residents will be charged applicable taxes. Offer not valid in Quebec. This offer is limited to one order per household. Not valid for current subscribers to Harlequin Romantic Suspense books. All orders subject to credit approval. Credit or debit balances in a customer's account(s) may be offset by any other outstanding balance owed by or to the customer. Please allow 4 to 6 weeks for delivery. Offer available while quantities last.

Your Privacy—The Reader Service is committed to protecting your privacy. Our Privacy Policy is available online at www.ReaderService.com or upon request from the Reader Service.

We make a portion of our mailing list available to reputable third parties that offer products we believe may interest you. If you prefer that we not exchange your name with third parties, or if you wish to clarify or modify your communication preferences, please visit us at www.ReaderService.com/consumerschoice or write to us at Reader Service Preference Service, P.O. Box 9062, Buffalo, NY 14240-9062. Include your complete name and address.

"Excuse me."

Jack pushed to his feet, his knee cracking thanks to an old rodeo injury, and faced the woman at eye level. Well, almost eye level. Though tall for a woman, she was still a good five or six inches shorter than his six foot one. He recognized her as the woman he'd seen earlier lurking in the foyer, practically casing the main house.

"Are you Jack Colton?" she asked.

"I am."

"May I have a word with you?" she asked, her voice noticeably thin and unsteady. She cleared her throat and added, "Privately?"

In his head, Jack groaned. *What now?*

"And you are...?"

He suspected she was a reporter, based on the messenger bag hanging from her shoulder. He had nothing to say to any reporter, privately or otherwise.

"Tracy McCain." She added a shy smile, her porcelain cheeks flushing, and a stir of attraction tickled Jack deep inside. Hell, more than a stir. He gave her leisurely scrutiny, sizing her up. She may be tall and thin, but she still had womanly curves to go with her delicate, china-doll face.

"Am I supposed to know you?"

Her smile dropped. "Laura never mentioned me?"

His ex-wife's name instantly raised his hackles and his defenses. His eyes narrowed. "Not that I recall. How do you know Laura?"

"I'm her cousin. Her maternal aunt's daughter. From Colorado Springs."

Jack gritted his back teeth. Laura had only been dead a few months and already relations she'd never mentioned were crawling out of the woodwork like roaches after the light was turned off. The allure of the Colton wealth had attracted more than one gold-digging pest over the years. "You should know Laura signed an agreement when we divorced that ended any further financial claim on Colton money."

Tracy lifted her chin. "I'm aware."

"So you're barking up the wrong tree if you're looking for cash."

Tracy blinked her pale blue eyes, and her expression shifted, hardened. "I'm not after money," she said, with frost in her tone.

Jack scratched his chin and tipped his head, giving her a skeptical glare. "Then what?"

"I wanted to talk about Seth."

Jack tensed, his gut filling with acid. He squeezed the currycomb with a death grip and grated, "No."

"I... What do you mean, no? You haven't even heard what I want to—"

"I don't need to hear. My son is off-limits. Nonnegotiable."

Don't miss
COLTON COWBOY PROTECTOR
by Beth Cornelison,
available June 2015 wherever
Harlequin® Romantic Suspense
books and ebooks are sold.

www.Harlequin.com

HRSEXP0515

HARLEQUIN®

A *Romance* FOR EVERY MOOD™

Love the Harlequin book
you just read?

Your opinion matters.

Review this book on your favorite
book site, review site, blog or your own
social media properties and share
your opinion with other readers!

Be sure to connect with us at:
Harlequin.com/Newsletters
Facebook.com/HarlequinBooks
Twitter.com/HarlequinBooks

THE WORLD IS BETTER WITH

Romance

Harlequin has everything from contemporary, passionate and heartwarming to suspenseful and inspirational stories.

Whatever your mood, we have a romance just for you!